A NEW AMERICA

A NEW AMERICA

The State of Independence

A Novel

———————

Aaron Morell

UNCONSCIOUS WILL
NEW YORK

UNCONSCIOUS WILL PUBLISHING

Copyright © 2024 Aaron Morell
All rights reserved
Library of Congress Cataloging-in-Publication Data

Names: Morell, Aaron, author
Title: A New America / Aaron Morell
Description: First Edition
Subjects: Novels
ISBN 979-8-218-98811-1 (hardcover)
ISBN 979-8-218-53975-7 (paperback)
ISBN 979-8-218-98812-8 (ebook)

Library of Congress Control Number: 2024916315

Published in the United States
1st Printing

Jacket design by David Provolo

INTRODUCTION

TRI-STATE NEWS Monday, Jan 7. Bonner's Ferry, ID. Early this morning, an unidentified group took over government offices and blockaded all inbound roads to town. The Boundary County sheriff reported that armed locals have also shut down the Eckhart International Airport and the county airport near Troy.

When the sheriff stepped out of his home that morning, four men were waiting. He later said they didn't "exactly" threaten him but a thirty-aught-six was enough to convey their earnestness. Junkyard cars and logging trucks blockaded the roads into town. Within the hour, revolutionaries had seized and occupied city and state offices.

By noon, CNN was broadcasting live with a bird's-eye view of the town blanketed in mid-winter snow. While the media centered its eye on Bonner's Ferry, similar events were unfolding in nearby towns. Municipal airports were shut down, courthouses occupied, and one National Guard armory was seized.

By two o'clock, I was on a flight from San Francisco to Spokane. The plan was to be in Portland by the weekend to report on a statewide redistricting dispute I had been tracking for three months. I made it to Oregon but not for another eight months and not for the redistricting issue. Instead, it was to cover diverging secession movements in the Northwest.

The events in Bonner's Ferry sparked a wildfire that would scorch the continent. It was unclear who was behind the seizures or what their intentions were until later that day when the local television station broadcast this statement:

> When, in the course of human events, it becomes necessary for one people to dissolve the political bands that have connected them with another and to assume among the powers of the Earth, the separate, and equal station to which the laws of nature and of nature's God entitle them, a decent respect to the opinions of humankind requires that they should declare the causes which impel them to the separation.
>
> Therefore, We, The People's Committee for Self-Determination, appeal to the good people of Idaho, Montana, and Washington, the people and representatives of the States and Federal Government, and to God, our Supreme Judge, for the rectitude of our intentions that these united counties are of right and ought to be free and independent, that they are absolved from all allegiance to the United States, and that all political connections ought to be dissolved, and that as a free and independent state, we have full power to contract alliances, establish commerce, and to do all other acts and things which an independent nation has the right to do.

The National Guard, FBI, ATF, and FPS were mobilized but the occupiers didn't budge. They would accept nothing less than sovereignty. At face value, it was an absurd, if not insane, demand. But it wasn't their immediate objective. They wanted to spark an uprising.

As the standoff—or standstill—continued into the weekend, supporters began showing up from all over the region. Braving the frigid temps, they amassed outside the police barricades with signs about freedom and tyranny. A violent collision seemed imminent. Violence or a mishap quelling the insurrection would have lit a fuse. Rather than put down the rebellion and risk casualties, the governors of the three states opted to negotiate.

Commentary and debate log-jammed media and social networks, providing a platform for anyone to channel their anger or general dissatisfaction with life into a cause connected with the standoff. For many, it was an opportunity to be a part of something growing more powerful daily.

The occupation inspired acts of defiance across the country. In Spokane, someone tossed a homemade bomb through the window of the FBI office. Authorities arrested three men. At the arraignment, the packed courtroom erupted when they saw bruises and scratches that one of them incurred while resisting arrest. Police were called to clear the room. The objectors gathered outside the jail and were joined by hundreds of others who arrived angry. It turned violent. They threw bottles, rocks, and bricks; broke out windows, flipped cars, and fought with the police.

Disputes over land use flared up nationwide. Some had been lingering for decades. In California, a developer named Henry Knox assembled a battalion of seventy-five men who called themselves The Continental Army. They defied a court order by draining eight acres of protected wetlands with a bulldozer. In New Mexico, hooded bandits pulled a Bureau of Land Management agent from his vehicle and then tarred and feathered him. A homemade bomb was detonated in the Land Management office in Carson City. In Utah, a dispute over creek usage led to the arson of a U.S. Forest Service building.

Since they believed the government represented an elitist minority, "public lands" was a misnomer. A common soundbite from those incidents was "we're reclaiming what belongs to the people." In reality, they were destroying what was allegedly taken from them.

Regardless if you agreed or not, their conviction was undeniable. This was clearly displayed in Arizona when hundreds of ATV riders and motorcyclists converged on a national monument that was closed to motorized vehicles. Following a fervent demonstration, they tore through the canyon. The sense of urgency was remarkable. It was as if sacred land was being taken away and riding off-road was part of their heritage.

When business magnates jumped on the bandwagon—or rather, upgraded it—they reframed the Panhandle Revolution as a populist uprising against government regulation and overreach. They took out full-page ads and bought prime time slots, spurring nationwide demonstrations demanding unprecedented government cuts. People were losing their minds over the national deficit. As tens of millions of people around the world protested against financial austerity, in the U.S. they demanded it.

Perhaps the most unexpected event was the New York City Soda Revolt. In response to the city's proposed restrictions on sugary drinks, industry advocates mobilized a coalition of anti-regulation, anti-government, and pro-freedom supporters. They came from everywhere, overrunning hotels in New Jersey, Pennsylvania, Connecticut, and the Hudson Valley. On Saturday morning, a mass of protesters poured into lower Manhattan, flooding the blocks surrounding City Hall and bringing the Brooklyn Bridge to a standstill. It spilled into Chinatown and down to Wall Street, where chants of "freedom" and "choice" roared through the narrow gorges of the financial district.

As I entered my third year as the Western correspondent for *The Atlantic*, I assumed the role of its de facto secession correspondent. Over the next seventeen months, I would chronicle uprisings and campaigns across North America, followed by another thirteen months covering similar movements globally. It seemed everywhere I traveled, contentious politics were bleeding into daily life and political identity was reforming values and relationships. Distrust was ubiquitous as people tried to discern one other's political leanings against a backdrop of misconceptions and half-truths. It seemed everyone harbored their own propriety blend of reality.

Like a Siddur for prayer and devotion, media outlets provided rituals of daily observance and social networks bolstered the faithful with conviction. Radio waves cracked with virulent exhortations and talk show hosts sermonized around the clock. A billion streams of cocksure postulations formed a rhetorical deluge of acrid words and indiscernible voices buffered in static.

We like to use the term self-determination when describing the desire for political freedom. The word control might be more suitable in this case. The American Secession Movement was a crisis on multiple levels—nationally, locally, communally, and individually. During those seventeen months, there was a tremendous amount of anxiety and not just about what was happening or would might happen. Anxiety was fueling the entire collective movement. At the root of it was the fear of losing control.

Small town and rural communities were the driving force behind American secession. They felt the world was changing fast and they were being left behind. They felt vulnerable and devalued. Simultaneously, countless voices were telling them—and they were telling one another—who exactly was behind the wicked crusade bent on destroying their way of life. It was a volatile mix.

I covered independence movements in Texas, Florida, Northern California, Utah, New York, Quebecc, Alberta, British Columbia, Victoria, and afterward in Spain, Belgium, the U.K., and Kurdistan, to name just a few. Not once did anyone suggest I should visit the High Plains region now known as Independence. For decades, people referred to that part of the continental U.S. as "flyover country." Throughout my secessionism beat, I crisscrossed the country nonstop and flew over the thirty-six counties of Independence on at least four separate occasions. Missing the Flatland Revolution bugs me to this day.

It's astonishing how little our coastal residents know about the interior states. Countless times I've seen this ignorance displayed like a badge of pride, often accompanied by disdain for people or places they view as below them. It evinces an elitist attitude that's been ruthlessly exploited for political purposes.

The events around the Idaho Panhandle and the path that led to the creation of Kootenai were well-documented. However, the origins of the Flatland Revolution are less understood. While in the country, I combed through libraries, historical societies, and private collections in search of documentation about local secession movements. None were as enlightening as the *Chronicle of Independence*, a collection of albums filled with newspaper clippings and magazine articles compiled by a group of librarians in Capital City.

Interspersed among the clippings were original flyers that had been posted in towns that are now part of Independence. The announcements were remarkably mild-mannered in contrast to the hyperbole and malcontent beginning to sweep throughout the nation. The collection began with local newspaper coverage of the Panhandle insurrection.

TRAITORS OR HEROES?
Come join us to talk about the Panhandle dilemma
Grant County Library 7 PM Tuesday

CRISIS IN AMERICA
Pastor Mosely will lead a discussion on the values and
principles at stake in the Panhandle Revolution
Soup and supper at 6 PM
Discussion to follow

LIBERTY AND TAXATION
Wednesday evening with professor Dave Newsome
6:30 PM @ Dodge Hilton Banquet Center

This last flyer refers to a series of regional tax referendums
that originated in Meade, Kansas. The town had a modest pre-
secession population of 1500 and a county population of 5000. Its
county commission and residents proposed radical reforms to the
foundational tax structure.

> MEADE – On Friday afternoon, the Meade County
> Commission held its third meeting in two weeks
> to address the budget shortfall. Once again, the
> board adjourned without a resolution. One
> councilman argued that deep cuts in funding—
> parks and rec, historical society, 4-H, non-essential
> school programs, and the library, to name a few—
> was the only way to save the county from going
> bust. Another councilman insisted that "tightening
> the financial noose" would bankrupt public morale.
> They agreed to hold another meeting, during which
> they will present a hypothetical scenario in which
> the "tax-and-revenue is restructured."

Beverly Frazer poignantly captured this meeting for her
Prairie Living column in the Wichita Eagle newspaper:

> It's safe to say that most of my readers had never
> heard of Meade, Kansas, until this week. Given the
> relentless barrage of national news stories, the
> developments in this small farming community
> might have slipped under your radar.

For those who have never had the pleasure of visiting Kansas, it could very well be the image of Meade County they conjure up. Here, the skyline is dominated not by skyscrapers but by grain elevators. Turn your back to the town and an unbroken horizon is a stark line dividing amber wheat fields from the vast blue sky.

Folks out there gripe endlessly about politicians and government. Political administration is, at best, a necessary nuisance. Shrinking tax bases and declining revenues are all too common across the rural Plains. Of course, this strains communities and intensifies their uneasiness with all matters financial. The budgetary shortfall, coupled with national unrest, created a perfect storm in Meade.

Dozens of regular citizens attended recent county commission meetings intended to resolve the budget problem. The meetings were often raucous as arguments broke out and demands were shouted. The commissioners eventually bowed to public pressure and agreed to hold a town hall to discuss the possibility of "restructured taxation."

Because of the expected turnout, the meeting had to be moved to the school gymnasium. I was in town visiting my mother at her retirement home. I had no expectations of what I would witness. To draw even sixty people to this sort of affair would usually take something extraordinary. Six hundred people came to this meeting! I've been covering rural Kansas life for thirty years, and I've never seen anything like this.

The mayor, commissioners, county clerk, and county treasurer sat at a folding table on the court. Mayor Steebs introduced them, but before he could present the agenda, a man in the crowd stood up and said there were no farmers on the board. "We're ninety-nine percent farmland, yet represented by one hundred percent city."

"We all know who runs this county, so just relax," the mayor joked.

There were a few chuckles from the crowd, but not from the farmer. "That's just not the truth. We don't run this county. That's baloney."

Opinions on this matter shot out from every section in the gymnasium. "Look here," the mayor shouted. "Can we go over the agenda first? We'll be here all night at this rate."

To paraphrase Mayor Steebs, the county was out of money, so it needed to raise more or cut back. The commission had previously discussed raising the property tax cap. The public delegates favored cutting services and lowering the cap. While he was explaining the nuts and bolts of the budget, collectively boring everyone to tears, a man with a long mustache and hair tied back under a cowboy hat stood up.

"If I speak only for myself, I'll hush up, but I think all of us are tired of can't-do-this and can't-do-that. We're here because, deep down, we know we're a dying breed. People are moving away every day, and the rest of us are withering away. We got committees for stimulation, renewal, and what have you, but it ain't doin' a lick of good. Is it God's will or the government's, whether or not we flourish?"

Commissioner Bolls, who was shaking his head emphatically, interrupted. "I thought we were here to balance our budget, not philosophize about the wealth of nations." A spattering of folks with serious expressions clapped sternly and then recrossed their arms. Not everyone there was caught up in the spirit of change.

"You think that's why half the dang county's here, to balance the budget?" the cowboy asked. "We want the kind of change they're demanding up in Idaho." This got near-unanimous applause.

Sitting with his head bowed and legs stretched out under the table, Commissioner Conner suddenly stomped his feet on the court and sat up straight. "Are we supposed to roadblock ourselves in and wait for them to turn off our electricity and water? Or wait till we run out of food, then shake our fists at them? You know, a lot of districts around here take in more tax dollars than they're paying out. The way this all works is that we help each other. Sometimes we gotta tighten our belts. This is one of those times. What else do you want, mister?"

The cowboy: "I want somebody who's not gonna sit there and give us a million reasons why we gotta live a meager existence. I want somebody who's gonna do what's right regardless of what the government says."

"It's not what the government says; it's the way things are."

The third commissioner, a nice-looking man in his thirties, spoke for the first time. "I know the government gets a lot of criticism at times, but the USDA and Farm Service are trying to figure out a way to give us all a boost. I grew up in a farming family. My grandparents and great-grandparents raised cattle here since the frontier days. We're still involved with that land. It's just different now. I want you to know you are represented."

The mayor nodded approvingly and said, "These trends happen in waves. Let the renewal plans work their course. There are no two ways about it; we live in a world where we pay for our goods and services and get paid for goods and services we provide. For right now, there's not enough coming in to maintain everything we'd like to have."

"That's the problem!" the cowboy shouted. "We never have enough, no matter what we got coming in or going out. Why can't we decide for ourselves what taxes we're gonna pay and where the money goes? We, the people. That's how it should be."

Commissioner Conner, the unrelenting realist, rebutted the agitators. "The market's not gonna change just because we, out here in Meade, Kansas, say it should."

"To hell with the markets, then. This town and county is built on farming. It's the purpose of our being here. Yet we're expected to feed the whole world while we live worse than just about anyone. The government's been tampering with the grain markets since I was yay tall with the Cheap Food Act and everything else they come up with in Washington. Expenses go up, but grain prices stay the same. People talk about all the subsidies, but I get little more than a pittance. Only ones benefiting are the conglomerates who got more than all of us put together. We should be deciding what our wheat sells for. Not Kansas City, not Chicago, not Minneapolis, not Washington, and not somebody in China. We shouldn't be paying for people's welfare in California. We're asked to make a lifelong sacrifice to feed everyone, and then they want to take away what little we got. That ain't right!"

"Why don't they pass a Cheap Computer Act?" someone called out.

"A Cheap Tractor Act!"

"Cheap Gas Act!"

Before long, folks were down on the court trying to say their piece. It appeared the whole thing was a bust. But the following day, I can tell you without exaggeration that everywhere I went, people were discussing the issues, be it taxation, spending, or Meade's place in the world. Later in the afternoon, the commission announced there would be a "special vote to amend federal and state tax payments." Well there you go, Meade County.

Three weeks later, the Realignment of Taxes and Expenditures passed with sixty-seven percent of the vote.

> We, The People of Meade County, have determined
> that if state and federal governments are going to
> manipulate markets by legislative means,
> international trade agreements, and by
> empowering massive agricultural conglomerates,
> we are no longer beholden to governments that do
> not represent our interests.

This marked the beginning of the Flatland Revolution, at least in hindsight. Dozens of small towns in the region began debating and sometimes passing similar resolutions. The national media still paid little attention until the Freedom 5 took over the courthouse in Garden City (now Capital City), which put them in the international spotlight right as Congress began debating secession. Before you knew it, they were part of the Secession Act.

Yet there was never a cohesive call for secession. Around the Panhandle, they *demanded* independence from the U.S. They went as far as to co-opt the Declaration of Independence! Although the Freedom 5 made Garden City the media epicenter of the Flatland Revolution, it was a rural movement. It might be difficult to see how a handful of small-town tax referendums could constitute a revolution. In the words of the local newspaper editor, "There's nothing more revolutionary than when municipalities stop paying taxes to the king."

Most people in Garden City never got on the secession bandwagon. That goes for most of the larger towns in the thirty-six counties. About sixty percent of the total population was against secession. But if you subtract the biggest towns—Garden, Dodge, Liberal, Dumas—eighty percent supported it. It's not a stretch to suggest Independence was created for people across the U.S. who wanted secession and not necessarily for the inhabitants of those counties.

The insurrection in Bonner's Ferry began with a shared idea that the government inhibited life, liberty, and the pursuit of happiness. The People's Committee gave form to the idea. It spread through media and social networks, where influential figures charged it with outrage. Secessionists across North America raged for seventeen months. Congress had to do something or the country would have cracked like an eggshell—neighbors against neighbors, family versus family. From the strife came Kootenai and Independence, two very different siblings.

PART ONE

Who Is Independence?

COLORADO BORDER STATION

Land flat as far as the eye could see. Alternating tracts of winter wheat stubble, green seedlings, and tilled dirt were laid out like a patchwork quilt. Crooked fence posts were like strands of yarn decoratively protruding from the seams.

It brought to mind a blanket my grandmother quilted for me when I was a young child. She spent her entire life on a farm in Oklahoma. My mother never took me to visit. This was as close as I'd ever been. As far as I know, my grandparents never traveled outside that rural microcosm. I imagine the quilt reflected the only land she ever knew.

As the shuttle neared the border station, I wondered how much the landscape influenced Independents' outlook. I could make out a tall chain-link fence spanning the horizon with its barbed crown arcing towards the new country. Nothing distinguished the new country from the rest of the arid pastureland. The crossing was just a scattering of simple prefab buildings. No one else coming or going. In the pasture, a dozen cows idled near a round water trough where a tin windmill quivered in the high plains wind.

"Are they closed on Sundays?" I asked but my humor fell on deaf ears. The driver was focused on maneuvering around orange traffic barriers, and the other passenger, an old farmer with a John

Deere hat and a face as windswept as the land, was preoccupied with what lay ahead.

Three and a half years earlier, I watched the moment of secession broadcast live. That midnight ceremony might have taken place at this same crossing but they all looked the same at night since the entire U.S.-Independence border cut through farmland. It didn't seem as isolated on television with all the media and officials awash in big production lights.

The van stopped in front of the customs station. The driver came around and slid open the door, letting in warm air and the sound of Old Glory popping in the wind. As a U.S. border agent directed us inside, he warned that if we hoped to "come back from that place," we had better have our exit papers.

A shopkeeper's bell above the door rang as we entered. A few moments later, an officer appeared from the back office. Judging by his sleepy eyes, he'd been napping. He took his spot at the counter and nodded to the old man, who humbly bowed his head and carried two bulky suitcases to the counter.

"Where you coming from?" the officer asked.

"Sugar City."

"What business you got in Independence?"

"Goin' to see my daughter's family."

"Where they at?"

"Independence City." The man unfolded his travel permit and smoothed it on the counter.

"Where's your Independence-issued visa?" the officer asked impatiently.

"Don't got one." He nodded toward the east window. "My daughter's waiting right over there."

"If they even let you in, you still need exit papers to get back or you'll be stuck."

"I understand," said the old man. "I got nothin' but my daughter and grandkids."

"Your life," the officer said apathetically and stamped the paper. "Next."

The open resentment toward Independence was jarring to see in person. In the weeks leading up to the historic separation, an enormous amount of animosity was aimed at the new country and its inhabitants. Perhaps it was a manifestation of our collective anguish. Seventeen fraught months ending with the loss of part of our nation were traumatic. Yet a year later, Independence goings-on disappeared from U.S. media. People didn't want to think about it. The U.S.-led blockade, coupled with Independence's own restriction on foreign journalists, made it easier to forget.

When I asked the agent outside if people around there disliked Independence, he muttered something about traitors. We heard this disparagement a million times after the Secession Act passed. It was meant to hurt the soon-to-be Independents. I can now say the insults hit their mark.

The gate clanked shut behind me as I left U.S. soil and the spiraling razor wire shivered atop the twelve-foot fence. I was stuck in No Man's Land momentarily while a young Independence guard fumbled with the padlock. It finally snapped open and dropped onto the asphalt with a thud.

The guard, really just a kid, leaned on his rifle when I asked if he ever spoke to the agents on the other side. His loose army fatigues flapped in the wind. Hand-me-downs from his father or an uncle, perhaps. "Nah. They think they're better than us but they're no different. We come from the same places, made of the same blood and bones. I got family that literally live a half-mile from the border and they won't talk to me and my dad and brother." He spat at the dirt and glared at his counterpart.

Inside the rudimentary Independence Customs building, a large man with a voluminous beard sat at a rectangular folding table. The hospitable welcome I received couldn't have been more different from the chilly reception on the other side. He was elated when I told him I was there to write a magazine piece about the country. He rattled off at least a dozen places I needed to visit.

His mood abruptly shifted when I tapped on the handwritten notice taped to the tabletop: *Visitors are strictly forbidden from engaging in trade activities. This includes buying, importing, or transporting goods for resell.*

"This seems a bit severe," I said.

"Talk to your government about that," he snapped. "Being cut off from the world by a blockade meaner than the Cuban Embargo isn't our doing. Everything up here," he said crankily as he slapped the table.

He unzipped my suitcase and slipped his hands into folded briefs and undershirts. While he searched for contraband, a pickup approached from the east. Men in camouflage and orange hunting attire rode in the back with rifles casually pointed upward. They stopped to visit with the young guard, who appeared to know them.

"What are they hunting?" I asked.

The agent glanced outside. "Illegals. They're volunteer patrol."

"Volunteer?"

"Volunteer," he repeated absently.

I gathered my belongings and walked outside just as the pickup was departing. The young guard stepped back and slapped the sidewall like a horse's flank just before it turned off the road and followed a rutted trail along the border fence.

The nearest U.S. town of La Junta was a distant cluster of trees against the hazy silhouette of the Rockies. Somehow the old man from the shuttle was already long gone but the ride arranged was nowhere in sight. No sign of the vehicle, or anything else for that matter, moving on the straight road. To make matters worse, I didn't have a cell signal and wouldn't for the rest of my stay.

THE BEEF EMPIRE HIGHWAY

By the time a little Chevy Spark showed up an hour later, I was at my wit's end. The driver explained he couldn't find gas. He got his mom to sell him a gallon but he had to walk across town to pick it up.

"How about a gas station?" I asked.

"Oh boy, this is your first time here, ain't it? You got a lot to learn."

We arrived in Las Animas ten minutes after my bus was scheduled to depart. The stop was at a former Loaf 'N Jug. Its store windows were boarded up and gas kiosks removed. Thankfully, my connection, a repainted school bus with a natural gas tank mounted on the roof, was waiting under the canopy.

I found a seat as the driver eased the Bluebird onto the street, mindful of bicycles. The number of Dutch granny bikes with baskets on the road was disorienting. Farmers and migrant worker types sitting upright on Opafiets was a sight unexpected. It was as if I had passed through a blundering time warp.

Of course I was aware of the blockade but not the profound effect it was having. I should have known it was being under-reported in the U.S. This was nothing new. The real-time impact of U.S. aggression and domestic policy has been back-page material for years. However, in this case, the Independence government was complicit in understating the blockade by being so restrictive with foreign journalists.

The bus rocked as it passed over a patch of eroded asphalt. Potholes and washouts were common but the driver seemed to know where they all were. The highway cut through sandy loam spotted with spindly soapweed and clumps of low-lying brush. To the north, a shallow valley with scattered trees and wild green grass split the arid plain.

We frequently left the main road for little towns and farming hamlets. The bus gradually filled up with adults ill-fit for the small seats. I watched two grown men struggle to angle their long legs in the tight space. Being well-mannered, the strangers made small talk but not so much that they came off as too friendly.

"Still feels unnatural not getting in my truck and driving where I want," one said as he stretched a leg into the aisle. "I'll never get used to it."

"Me and my partners feel like we planted enough soy to diesel the whole country for a year."

"I know some folks out in Kiowa County growing two thousand acres of hemp. Next thing you know…."

The two men chuckled and shook their heads.

About fifteen miles east of the former Colorado-Kansas border, we stopped at a cinderblock building with a massive heifer mounted on the flat roof. Across its plastic torso were magnetic letters: THE TRADING POST. Inside, classic country-western tunes played on a transistor radio. Shelves were packed floor-to-ceiling with teapots, cookware, tools, bags of plastic bags, empty medicine bottles, soda bottles, antiquated cooking books, and lots of blankets. There was an abundance of miniature wood carvings of wheat, cattle, crossed pistols and engravings of various secession mottos and epigrams: LIVE FREE OR DIE; THIS LAND IS *OUR* LAND; THE UNITED **STATE** OF AMERICA.

One particular section was given reverential consideration amidst the clutter: THE WALL OF INDEPENDENCE. Its shelves displayed framed photographs from the Flatland Revolution. I recognized the picture of the county courthouse with the banner, CITIZENS RECLAIMING GOVERNMENT, hanging from the second-floor windows. The star of the tribute was Major Krug. He and his fellow National Guardsmen took over the local armory and plowed through police barricades surrounding the courthouse. The last I heard of Krug, he was in Leavenworth Penitentiary.

At the counter, I asked about a map. There were none for sale but the storekeeper rummaged through a cabinet and emerged with a worn roadmap. He unfolded it and stuck a crooked finger on our location in Southwest Kansas. The Independence border was traced in yellow highlighter: the adjoining corners of Colorado and Kansas, the Oklahoma Panhandle, and half the Texas handle. A nation-state the shape of Arkansas with the landmass of Maine. The Beef Empire Highway crossed the northern part of the country. We were at its midpoint.

I walked outside to the edge of a freshly cut field of alfalfa. Haystacks were picturesque against the sky, so vast and opulently blue. Bruce, a man I met on the bus, walked up behind me with a hand-rolled herbal cigarette.

"No one ever thought twice about seeing cut hay until they started piling it into stacks like that," he said. "They don't have fuel to use the balers anymore."

"It's like a painting," I said.

"I see jobs when I look out there."

THE WALDORF OF THE PRAIRIES

Ninety minutes later, the sun set behind abandoned feedlots outside Capitol City. Long rows of empty metal troughs dully reflected the lavender sky. The sight starkly contrasted the highway's namesake: Beef Empire. The name harkened back to pre-secession days when the region's agricultural industry thrived. During the Transition (the period before the border closed), the packing plants shut down and cattle were trucked away. Ranchers who remained in Independence realized prices would plunge so they liquidated their stock. The lingering stench didn't seem to bother anyone besides me.

The straight road and the engine's steady rpm induced a calmness that was broken by a woman up front. "Look what they're doing!" she exclaimed. I ducked down so I could see a billboard that spanned the top of four conjoined feedlot silos. Two people were on the catwalk working on the sign: OUR FREEDOM = SECURE BORDE. They were working on the final R. For a half century, the sign had read EAT BEEF KEEP SLIM. This recent development bothered some and amused others.

Along the way, I had noticed dozens of revised billboards tagged with patriotic slogans and border security messages. Given that Capital City was the nation's political center, it wasn't surprising that the closer we got to town, the more varied and pointed the signs were. OUR NATIONAL RESOURCES BELONG TO US!; CONGRESS **MUST** ACT NOW; WASHINGTON = USA = VOTE GRADY OUT!

I quietly asked Bruce, "Who's Grady?"

"President Washington," he said. "Some people don't like him. They think he's trying to turn the country into a mini-U.S."

"What do you think?"

Bruce looked around, gauging whether he could answer honestly. He shrugged. "It's a tough job," was all he would say.

We passed a desolate stretch of abandoned strip malls and shopping centers but as we drove deeper into town, I could see its heart was still beating. Enormous trees, old homes, and kids playing outside gave the neighborhoods life. Familiar franchises had been repurposed Independence style, like Maria's Café, where the McDonald's sign was repainted with a barber shop swirl.

More than half of the passengers disembarked on Main Street. Like everywhere else I'd been so far, the dearth of cars on the road was conspicuous. The broad four-lane street with angled parking on both sides was like a parched riverbed.

The Hotel Windsor stood out from the ordinary downtown buildings in size and style. It opened a year earlier after being shuttered for decades. I had been looking forward to visiting the hotel since reading about it in an Independence-Kootenai edition of *Architectural Digest*. It didn't disappoint. Arched stone lintels topped long and slender room windows. A limestone cornice and parapet spanned the roof edge. An ornamental tower with a sloped roof and gabled dormers punctuated the hotel's presence on the northeast corner.

A young man in a blue denim vest stepped out to open the door and I stepped into another time. The place emanated century-old authenticity with plank wood flooring and mahogany-framed arched doorways on both sides. Gaslight wall sconces and a crystal chandelier illuminated the narrow lobby. I peered into the room to the left, half-expecting to see men in bowlers and top hats. An elderly couple in white sneakers marred the illusion but the impressive atrium made a stronger impression. On opposite corners, solid wood staircases rose to second and third-floor balconies. Skylights covered the entire length of the gambrel ceiling and the waning twilight created an ambient violet glow.

A lanky bellhop led me to my third-floor room, leaving me before a painting of a Hereford bull that matched the cowhide under my feet. The room was furnished with an antique dresser, armoire, and a walnut four-post bed. A washstand served as décor and a resting place for a boudoir bed doll. When I turned the metal key on the bedside lamp, the mantle burned brightly, casting the room in an orange-yellow glow.

My window looked down on Main Street, where disabled traffic signals hung over the intersection. The road was lit solely by light from the hotel. Nothing but silhouettes existed beyond downtown.

When the Windsor was built in 1889, it was nicknamed the "Waldorf of the Prairies." After it closed in the 1970s, preservation groups saved it from condemnation but couldn't bring in the millions of dollars needed to return the hotel to anything close to its original splendor. Considering the dilapidated state of the Independence economy, the hotel's rehab seemed miraculous.

A group of local entrepreneurs, who came to be known as the Windsor Founders, saw its potential. It was their version of a public works project. The economy was stagnant and the few banks still around weren't lending money. Those with capital were reluctant to part with it. Money needed to move. People needed work. And the nation's capital needed a first-rate hotel.

The government refused to assist the restoration (taxation was heresy). The founders requisitioned the public for investments and donations of any size or shape. Their crews scavenged scrap piles, warehouses, barns, sheds, and abandoned homes for anything that could be reused, repurposed, or reformed. They developed a barter system that grew into its own micro-economy. To offset low wages, the workers earned equity in the hotel. They also received Buffalo Bucks (named for the town's founder, Buffalo Jones) that were used at the trading tent where workers could request items or services they needed—food, clothes, paint, a pot, a plumber, a chair, you name it. It kept a full-time trader and support staff busy six days a week.

This line from the pamphlet in my room doesn't seem the least hyperbolic: "The reconstruction was a spirited testament to the people of Independence and the potential of our new economy."

However, looking through the newspapers from those early days, it was clear not everyone held the project in high regard. To many, it seemed idiotic to waste so much effort restoring a decrepit hotel when the country was coming apart at the seams. Food was scarce and farmers were still struggling to adapt. Utilities and streets were in disrepair. The natural gas infrastructure needed to expand fivefold, but the country lacked the resources to make even a minimal expansion. Some perceived the founders as barons exploiting a depleted population. The hotel was their Sphinx and the people their slaves. For what it's worth, I never heard anyone complain about the hotel while I was in the country.

THE END OF INNOCENCE

Travel fatigue reminded me that this wasn't Kansas anymore. It felt like I had journeyed to another continent. It took five hours to get from San Francisco to Pueblo, three hours to get to La Junta via bus, another hour until I arrived at the border, and from Las Animas, a three-and-a-half-hour bus ride to Capital City. I was fortunate to wake up in time for breakfast.

The hotel was a block from Independence Plaza, where federal and local governments were located, so the restaurant was busy. I sat at the bar, which looked exactly like a framed *New Yorker* cover from 1965 mounted on the back wall: carved dark walnut, mirrors behind glass shelves, bottles on the left and right, glasses in the middle, and a brass foot rail to boot.

When I ordered coffee, the waitress gave me the exact look I got from the desk clerk the night before when I handed him my credit card. It might as well have been a slab of stone. Because of the embargo, coffee was almost as rare. The unofficial national drink was roasted dandelion tea blended with black tea. A touch of cream was enough to trick the palate. It wasn't bad at all.

Breakfast wasn't bad, either. A government woman at the bar told me one thing that improved after secession was the food. "Getting cut off from factories brought out the people who could actually cook. You can't run a restaurant anymore with #10 cans of green beans and processed chicken fingers." What she didn't mention was nine out of ten restaurants closed nationwide and never reopened.

I spent the morning reading the local paper and listening to conversations undulate around me in a dialect formed by the land: words rounded by the winds and sentences that unfolded across vast plains, in no rush to make a point. The *Capital City Gazette* used the thinnest newsprint I'd ever seen: two sheets of standard newsprint folded to make eight pages. The margins were razor thin and every space was utilized with few illustrations and no photographs.

While I was traveling from California, a pivotal story had been developing that made the next day's front pages across the country: the nation's first homicide. It happened on a rural road near Las Agoras, a town two hours south of Capital City. The victim, Daniel Velasquez, started a business after the secession, building greenhouses and various structures with foraged materials. He was working late at a job site fifteen miles away but never made it home. Early the following day, a natural gas technician found him on a dusty farm road.

The story broke on a local radio show that morning. Initially, there wasn't much to report except that a body was found on the side of the road. The victim hadn't been identified, but as the news spread on regional radio, reports suggested he was a U.S. fugitive, an illegal border crosser.

Before I continue, I should explain who the militias were and why they existed. The economy collapsed in Independence within days of the border closing. Like everything else, public services were cut and law enforcement took a big hit. Police and sheriff's departments became skeletons of what they once were. Along with the gas shortage, patrolling rural areas and responding to calls was exceedingly difficult.[1] Rural crime wasn't a major issue, though. At least not until two years later, when a particular New York Times article reached Independence.

The *Times* piece reported on asylum seekers from Central and South America who had been amassing at U.S. border points. These were mostly refugees fleeing persecution and violence. The political climate in the U.S. had shifted so it appeared the country no longer wanted the tired and poor masses yearning to be free. The migrants came anyway. They were desperate. The *NYT* article focused on new hope that had sprung up among those itinerant communities: Independence. This new country carved out of the interior states embodied the noble belief in the freedom to pursue life, liberty, and happiness. Independence, not the old America, was the land of opportunity.

If Independents reading the *Times* article felt pride, a twist quickly spoiled the flattery. Sources told the reporters that U.S. Customs and Border agents were busing asylum seekers directly to Independence from U.S.-Mexico ports of entry. It was also alleged that illegal immigrants caught in the U.S. were being brought secretly to the border.

The reportage caused an uproar in Independence, especially along the southern border around Dalhart, Dumas, and Perryton. Within weeks, volunteer border patrols began forming. It's not surprising that the thought of tens of thousands of refugees coming up from Central America frightened Independents. For one, they distrusted the U.S. They were also worried the influx would strain

---

[1] It was virtually impossible to acquire parts for natural gas converters. Gerry-rigged conversions were outlawed in the first year after a spate of explosions injured many and killed one person.

the country's beleaguered resources. Communities had already suffered critical food shortages.[2]

The militia movement gradually expanded to the interior. Leading up to the Velasquez homicide, rumors were spreading about a significant uptick in rural thefts that were linked to illegal immigrants. Livestock, equipment, and fuel were supposedly the primary targets. This was why local militia leaders were patrolling the area around Las Agoras.

Along with misinformation about Velasquez's identity were allegations that Las Agoras had become a "safe haven for illegals." This infuriated townspeople. Despite their vehement refutation, the characterization stuck, even after the claims about Velasquez being a border crosser were debunked. A murder in their community was already taking its toll. The rhetoric voiced on the radio intensified the anguish, confusion, and anger.

I contacted the *Gazette* editor, who got me in touch with Juan Diego Morales, one of the journalists covering the Las Agoras events. Pre-Independence, he covered regional secession uprisings for the *Topeka Journal*. Since the nation's inception, he had been freelancing for the *Gazette* while running a biweekly paper called *The Weekly Independent*.

After he returned from Las Agoras, we met at a little bar near the Plaza called Zapata's. Smooth skin and round wire glasses gave him a youthful appearance that belied his age. Morales spoke with a slight accent but his elocution was clear. He was born in Michoacán and moved to Kansas when he was nine years old to be with his father, who worked at a nearby slaughterhouse. The plan was for his mother and three sisters to join them. After the post-

---

[2] The first winter was especially hard for Independents. They were unprepared for the self-subsistence needed to feed themselves since no food was imported. I heard many stories about suffering, malnutrition, and even starvation. International organizations started flying in food shipments the following spring.

NAFTA surge of illegal immigration, the border had become militarized and immigration was a frustrating morass.

It had been four days since Daniel Velasquez's murder. Town leaders had demanded a public apology from those who claimed he was a non-citizen. In a radio interview, a county militia leader said that was unwarranted since the circumstances around the homicide looked like a "mercenary execution." He declared, "This is no longer a border crisis. It's a national crisis."

Armed squads in pickup trucks cruised through town. These were clearly acts of intimidation. Having learned Las Agoras was overwhelmingly Latino and the surrounding county was primarily white, I asked Morales if he thought it was racially motivated. Surprisingly he said no. He believed a rural-urban divide over the fear of criminals migrating from Mexico and Central America was the root of the contentiousness.

"When volunteers first mobilized at the border, they wanted to stop U.S. criminals who were fleeing the authorities.[3] But it didn't take long before we realized most of the border crossers weren't criminals. If they were coming from outside the U.S. illegally, then yes, they were technically fugitives. But mostly they were refugees escaping bad situations in their home countries or they were coming because they already had family here."

Ever since the *New York Times* article hit Independence, militia recruiters had been spreading the message about waves of fugitives pouring through the border. Talk radio hosts took up the cause early on and joined them in their anger toward anyone and everyone who didn't stand against the insurgence. Morales thought this emotional rhetoric created the rural-urban divide in the South. They *insisted* the border crossers *must* be feared. "You can't listen to

---

[3] Countering the kneejerk reaction to the *NYT* story were those who insisted it was a moral and Independent duty to welcome anyone wanting to participate in their "democratic experiment." The compromise was that fugitives of the law would be prohibited from entering the country.

the radio for more than an hour down there without hearing it mentioned," he told me.

"People who live out in the countryside are afraid of criminals breaking into their homes and taking them hostage, or worse."

"Because...?"

"For safe houses," Morales answered. "The idea is they're going to break into your house, hold you and your wife hostage, and force you to keep up the appearance that everything is okay so they can hide their people there. This has never happened but the rumor started with a grain of truth. About a year ago, a militia group discovered immigrant families living in an empty farmhouse close to the border.

"Radio hosts talked about it nonstop, day and night. Instead of instead of considering why the families came to Independence in the first place, the radio hosts made it appear they committed a horrible crime. They speculated nonstop about hypotheticals involving terrible criminals breaking into rural homes in the middle of the night."

Morales said it was hard to blame farmers for being afraid of food and fuel theft. Biodiesel production was an integral part of farming. Even those who primarily used workhorses, mules, or oxen still needed to get their product to town. The farmers lacked police protection and listening to the radio reinforced their fears all day and all night.

"When you were young, did you experience hostility for being an immigrant?" I asked. That was a time of transformation. Large-scale slaughterhouses brought tens of thousands of immigrants from Mexico, Central America, Southeast Asia, and cities like Houston and L.A. Before that, the region had been racially homogenous for as long as anyone could remember.

"No," Morales said with a note of exasperation that suggested he had tired of discussing this long ago. But after a contemplative pause, he admitted the racial makeup of Las Agoras had shifted dramatically, and more than once. He also suggested there may have been some racial friction during the Flatland Revolution. For the moment, this was all he would say.

I needed to travel down there to see for myself what was happening.

IN COLD BLOOD

I spent the first couple days exploring Capital City and talking to as many people as possible. I was eager to get down to Las Agoras, though. The Independence Arrow bus came through three times a week so getting there wasn't a problem. I needed cash, but for that, I needed a wire transfer, which had to be authorized by the State Department.

Their offices were on the second floor of the Federal Building. I paused in the hallway to look at photos of Independence dignitaries posing with foreign officials from China, Mexico, and Venezuela. China was one of the few economic powers still willing to deal with Independence. Mexico hosted early negotiations to run an oil pipeline through Texas but the embargo shut it down. Venezuela was involved in the project talks. They had donated desperately needed agricultural supplies to Independence, including non-sterile seeds. Their own political crises eventually stunted trade possibilities.

After I filled out an application, the secretary led me to a tiny office where a tall man with red hair parted down the middle sat behind a metal desk. He stood and introduced himself as Jon

Becker, Assistant Director of Consular Affairs. "Tell me about what you're writing," he said as he looked over my application.

"The state of Independence." I hoped this would be enough but he waited for me to elaborate. It made me nervous. I exhaled forcefully, as though he had asked me to describe my life purpose.

"'The Spirit of Independence,'" he read from my press visa application on his desk.

"The working title," I said. "I'm here to learn about the people. Who is Independence?"

"I know you wrote a ton about the movements for *The Atlantic*." He counted on his fingers, "The Panhandle Revolution, California, Texas, Utah, Florida, Staten Island, the U.P., Quebec, British Columbia, Victoria...."

"Spain, Ireland, Taiwan, Hong Kong," I added. Most Americans stopped paying attention once the independence movement left its shores.

"Now you're putting it all together," he said. "That's why you're here?"

"Yeah, sort of," I answered. "I'm working on a book."

"What would you say was the common denominator in all the movements?"

"Self-determination," I answered without hesitation. "The fundamental principle was the same everywhere. People wanted control of their own governance because they felt their government didn't represent or care about them."

"That much is obvious," Becker said with a smile. "But what was *really* going on? I ask because in one of your articles, you said the true source of secessionism was here inside of us." He tapped his chest.

I wrote something like that in one of my last pieces for the magazine. What I meant and what I told the consulate was the real reason we desire self-determination is because we're not in control of our own destiny. That anxiety permeates our lives. For separatists, it manifested as anti-government.

"Then what does that say about us Independents?" he asked.

"That's what I'm here to learn. This is what secessionists everywhere wanted."

Becker sat bolt upright. "Hold up." He leaned forward in earnest. "We didn't ask to be cut off from the rest of the world or burdened with crushing debt. We didn't ask to be deprived of light bulbs, books, car parts, furniture, freon, clothing, pens, pencils, computers, electronics, lumber, toilets, fans, eyeglasses, medicine, doorknobs, clocks, phones, batteries, blankets, beer, cigarettes, tractors, oil, groceries—"

"Secessionists demanded a separate state and received Independence and Kootenai," I said. "They had the opportunity to move here. But would it have mattered? Does the anxiety of not being in control go away after secession? I'm guessing the secessionists knew this intuitively or else this would be the most populous region on the Great Plains."

Becker leaned back, crossed his arms, and looked at me. "You familiar with Truman Capote's writing?"

"Very much so."

"Then you know this is where...."

"Of course," I said. "I saw the *New Yorker* cover in the Windsor lounge. September 1965."

"Yep." He slapped his leg, suddenly coming to a decision. "Even though the U.S. granted you a special passport, they won't authorize a wire transfer. They don't want cash coming in here. Most of the transfers we do are through Kuwait or Turkey. It's a bit of a process. Come back, say, four o'clock. How's that sound? Don't worry, I'll take care of this." He gripped my hand and looked me in the eye in a way that assured me he meant what he said.

35

I returned at the appointed hour. The secretary telephoned Mr. Becker. A few minutes later, he came out with his suit blazer half-on. "Come with me," he said. He switched his briefcase to his other hand and slipped his arm into the loose sleeve. "I want to show you something."

We walked through the Plaza to Presidential Hall, which used to be the county courthouse. Under the soffit of the regal neoclassical building, PRESIDENT OF INDEPENDENCE was set with charred wood. Interspersed gray and buff stones lay horizontally across the marble-smooth façade and in pilasters. Dark steel-framed windows reflected the deepest hues of the blue sky.[4] On the front lawn was a statue of Buffalo Jones, the town's founder. He wore a wide-brimmed cavalry hat and cords strung crosswise on his chest. He was removing his gloves mid-stride as he looking out with a satisfied grin, apparently unfazed by the state of his town and country.

After showing Becker his credentials to security, Becker led me up a bifurcated marble staircase to the second floor. In the north wing was an unmarked door. He opened it gently, even reverently, and entered a courtroom. It was lit by tall windows along the outer wall. The judge's bench, witness stand, clerk and counsel tables, swivel chairs in the jury box, and gallery pews had been left intact.

"Am I on trial for something?" I asked.

I couldn't see Becker's reaction as he opened the gate to the courtroom well. He approached the bench and turned to face the gallery where I stood. From his briefcase, he removed a tattered hardcover book. "A lot has changed since this was written." He held it up so I could read the title: *In Cold Blood.*

---

[4] I'm not sure what this says about the nation, but the courts—municipal, district, and federal—were relocated under one leaky roof: a schoolhouse that was condemned decades ago but escaped demolition when it was listed on the historical registry.

"'An unspeakable crime in the heartland.' Happened six miles west of here. The killers came at night and were gone by the morning. A nightmare of the severest degree. It shook this entire region to the core. This is where the trial took place." He walked to the defendants' table. "Perry Smith sat here. Dick Hickock here. Some people have disagreed with the way Capote told the story and some things he wrote, but like it or not, he played an important role by giving life and complexity to the Clutters and the community. I've read this probably twenty times. A few folks over in the Sheriff's Department might know more of the trivial details of the case but few appreciate more the emotional impact it had here. It's part of who we are. I genuinely believe it scarred our psyche. It's no wonder rural folks are spooked these days.

"Some say we lost our innocence in November of '59. What are we going to lose this time if things get worse? Our trust? Our community? Roman, we need you to write about us so we don't forget, just like we needed Truman Capote. We can't lose our faith in one another. But if we do, if things don't go so well, we need to be able to look back to see the how and why. Will you do that?"

"Of course," I answered, although I wasn't certain what was being asked of me. "Six miles, you said? I should go have a look."

"Now listen here," Becker said in a scolding tone. "Leave that be. There are still people around who harbor animosity toward the author. It would be best if you were careful in general. You're not from here, and like Capote, some may hold that against you, especially if you get too personal. People don't want to be turned inside out." He checked his watch. "You're staying at the Windsor, aren't you? It's a great place but you need to move to Wheat Lands. That's where Truman stayed. I called the manager and arranged for them to get the room ready for you."

"Can I ask you something? Between you and me, is there something going on?" Becker looked confused by the question. "I mean, are things worse than they appear?"

"How do things appear to you?"

"Las Agoras, the border, the militias…."

"There you go."

WHEAT LANDS MOTEL

I was perfectly happy at the Windsor but I felt that Jon Becker's suggestion was more for him than for me. I would've hated to let him down if I needed his help again. My new lodging was a mile east of downtown.

Pulling my rolling suitcase with one hand and my laptop bag slung over the other shoulder, I walked down a broad avenue of empty parking lots, barren dealerships, desolate lumberyards, and closed auto shops. The emptiness pricked at me, as though I'd missed the boat out of the apocalypse. On one office window, the lettering had been scraped off but I could make out U.S. ARMY RESERVE in the glue residue. The only piece of furniture left was a green vinyl chair with a torn seat. A copy of the *U.S. News & World Report* was splayed open on the floor.

HEATED POOL • REFRIGERATED • FREE TV • RESTAURANT — Wheat Lands may have been the real deal back in the sixties but it lost its allure over the decades. The pool was empty and the disassembled slide lay inside the fence. Like most places in town, the motel had a spacious lot with generous parking but there were only two cars and one of those had four flat tires.

The manager was expecting me. Don was his name. He was a squat man, around sixty years old, with an overgrown combover that reached past his opposite ear and was too wispy to cover his bald dome. At a snail's pace, he led me past a row of unoccupied rooms. I couldn't tell if it was because he was gimpy or just wanted to chat.

"Business has been down since the Windsor opened," he said. "Plus, people don't have the means to travel anymore, and when they do, they find alternative lodging. You can rent a room in someone's home for twenty dollars. How am I supposed to compete with that? Good thing there are still folks like you who appreciate their own space and the amenities of a decent motel."

He unlocked a door and pulled back the window curtains. It was a basic room with cheap mid-century furniture.

"This is where Truman Capote stayed?" I asked.

"That's what they say."

"Is this the desk he used?"

"Oh, sure," he said unconvincingly as he scratched his neck.

"Is there a restaurant here?"

"CJ's Saloon is just down the street. That's where we send everyone. Kids are welcome too. There's a Vietnamese place about four blocks that way," pointing downtown. "Chuck Wagon on Independence Avenue is real good but it's a ways away. You don't have transportation, do you? Tell you what, I'm gonna sweeten the deal. This is a limited-time offer. With this room, or any room for that matter, you get free use of a bicycle. They aren't easy to come by."

A few minutes later, he rolled a ten-speed bicycle out to the parking lot. It was rigged with a square wire basket in front and a rectangular basket behind. The shifting levers were mounted on the down tube. It looked as though rusty spots had been painted with an enamel finish glossier than the rest of the bike. He handed me a heavy chain and padlock.

"Make sure you lock it up in plain sight, and whatever you do, don't leave it out at night. These are in high demand."

The gears were tight and the brakes squealed but it worked. I circled the parking lot a few times before riding into the street.

"Okay, see you later then," Don yelled when he realized I wasn't returning.

The outskirts of town were only a few minutes away, where I turned onto a northbound road. At Independence Avenue, I coasted through an empty intersection with dead stoplights swaying in the wind. It was like an emptied floodplain with abandoned office buildings and big-box stores with barren lots spotted with weeds. Closed restaurant franchises still smelled of charbroiled meat. At the highway overpass, I peddled up the ramp. It felt strange being alone on a highway on a bicycle. The only sound was the wind in my ears and the tires on asphalt.

JOIN THE FREE MAN'S BATTALION
OUR INDEPENDENCE IS UNDER ATTACK
✓FIGHT FOR YOUR COUNTRY!
✓FIGHT FOR FREEDOM!
SATURDAY AT FINNUP PARK CANNON MEMORIAL

These announcements were popping up around town so I postponed my southern trip. Free Man's Battalion was a local militia. Although the interior counties had militias, they weren't as robust as the border groups. The Las Agoras situation was intensifying interest. Recruiting rallies were happening everywhere.

On the morning of the rally, I rode toward the park on a street with big gangly trees draped over yards barren of grass. Cracks sealed with tar interlaced the streets like varicose veins. I imagined the neighborhood having a name like Old Town, where folks passed the time on the front porch chewing the fat and partaking of sweet tobacco.

After passing under a limestone archway, the road narrowed and curved through the park. Near the entrance at the adjacent corner were several hundred people, mostly men, already gathered around a World War I cannon. Beyond the park was the ochre-hued prairie with its smattering of unimpressive trees. Further south was a preserve where descendants of Buffalo Jones's original herd still lived.[5]

At 11AM sharp, a man in a trucker's cap, plaid shirt, and cowboy boots climbed onto the cannon carriage. "Who wants to know about the Free Man's Battalion?" he shouted. People stopped talking and turned to listen. "My name's Bud Keller and I'm one of the founders. The Free Man's Battalion is an organization of citizen

---

[5] Three years earlier, there had been a campaign to free the buffalo (*O give me a home where the buffalo roam....*). The movement abruptly ended when two men killed a bull for its meat.

soldiers formed by people born and raised here, whose families go back generations, who love this land, who farm this land, who believe in its people. We didn't secede from the most powerful country ever to get our rear ends kicked and chased away."

About a dozen men behind the cannon were part of his so-called battalion. They looked on without emotion, as if they already knew what he had to say. Judging by their hardened, deadpan faces, his message wouldn't be for the faint of heart. One of those men, with long stringy hair under his trucker's cap, made eye contact with me as he scanned the crowd. Out of the corner of my eye I saw him lean forward and spit tobacco juice in the grass as he grimaced at no one in particular.

"I'm sure you've all heard what's happening down south. It isn't just a border crisis anymore. It's spreading north and coming this way. The murder down by Agoras, we don't know exactly what happened. We do know their county militia mobilized a month ago because there'd been reports of strange figures roaming the countryside at night.

"Uninvited illegals have been coming in from the U.S. since the Transition. They've been coming from places in Mexico and Central America already gutted by drug lords and gangs. Towns where police have been driven away, leaders assassinated, and businesses destroyed. You thought they were coming here to *escape* that, right? Well, now we know they're coming here to do exactly what they did down there. They're coming to claim Independence as their own. We're not talking about an invasion to take over our jobs and schools. Their mission is to bring their reign of terror here."

This sent a tremor through the crowd. In its wake, dozens of agitated discussions forced Keller to yell over the chatter.

"They're bringing drugs and amassing money and weapons. They're coming, people, and our border patrol can't stop 'em. No one's coming to save our rear ends. It's up to us."

Many in the crowd were ready to sign up then and there, no questions asked. From his back pocket, Keller unfolded a sheet of notebook paper from which he read at least a dozen instances in which border crossers had been apprehended and extradited to the U.S. Some charges were genuinely grievous, e.g., murder, rape, and armed robbery.

Juan Diego Morales had told me militia leaders made sure a bright spotlight was cast upon those incidents. The Southern radio media was more than happy to oblige them. Keller was using their playbook.

"Is there anyone here who's okay with them coming in and taking over your land, your wives, your kids, your country? Anybody okay with that? If you are, raise your hand so we can see who you are." Of course no one raised his hand. "We need to mobilize fast. We've got to be ready. If we wait too long, it'll be too late. Our backs'll be broken. I got three girls and two boys at home. When I think of what'll happen to them if I do nothing…I swear to you right now—" The thought choked him up. "I swear to everyone here that I'll do everything in my power to stop them before they get to my family and yours. So tell me, what are we gonna do?"

The crowd was silent. The sound of the wind blowing across the prairie was pronounced. I realized for the first time how quiet the town was. There were few cars and trucks, no lawnmowers, and none of the industrial rumblings of a typical municipality.

"I said, what are we gonna do about it?" This time, he looked right at me. "How about you?"

"Uh, me?" I asked as I looked around.

Thankfully someone shouted, "We gonna fight," and shifted his attention away from me.

"That's right, we're gonna fight if we're gonna survive," Bud yelled. "I am a survivor! I will fight for our land, fight for my family, fight for our freedom!"

He jumped down from the cannon and his fellow militiamen stepped forward with clipboards. The man with the stringy hair troweled the chaw from his cheek and flung it on the ground. He raised the same hand above his head and beckoned new volunteers to him.

Bud Keller spoke for fifteen minutes. That was all it took to convince at least a hundred men and a few women to sign up. As they clustered around the militiamen, I could see the confidence that comes from the security of camaraderie. But many people were still grappling with the vague allegations, including most of the Latinos present. They were well-represented but not in proportion to the town's population. Throughout the spiel, they looked to see how others were receiving the pitch.

"What are the requirements to join?" A Latino man asked Keller and then crossed his arms as if expecting an answer he couldn't accept.

Keller neutralized his distrust. "Be of able mind and body and be prepared to fight."

"Why would we be hearing it from these guys first instead of our own government or even a newspaper?" I heard several times as I walked around, listening in on conversations.

"What's a militia supposed to do?" a short, roundish man whined. "This isn't the 1700s! We need professionals."

"What about Al-Qaeda?" I asked him. "They basically started as a militia, right? They've left their mark on modern history. The Bolsheviks started with workers' militias."

"Al-Qaeda!" the roundish man rasped. "They're terrorists! It's not even close to the same thing!"

Close by, a solid and stocky young man with a broad face and squinty eyes overheard what I said and turned from his buddies to glare at me. He looked like he could lift a full-sized cow. He adjusted his cowboy hat and spat on his boot. "What are you trying to say?" he asked as he stepped closer.

"I'm only saying militia doesn't mean farmers with muskets and pitchforks."

A skinny man with a fluffy beard and bulging eyes nodded eagerly in agreement. "It'd be better if they called themselves something other than a militia," he said. "But the main principles of fighting haven't changed since Cain killed Abel. You fight according to the world you live in. This is our world, intruded upon by Mexican cartels."

"Who said anything about cartels?" the roundish man asked.

"He did!" the skinny man said, pointing back toward the cannon.

They briefly debated whether Keller specifically referred to drug cartels. It was the most surprising and possibly most contentious point made to date in the years-long refugee-fugitive debate. Although we didn't realize it, that message was spreading across the entire country.

A man passing by interrupted the discussion. "They want us to drive all the way past Plymell!" he exclaimed. "Do they expect us to travel all over the country on hamburger drippings?"

"You can't have a modern army in this world without oil," the roundish man said matter-of-factly.

The bullish young cowboy was still glaring at me. I nodded peaceably, hoping to pacify him. It had the opposite effect. I thought it best to get out of his line of sight, but as I slipped away, he called after me.

"Hey you, Al-Qaeda man," he said in a booming voice that halted all nearby conversations. "Why didn't you answer when he asked if you were gonna fight?"

"I didn't know who he was talking to," I said, exaggerating my innocence.

45

"You think your smart-ass Al-Qaeda jokes are funny?"

"It wasn't a joke."

"No one's laughing."

My bicycle was leaning against a brick barbecue pit about twenty feet away. A gut feeling told me I should get on it and go. The man followed with his two buddies in tow. I'd been in uncomfortable situations before. I attended a county commission meeting in Yreka, California, where they were debating whether to join other counties in the region that hoped to collectively become the new nation of Jefferson. Mid-meeting, an anti-secession mob stormed in, overturning tables and throwing chairs. I was pulled into a brawl as it spilled into the hallway but I escaped mostly unscathed. The confrontation with this cowboy was the first time the threat of violence had ever been pointed at me.

"Is this what you do?" he asked, sneering at my bike. "Ride around with your faggot baskets, staying stupid shit?"

"I didn't mean to offend you, man."

As I mounted the bike, he grabbed the handlebar joint with his brawny arm. "Where do you think you're going?" He turned to the crowd, "People, we have here an Al-Qaeda sympathizer! You like terrorists?" he asked me. "Are you a terrorist?"

"I'm a journalist," I said with as much poise as I could muster. "Will you please let go of my bike."

"A journalist!" he scoffed. "Where from?"

I had the feeling my answer wouldn't go over well but I had nothing better to offer. "California."

"California!" He looked like he stepped on a live wire. I might as well have said I came from the caves of Afghanistan. His eyes bulged and his jaw quivered. He looked at his friends and people around us with utter confoundment.

"Clint!" A man wearing a suede blazer with a Western yoke came toward us. His clear voice and dapper appearance gave me a glimmer of hope. "What is going on here?" he asked the young man in an admonishing tone.

"This guy's been making fun of our militias, talking about how great Al-Qaeda is. He got asked what he was gonna do about the Mexicans and he just stood there. Didn't say a thing. He's not even from here. He's from California!"

"He didn't call anyone here Al-Qaeda," the short, roundish man said. "Take it easy."

"And who cares if he's from California!" the man in the blazer exclaimed.

"Call us Al-Qaeda again, you fucking faggot."

He jabbed me in the chest with his index finger. It was enough to knock me off balance. Gripping the bicycle handles, I tried to catch myself but my shoulders swayed too far. My hips followed so I let go of the bike but then stepped on a tire, which caused me to topple backward. A bolt of pain shot through my lower back as I landed on the pedal. I ended up on the rear tire with one arm over the basket.

"Get off the ground, bitch!"

A stranger came forward and offered his hand. Others came to help me off the ground.

"Come on, you fucking coward!"

"Clint!" the man in the blazer barked. "Calm down."

"Who you calling Al-Qaeda now?" Clint taunted.

"You're the only terrorist I see around here," I said through clenched teeth. Not the wisest thing to say, I admit. It must have been the blinding pain.

Clint's face enlarged and his neck veins bulged as he charged into the men who stood between us. The barricade stumbled back and I nearly fell over the bike again. Again he tried to plow through but the men held the line against the maddened earthshaker.

Bud Keller plowed through the crowd with a stalwart partner. "That's enough," he shouted. "Save it for the real enemy."

"We got the real enemy right there." Clint pointed over the human blockade.

Keller gave me a quick once-over. "What's your name, sir?"

"It's Roman Wolfe," I replied as I rubbed the throbbing spot on my back.

"Does he sound foreign to you?" he asked Clint. "Does he look Mexican? We can't pick each other apart. That's exactly what the enemy wants."

A woman picked my bike up and tilted her head toward the street. I gleaned her suggestion and walked away.

"Next time I see you," Clint yelled, "I'm gonna shit in your mouth."

"Oh, come on," an onlooker said with disgust.

I was planning to sign up for the Free Man's Battalion to learn more but by this point I just wanted to get away. A part of me wanted to fight back but I knew I wouldn't stand a chance against the raging cowboy. Without knowing or caring why, he'd probably die before he backed down to reason.

At the park entrance, a man with a wild reddish-gray beard was facing the oncoming foot traffic. "We need to talk about what's happening," he declared. When I was sure the cowboy hadn't followed me out, I moved out of the way to listen to the man. "We need clarity and thoughtfulness. Militarizing ourselves is not the answer." He cupped his hands to his mouth and swiveled back and forth. "If you truly care about freedom and justice, then you understand that hunting people down like savage animals isn't the way forward. Please attend our emergency community meeting tonight at 7PM at the American Legion. It's important to discuss what's going on before paranoia tears us apart."

"Are you a Legionnaire?" a gravelly voice demanded.

"We're just using the space," the red beard answered and continued speaking to the crowd. "Congress and Presidential Hall is allowing this to—"

Another man with a Rasputin beard stepped forward and interrupted. "Who gave you permission to use the Legion?"

"The custodian."

"That's Legion property," stated the owner of the gravelly voice.

"No, in fact, it's not."

"You're saying the Legion isn't Legion property?"

"The American Legion is a U.S. organization and that building is owned by a rancher who lives seventy miles away."

"I've been a Legionnaire for thirty-five years," the Rasputin man snapped. "Don't tell me who runs it."

"It's obviously not that important if you're just finding this out," said the red beard.

Agonistic yipping and growling and teeth bared in thick manes impressed that in this nation of unshaven men, the size of one's beard represented strength and masculinity. Recalling the clean-shaven cowboy flew in the face of this notion. I left before he showed up.

MEXICANS OR MYTHS

The Legion building's Art Deco façade didn't match other architecture or color palettes around town, although the sandstone bricks, with their light brown and powder blue ornamental masonry, evoked the land and sky of the High Plains. The building occupied the corner of an otherwise empty triangular lot. Presidential Hall was on the adjacent corner and would be the target of the organizers' ire.

Hundreds of people were already packed inside when I arrived. At the back was a low stage where a few people were fiddling with the PA system. They eventually gave up and took the microphone stand away. The red-bearded man I'd seen outside the rally remained on stage with a well-groomed silver-bearded man with matching hair combed straight back. The latter gentleman began the meeting.

"I hope everyone can hear okay. My name is Carey Dobbs. I served three terms on the city council before the secession. And this is Todd Leiker. Before secession, he taught political science at the community college."

A woman in the audience shouted at Dobbs, "You're the one who voted against independence."

"City council never voted for or against it," Dobbs responded.

"You voted against tax abatement."

"You mean to stop paying taxes and lose public funding? No, we didn't vote on that either."

"That's as good as a vote against secession!"

His partner intervened. "You can't challenge the loyalty of anyone who's here. He could've left just like you could have. He stayed, you stayed, we all stayed. We didn't come here to measure our commitment. We're here right now because we need to talk about what's happening in our county and country."

Leiker was imposing with his size, big beard, fiery eyes, and booming voice. He reminded me of the famous painting of the abolitionist John Brown, in which he's standing with arms outstretched, a rifle in one hand, a bible in the other, and a tornado stirring up the Kansas prairie behind him.

The early interruption set the tone for the rest of the night. From the get-go, a combative minority opposed Dobbs and Leiker. It seemed more like a debate between adversaries than the community discussion organizers had in mind.

The agenda revolved around the militias and their motivations. To say Dobbs and Leiker were concerned about the militia movement is an understatement. Throughout the meeting, they referred to the "militarization of Independence." They saw the county militias as reckless, untrained, and unbound by law. According to Dobbs, there had been multiple reports of militia-led roadblocks used to search vehicles and riders against their will.

"Control and domination define these groups. It's their nature," Leiker lectured. "Right now, they're autonomous but united by a common cause. When the current threat—regardless if it's real or not—is no longer relevant, do you suppose they'll just disband and let go of their collective power? Only if they lose the battle against truth. Another likely possibility is they will unite as a hierarchical organization. It would create an army independent of our government."

"As it should be!" a woman shouted. "Power to the People!" The vocal minority repeated this sentiment.

"Our government is the people's government!" Leiker responded and reiterated this until he was blue in the face. "Government of the People for the People. This is what's supposed to define this nation. It's the purpose of secession. Hopefully you can understand that government is not nefarious by nature, as so many have been conditioned."

"It's the managing structure," Dobbs added.

The naysayers disagreed. Leiker attempted to establish common ground. He believed—and this angered him more than anything else—that Congress and Presidential Hall were to blame for what was happening in the country. "They have the power to oversee these militias and stop the roadblocks but they don't. They let it persist because they want discord and to deflect attention away from how bad things are here and how little they've done. The administration's total lack of transparency and communication shows they don't give a damn about you and me."

He had to shout to be heard over the opposition. The vehemence of the vocal minority was noteworthy. They were possessed by outrage so forceful that it put their opponents on their heels. Even Dobbs, who appeared innately patient and tolerant of opposing viewpoints, grew visibly flustered as the dissenters rallied behind the Free Man's Battalion's allegations of a criminal incursion. Some took it further, saying it would soon amount to a full-blown foreign invasion.

An old man with deep wrinkles was helped onto the stage. Unsteady for a moment, he glared at Leiker and Dobbs before scolding them in a strained voice. "It's not right to stand up here and attack the president. We should all be working together. This'll be Vietnam all over again if it turns into an in-fight. We need to come together and do something about the Mexicans."

"The Mexicans?" a Latino man near the stage asked. "Like me?"

"The Mexicans from Mexico."

"My eighty-year-old mother is from Mexico. What you got against her?"

"You know what I mean," the old man moaned.

"The gangs, asshole!" someone shouted.

From the back corner, someone yelled, "The Black Hand." People turned to the speaker but he said nothing more.

A young woman sprung onto the stage after the old fellow was helped off. "I've been hearing a lot about how Mexican immigrants came up to steal people's jobs and take over their towns. My grandpa came here thirty years ago to work in the slaughterhouse doing a job no one else wanted. Because of him and people like him, places like this prospered." With emotion quivering her voice, she asked, "How can you be so disrespectful of people in your own community who've given so much and sacrificed so much? Look around you. We make up half the population of Independence. Half!"

"This isn't about good-intending citizens," a man in the front said. "It's about those coming here to hurt our country."

"Then call them the enemy," the young woman replied. "Call them evildoers. Call them anything you want but don't throw us under the bus."

Dobbs tried to re-center the focus on Congress and Presidential Hall. "They gave the gas companies our most abundant, most critical resource. They didn't have to do that. The natural gas belonged to us, the people." His opponents heckled him mercilessly for this. "Yeah, yeah, yeah, call me a socialist or what-have-you but we chose to be Independents so that we could live in an equitable society. The fact of the matter is natural gas is the foundation of our security."

From the back, a man again shouted, "The Black Hand," but no one seemed to notice or care. I meant to ask someone what this meant but I quickly forgot about it until the name resurfaced much later.

The meeting began descending into mayhem. The naysayers were growing angrier and more turbulent by the minute. They jeered at Dobbs while their opponents in the crowd fired back at them with equal ferocity. Todd Leiker was shouting over everyone. "We were used to being inconsequential, and those in power decided everything behind closed doors. Now it's happening here! Right here!" Dobbs was lecturing in his even-tempered manner but there was desperation in his eyes and beads of sweat on his forehead. "A handful of individuals were given our greatest resource."

A man nearby began yelling excitedly at me, even though we hadn't spoken up to this point. "Washington promised us gas!

That's all he talked about during his campaign. The stupid pipeline fell through and he ain't done nothing about it since."

But this wasn't what Dobbs was talking about. He was referring to natural gas properties and rights handed over to private companies during the first days of Independence. Those companies took over the payments to the U.S. that were negotiated during the Transition. Industry insiders then worked with the administration and Congress to create legislation that gave them the power to determine the market value of natural gas.

The consumer cost of gas and electricity (from gas-powered plants) was less than pre-secession but relative to income, it was exorbitant. Many residents created their own closed cooking and/or electrical systems using homemade fuel, natural gas tanks, or solar for the lucky few.

Congress's answer to criticism was to hold a public hearing addressing the gas industry's lack of transparency about the prices they were charging. Gas executives broke down operational and delivery costs and pointed out that they took on a burdensome loan when they received the properties and rights. In the end, nothing substantial changed. Rates dropped slightly and companies agreed to explore "municipal energy alternatives." No one could tell me with certainty what this meant.

Independents accepted their lot and carried on as usual. Dobbs and many others never forgave the Washington administration. At every opportunity, they reminded people of what they considered the government's original sin but I don't believe they intended it to be part of this discussion at the Legion.

The failed pipeline and fuel shortage were also beside the point but once people got going, the emotional intensity in the room ramped up. There were moments when I thought we were barreling toward a violent clash. Even attendees who weren't visibly engaged in the rumpus looked on with rapt attention, their expressions fraught with past anger, humiliation, and suffering.

It had been over three years since talks to build an oil pipeline (with natural gas flowing in the opposite direction) from Mexico fell through. Solutions to the fuel problem were bandied about but nothing came to fruition. "They've always got a new idea, a new plan, but nothing ever happens," one lady told me. "It's a sad thing."[6]

Much of what I witnessed that night was almost certainly frustration from years of bitter struggles and broken promises. The militia supporters, who made up the vocal minority, pushed back against blame aimed at President Washington for his perceived fuel failures. They were as hot-blooded and forceful in their defense of the president as Leiker and his allies were in condemning him.

Later on I spoke with some agitators outside to see how they viewed the country's inability to set up a comprehensive fuel system. "We're as frustrated about it as anybody. But blaming the president and the people working their butts off to figure it out is just plain idiotic." This was said with more exasperation than contempt. He looked over at a group of Leiker-Dobbs allies. "They've been breathing too much homemade gas fumes."

The others in the circle nodded in agreement, except for one man with a peculiarly expressive grin. He looked like he might burst into laughter at any moment. He was one of those people for whom the world's a stage…in a comedy club. I've sometimes wondered if they know more than the rest of us. He laughed and said to his friend, "Lance, you were so mad back then you would've thrown your boots at Washington if you had the chance."

---

[6] The most promising proposal was the Farmers Fuel Independence initiative. In theory, it would have established large-scale feedstock production and created ethanol and biodiesel facilities in every county. It never got off the ground. Farmers were skeptical from the outset. They worried the end product wouldn't be worth the time and effort.

"I was just frustrated!" his friend snapped. "It's different from what they were saying in there. They're taking the insurgents' side over our own!"

During the meeting, the militia supporters spoke of the incursion with dread and urgency. I seemed that many of them had seen it firsthand. But among those I spoke with afterward, none had witnessed anything compelling. It was mostly hearsay. And the secondhand accounts were dubious at best.

"I was down in Texhoma, visiting family," one man told me. "They'd been saying for a long time that more and more of 'em are coming up. The sheriff, it's just him. He can't do anything alone. He needs the militia."

"Seeing who more and more?" I asked.

"The Mexicans!" the man exclaimed irritably.

"And you believe they're criminals?"

"It's so obvious. They stick out, wearing their tank-top undershirts and baggy pants and bandanas on their heads."

A Latino man standing nearby chimed in with exaggerated disbelief. "Bandanas! Like John Wayne?"

"Oh! People up here don't get it!"

The constant references to "the Mexicans" undermined Juan Diego Morales's belief that tension around militia activity had no racial bias. Later he would admit he was wrong but by then it was glaringly obvious. Morales knew Independence intimately but he was in denial or naively unaware. It's possible the bias and vilification had been sequestered behind closed doors and ever-present predilections were lying dormant, ready to be awoken by the right signals.

DISAPPEARING CITIZENS

The southbound Independence Arrow was scheduled to depart at noon on Saturday. I walked downtown to have brunch at the Windsor beforehand. All the talk at the bar was about a gathering outside the Law Enforcement Center. A caravan from Las Agoras had arrived early that morning and they were demanding the release of certain detainees. It appeared the Las Agoras turmoil came to me before I could make it down there.

I cut my brunch short and headed to the jail, where I found an audience surrounding a rumpus at the entrance. Pressed against the double doors were about forty Latino men and women shouting at a fortified line of officers inside. For twenty solid minutes, they yelled through the closed doors, demanding to see detainees. The scene settled but the group didn't leave—for five days.

Here's what happened: At 2AM the previous night in Las Agoras, six men and one woman were apprehended in a bizarre covert sting. There was one consequential witness. Sam Delgado was awake when it went down, not because he heard anything, but to answer the call of nature. As he was returning to bed, he noticed two black vans parked in the front yard of his cousin's house across the street.

"I saw flashlights and dudes with machine guns. They were bringing everyone out cuffed and threw them on the ground. I was like, oh man, this is some militia shit. But they didn't look like militia at all, you know. They were dressed all in black, like combat gear or something. The way they moved seemed more like a SWAT team. It happened so fast. They put 'em in the vans and just like that, they were gone."

Delgado quickly dressed and ran outside to the garage, where he kept his motorcycle. He followed the vans out of town and all the way to the Finney County jail. Fortunately he had enough fuel. The headlamp on the older model Yamaha could be switched off so he could follow them from a safe distance. After the Sallyport doors closed behind the vans, Delgado found a phone and called his aunt. Ninety minutes later, the caravan departed Las Agoras.

What made the situation on the Plaza especially controversial was that neither jail officials, the Sheriff's Department, the County Attorney's Office, nor anyone else in an official capacity would confirm or deny whether the alleged arrestees were at the jail. This was a big reason the family members were so upset.

It took another twist when a local newspaper reporter, Meg Miller, appeared on the *Gazette Radio Hour*. She had spoken to the sheriff and quoted him as saying, "We have a transparent booking process that was established when this was still Kansas and the law was the law. So you can ask me about anyone who's been legally admitted to this jail." Reading between the lines, Miller saw evidence the captives were there and that it had caused dissension in the law enforcement ranks.

The following day, *Gazette* Editor and *Radio Hour* host Colm O'Brien offered a what-if scenario. Two years earlier, Congress passed the Home Defense Act. It established the National Intelligence Agency (NIA), a modest equivalent of the FBI.[7] But it appeared as though the program never came to fruition. Considering they went through the trouble of getting the legislation passed and then funded it with various tabooed taxes, O'Brien suspected the NIA existed unbeknownst to the public. And who better to execute a covert sting than the secret police?

The afternoon announcement from Presidential Hall gave hope that everything would soon be clarified. The president was going to address the nation on live television. When I returned to

---

[7] The NIA was part of the National Security Department, which was run by the Flatland Revolution hero, Major Krug. Turned out he'd been released at the border a year after the secession, escaping a military court martial.

the motel, Don was worked up about this breaking news. It meant something big was happening.

A RARE APPEARANCE

At CJ's Saloon, two blocks east of the motel, people crowded around the bar where a tube television was mounted. We stared at a static shot of the Presidential Hall press room for at least a minute. Moments earlier, the barroom was buzzing to the tune of local beer. Cornsilk and tobacco smoke diffused the last light of day coming through the stained dormer glass. The three pool tables were busy and conversations full-hearted. Now, all was still.

At last, President Washington appeared. He was short in stature and wore blue jeans, a brown Western blazer over an open-collar shirt, and boots. The casual look was surprising. I guess I had a preconceived image of the president based on a lifetime of seeing political leaders in business jacket-and-tie uniforms. Washington winked at correspondents in the front row before he arranged his notes on the podium. When he looked at the camera, his nonchalance dissipated and his gaze was lost in the lens for a long, awkward moment.

"Friends and family," he began, "Citizens of Independence. Hardship has been a rite of passage for us Independents. We have suffered but we have persevered. Sometimes dark clouds hang low and it's hard to see the light. But we keep our faith because the sun is always close. This is one of those moments.

"Many of you have been hearing about secret routes running from Mexico to our southern border." He shook his head and seemed to struggle with what came next. "I'm sorry to say it's true."

The bar erupted in astonishment, drowning him out Washington until shushing prevailed. "These networks are funded and operated by organizations whose deeds can only be equaled by the devil himself. These underground routes flow with drugs and guns and people connected to thousands of brutal killings. We believe they're attempting to make Independence a centralized drug haven with their greatest consumer, the U.S., on all sides.

"The first militants came through during the Transition. They've been patiently planning and quietly building. Sadly they are often harbored by families blinded by their desire to help, just as they were taken in when they came to our land. But back then, they came for opportunity and lived decent lives within our communities. The aliens they now shelter are not here for the betterment of anyone except the demons who sent them. They are assassins of liberty and justice and they are here to perpetuate the misery that is their Godless existence.

"Some think being surrounded by an empire insulates us from the outer world. But within that mammoth beast, dangerous networks thrive. They get lost in the vastness and feed on the strife our former country propagates. These malignant cells have the potential to spread that cancerous culture through our borders and disease our nation. This is why, two years ago, Congress passed the Home Defense Act, which created the National Intelligence Agency. The NIA is a highly skilled body created to coordinate intelligence functions to seek out those who want to inflict harm on our country and way of life. Centralized intelligence is critical for any modern nation's survival and freedom.

"Through comprehensive surveillance, agents identified the insurgents' smuggling routes and safe houses. Last night, the NIA raided one of their operational headquarters. We now have in our custody dangerous individuals who are critical components of the network that threaten our existence. In due time, they will be brought to justice."

Gripping the edges of the podium, his eyes hardened and his jaw trembled, making it look like words were trying to punch their way out of his mouth. The bar crowd was stunned and silent.

"They're not coming; they're here. If you see something, don't keep it to yourself. Beware of homegrown seditionists who the evildoers have turned. Their faces you'll recognize but their hearts you won't. Stay vigilant. Our bright future lies ahead. The American dream of prosperity and security is alive and well here in Independence."

He flipped to the next page and his grave expression gave way to one unexpectedly humble.

Emotions gust like the south wind,
Swaying like a young cottonwood.
You feel your roots pulled up,
Ripped from the soil of our ancestors.

North, South, East, and West
The Earth trembles beneath our feet.
Independents! Patriots! Come forth!
The citizen is in need. Run, don't wallow.

Hellish flames burn with vicious might.
But not even a devil'd dragon breathing spite
Could char the spirit of God's light.
Independence will shine, shine into the night.

"Thank you and God bless."

The screen went blue and the saloon blew up. "Wow," I said to Gus, a regular I was speaking to before the broadcast.

"I can't believe I just heard that," Gus said as he numbly combed his beard with his fingers.

"We knew the risks," said Steve, another regular standing behind us. He compulsively rocked from heel to toe with his hands in his khaki pockets. "This is what we get for being so lax at the borders. A hundred miles between checkpoints, with one or two agents in between."

"I'm speechless," Gus said. "NIA, cartels. Say what?"

"Who said anything about cartels?" Steve asked.

"Well, who else could it be?"

"The president would've said cartels."

"Let's talk about the NIA," the bartender demanded as he refilled a line of mugs. "I mean, holy shit!"

"I don't understand why we need them," a longhair in a green army jacket whined. "Shouldn't we be using our own police to police ourselves?"

"That wouldn't be policing ourselves, would it?" Gus asked.

"We already have police. That's my point."

A long drink from a freshly poured beer energized a wild-haired, red-faced woman down the bar. "I don't know nothing 'bout the NIA but if they kick the shit outta them Mexicans, I'm one hunerd ten percent behind 'em."

"But if they're taking power away from our local law enforcement and giving it to some federal agency, doesn't it go against what we believe in?" the longhair asked.

"This ain't the time to start pissing on our troops," the red-faced woman shot back. "They need our support."

"They're not troops, lady," said Gus.

"Mister Know-It-All!" she barked. "Just yesterday, you was saying the cartels was a hoax. You too," pointing her chin at Steve. "You both need to shut your mouths about things you don't know nothing about."

"Nobody said anything about cartels!" Steve exclaimed with exasperation.

"When you think about it," Gus said, turning back to Steve and me, "they smuggle drugs and people into the U.S. nonstop. The money has to get back through somehow. Maybe it's easier to smuggle the money here and fly it back to Mexico."

"I just think we should use our own police," the longhair said.

A rawboned man with deep eye sockets was glowering at the conversation from the pool table. Suddenly he let loose and stormed to the bar. "The police stood by while we was fighting for our independence," he yelled at the longhair. "You forget that? They don't deserve shit! Fuck them!"

The bartender, caught up in the emotion, hammered the bartop with his fist. "This is where it all began. Right here in this room. Don't forget that."

The wild-haired woman's old man lumbered back from the restroom. In one motion, he finished his beer and turned to everyone with a gnarled alcoholic face. "I wanna see them motherfuckers strung up and raked so their shit spills on the street."

"Pry out their fucking eyeballs like an oyster and watch 'em scream like the shit-eaters they are," his old lady added.

This wrecked the discussion beyond repair. The bartender turned on the music. From the speakers, a singer crooned about a woman he couldn't stop thinking about. Even if a fence couldn't keep them apart, his love of freedom and independence would. I wasn't sure if that was independence with a capital or small i.

"They've told us so little," Gus said. "Is it so bad they don't want to cause a national panic? I expect they'll give us more information in the coming days."

"He read a poem at the end," I said. "Didn't expect that."

"During his campaign, he would read his poetry. I guess it made him stand out."

"He doesn't come across as the poet type. Where's he from?"

63

Gus was still reeling from the speech. He massaged his forehead for a moment, redirecting his thoughts. "Arkansas. He owned a chain of lawnmower stores. But his family comes from oil."

Down the bar, the wild-haired woman was leading a toast. People around her raised their shot glasses. "Here's to the N-S-fucking-A. Whatever it stands for."

"That woman and her man do not represent the people here or this town," Gus said. "A filthy mouth on her."

"What did the bartender mean when he said this is where it all started?" I asked.

Gus was surprised. "I figured that's why you were here. This is where the Freedom 5 came up with their plan to take over the courthouse."

Gus and Steve told me the story of how five men, who would become the Freedom 5, were drinking one night after work and got themselves riled up talking about current affairs. It was an emotional time with the Panhandle Revolution and other secession movements. They wanted to make a statement like the People's Committee did around the Panhandle. So they hatched a plan and swore a blood oath to carry it through. They drew blood and shook on it. The joke was they were too hungover the next day to do anything.

You would think they'd be national heroes or at least revered figures at the saloon. In actuality, they were rarely seen in public. One of them was involved in a bad situation. He was driving drunk one night and hit a lady crossing the street. Killed her. The law on driving under the influence at the time was unclear. It was late at night. It was raining. They didn't test his blood alcohol. No one at the bar knew what happened to him.

Another one completely disappeared. His wife allegedly moved to Iowa with their kids during the Transition while he was in Leavenworth Penitentiary. The day after Independence officially seceded, he and the other Freedom 5 members were released at the border. It was assumed he left the country to find his wife.[8]

Gus pointed toward a round booth in the back corner. Framed headshots of the five men hung on the wall. I walked over to get a closer look. The two couples sitting at the table turned around to see what I was staring at.

"Whatever happened to them?" one lady asked.

"Jerry's still down at Fulton Auto Shop," her man answered.

"Doing what!" the lady guffawed.

THE FREEDOM 5

The repair shop wasn't far from the motel. I passed it many times but it looked closed down, like everything along the avenue. I called the next morning, not expecting anyone to answer. Lo and behold, Jerry Hickman himself picked up. After talking for a bit, mostly about what I was doing, he suggested I come to the shop.

He left a garage door half open. The only vehicle inside was a '49 Packard Super 8 with a body sanded down to bare steel. The interior had been gutted. No seats, door panels, or dashboard, but the steering column and shifter were still intact. Jerry scooted out from under the car feet first and wiped his hands with a red rag.

"It's a labor of love," he said. "Sat in my uncle's garage for twenty years. He gave it to me when he left four years ago and I've been working on it ever since. It's my symbol of hope. And it gives me something to do."

---

[8] The five men gave themselves up to authorities, ending the courthouse occupation. Major Krug and most of his fellow guardsmen were also arrested. They were eventually pardoned by the president.

We sat in the small office. The smell of grease was stronger than in the garage. The desk was covered with spark plugs, ball bearings, and rubber gaskets. An outdated, obligatory classic car calendar with pin-up models was on the wall.

"So is it true it all started one night at CJ's Saloon?"

Jerry rocked in the padded desk chair and nodded his head. "The real credit belongs up in Bonner's Ferry. That's where it all started. We were caught up in all the secession talk around the country. The difference between us and most other people is we took action. Five regular guys. Luke Patterson, Randy Harrell, Bob Bowman, Gunner Romero, and me."

"You just decided one night you wanted to do something?"

"We were bellied up to the bar talking about the direction the country was headed: down. I looked them all in the eye and said, 'Do you truly believe in what you're saying right now? Or are you just mad at your wife or boss so you gotta complain about something?' They all swore they were speaking from the heart."

"About what?"

Hickman counted on his fingers. "The government being run by elites, foreigners meddling in our affairs, over-taxing workers, the erosion of American values, jobs being sent overseas. Nobody felt good about the future. I was like, 'If you really feel how you feel, then let's do something about it.'"

"And you made a pact."

He showed me the scar on his palm. "We were gonna make history or go down trying. We met at my house on Sunday after we'd shaken our hangovers. I don't know if everyone believed it would happen. We were bound to the promise we made to each other."

"To take over the courthouse?"

"To take a stand. To make an impact and not by blowing shit up or killing people. We weren't terrorists. The courthouse was the best we could come up with. We planned it out best we could but it wasn't like any of us had ever taken over a building. We weren't Delta Force. We were regular people but we had something special: heart and love for our country.

"You still keep up with the others?" I asked.

"I see Gunner from time to time. He used to work here. After secession we had to cut down to me and the owner. He's still bitter about that. He and his old lady have had a rough go of it. And Luke, he had an incident the first year. He hit some lady crossing the street one night. It was raining and the streetlights were off so it was dark as pitch. He didn't go to jail but it messed him up. He ended up moving to Bucklin to live with his folks. Randy's still around. He used to come by but I haven't seen him for a while."

"You guys don't hang out at CJ's anymore."

"It's a historical place. History I was part of. If I'm hanging out there, it looks like I'm trying to wallow in my fame. It would ruin the sanctity of the place." He tried to smile but his eyes betrayed his sorrow. "I don't know. If things were better here, I'd feel a lot more heroic about it all."

The phone interrupted us. Jerry's friend called to report that the gathering outside the jail had ballooned into a full-blown demonstration. Jerry frowned after he relayed the news to me. "Demonstrating what?" he said spitefully. "They're upset we caught criminal intruders who want to destroy our country and our hard-earned freedoms?"

It made him sick to his stomach. For several minutes, he reclined in his chair. His face was pallid and he covered his eyes with his hand. In this weakened state, he told me he was worried too many people who moved there didn't represent or appreciate the values he had fought for. He had regular nightmares about Independence becoming a socialist utopia or a state of anarchy.

"What about a drug haven?" I asked. He groaned.

When Jerry and his drinking buddies took over the courthouse, Congress was already debating secession. The Flatland Revolution didn't exist yet. There were at least a dozen more prominent and robust campaigns across the country. Yet the counties of Independence accomplished what only one other movement could. This made Jerry Hickman one of the most pivotal individuals of the North American Secession Movement. He was a seminal figure who would go down in history. He was proud of what he accomplished but I saw melancholy in him. His irrelevance was striking. The same could be said of Independence, I suppose.

ZAPATISTAS

When Hickman told me the demonstration at Independence Plaza had grown, I envisioned maybe a couple hundred people. When I rounded the corner, I was shocked to see about five hundred protesters spilling into the street. Buses coming up from Las Agoras that morning had contributed to the growth but most of the people were from Capital City.

Todd Leiker and Carey Dobbs, who organized the meeting at the American Legion, were there with dozens of supporters calling themselves the New Legionnaires. Leiker stood at the center of the gathering with a bullhorn. "If our rights are under attack, then we are under attack. Unless they release the names and bring the prisoners before a judge, we will take this as a declaration of war against our democracy!"

Another group had hoisted a colorful pennant for THE HISPANIC-INDEPENDENT JUSTICE LEAGUE. That's where I found Juan Diego Morales pleading with their members. Whatever it was he wanted, they did not, and they soon turned their backs on him. He told me afterward he was trying to persuade them that by making it a racial issue, they were separating themselves from the rest of the people and weakening the solidarity. "This should be about all Independents. It's not a racial issue."

I looked over at the families near the entrance. "Are you sure about that?"

"People are using this moment to voice their bigotry," he said. "We can't take their bait. We can't divide into racial or cultural bands. This is about democracy and justice for *all* citizens. If the prisoners were white, nobody would be out here protesting for Caucasian rights." He was afraid that if the governmental misdeeds came to be viewed as racially motivated, it would diminish the collective outrage.

Todd Leiker walked past with his bullhorn. "Honesty and transparency in a democracy are like bread and water and we are in a famine. Our Constitution says clear as day that government shall derive its power from the consent of the governed. We're staying here until we get answers. We'll stay until starvation thins us and the winds blow us away."

"Seems counterproductive," I joked.

Morales and I made a plan to meet back there in the evening. I left in search of a recommended restaurant. A brick road led to the west side of town, where streets were laid out symmetrically with alternating dirt alleyways. Between those straight roads, conformity was abandoned. There were Spanish revival homes with red-tiled roofs, Craftsman houses, and an array of Victorian styles spread out on uneven lots. Backyards abutted against front yards, some houses were built close to the street, and others near the back. There were grass lawns with hundred-year-old trees, dusty yards with dead craggy trees, perfect picket fences, rotting wood fences, chain-link, and yards without fences.

Vegetable gardens that had replaced front yards were common in Capital City. There were entire blocks where trees were cut down and stumps shaved to the ground. Undeveloped lots were converted into community gardens with plots separated by makeshift fences of chicken wire and scrap lumber. A few people were out gardening in the warm midday sun.

El Restaurante Zapatismo was next door to a gardening store that sold seeds, compost, and used equipment. The faux-adobe building had once housed a Mexican bar and grill that was abandoned in the Transition. It hadn't achieved its predecessor's popularity but I was told it was the best food in the entire country.

The waitress told me my eyes would adjust to the poorly lit interior. I opted for a window table where I could work on my notes. As promised, the darkness lifted, revealing framed black-and-white portraits mounted on the walls. They were skillful exposures of men and women wearing black masks or balaclavas pulled over the nose. My first thought was they were part of the Flatland Revolution but I realized they were Zapatistas, the restaurant's namesake.

A woman came out from the kitchen and saw me studying the photographs. She wore black slacks, a long wool cardigan over a white blouse, and a necklace of rough-cut jade beads, Mayan perhaps. Her name was Consuela.

"I like the revolutionary theme," I told her.

"Oh, it's more than a theme," she answered.

"How so?"

"We *are* Zapatismo," she said proudly.

"From Chiapas?" I asked, surprised.

"We're part of the international movement."

During the Transition, she moved from New Mexico with her husband, sister, and other Zapatistas. They saw Independence as an incredibly rare opportunity to be part of a genuine egalitarian society. Consuela was unpretentious and confident in her beliefs.

When I told her she didn't fit my image of a revolutionary, she gave me a curious look.

"Why do we still consider equality and fairness such radical ideas?" she asked. "And that anyone who would believe in those ideals must have a crazy streak?"

The food didn't disappoint. The *enchiladas quelites con salsa roja* were as good as anything I'd ever had in the Mission District.

PROTESTS ON THE PLAZA

When I returned to the Plaza, there were at least a thousand people there. Long tables were set up in the street with big pots of stew and beans; double-handled pans with enchiladas; rondeaus filled with ground beef and potatoes; casseroles of corn, broccoli, and cheese; and other homemade dishes. Speakers took turns atop a stepladder on the sidewalk. Todd Leiker played heavy in the rotation. I watched him whip himself into a frenzy.

"We want answers! We didn't sacrifice everything to be peons. We fought for the power. It belongs to us! This is our country!" He pointed down the street toward Presidential Hall. "Grady Washington promised he'd be the person to fulfill the promise of democracy and self-sufficiency. What has he done for us? Nothing! He has done nothing for the people and everything for the cronies."

We could hear what sounded like an enormous choir but nobody could tell where it was coming from. People at the northern end of the Plaza were the first to hear the singing. Soon, a parade appeared a block away as slipshod lines a dozen marchers wide swiveled around the corner. A hundred-fifty strong advanced toward the Plaza.

A single voice rang from the front line. En masse, the group belted out the chorus behind him.

> *Glory, glory, hallelujah!*
> *Glory, glory, hallelujah!*

Police moved the barriers and the cavalcade came marching in. They sang with gusto. Hundreds of the Plaza demonstrators joined in.

> *I have read a fiery gospel*
> *Writ in burnished rows of steel,*
> *As ye deal with my condemners,*
> *so with you my grace shall deal.*
>
> *Let the hero, born of woman,*
> *crush the serpent with his heel,*
> *Since God is marching on.*
> *Glory, glory, hallelujah!*
> *Glory, glory, hallelujah!*

All at once, the marchers brandished signs they had kept concealed: IS THIS INDEPENDENCE OR MEXICO?; SUPPORT OUR GOVERNMENT; SUPPORT THE NIA; LET'S WIN THIS WAR.

Gasps and groans tore through the crowd. "Stop singing. Everyone stop singing!" But many who knew the verses couldn't seem to stop themselves.

> *He has sounded forth the trumpet*
> *that shall never call retreat.*
> *He is sifting out the hearts of men*
> *before his judgment-seat.*
> *Oh, be swift, my soul, to answer him!*
> *be jubilant, my feet!*
> *Our God is marching on.*

When the marchers reached the center of the demonstration, they did an about-face. The conductor ran to the other end, waving his hands and yelling, "Once more!" Against a chorus of boos and sneers, they sang louder than ever.

The counter-demonstration was impressive. It clearly took a lot of planning and it looked like they also tipped off the local news station because when the song ended, a *Channel 7* cameraman was waiting. He sidestepped in front of them, creating a dramatic tracking shot of the group. When he reached the end, reporter Jill Nguyen stood with microphone in hand.

"First, what do you call yourselves?" Nguyen asked the conductor.

"We're Independents. We're parents. We're grandparents, children, sisters, and brothers."

Nguyen asked him and the group, "Are you protesting the protesters?"

"We're not protesting," a woman beside him said. "We're supporting our country. We're supporting our president. God bless him and Congress for having the foresight to create an agency to protect us. Without them, we'd be...." The woman shook her head at the horrific thought. "These protesters are a disgrace. I understand the families of the accused coming here. They want to understand what's happening. Family is family. But the rest of the people here—yeah, you!" she shouted at two hecklers. "They don't even know what they're doing. They need to realize their actions undermine our lawmen."

Jawing back and forth disrupted the interview. The news crew eventually gave up and the counter-protesters ended their demonstration. Many of them remained on the Plaza and dispersed into smaller groups.

A vigil began after sunset. Lights were off in the law enforcement lobby. The vocal protesting had ceased and people were spread out on the grass. A violet luminescence glowed above the trees and hundreds of candlelit points charmed the Plaza.

I walked through the gathering until I found Juan Diego Morales. He was sitting in front of Presidential Hall with his friend, Tommy Jones, who helped with his newspaper production and distribution. Jones wasn't a newsperson by trade. He made a living making spirits—gin, whiskey, vodka—and helped his friend on the side. It was obvious he was as passionate about the paper's subject matter as Morales but his temperament couldn't have been more different. His hazel eyes were intensified by his dark beard and thick hair that stuck up from anxiously running his hand through it.

We sat and chatted quietly about the current events. The most confounding aspect of the jail imbroglio was the lack of basic information being conveyed by public officials. "Am I missing something?" I asked. The president's brief television address was all the information we have. "Did you hear what the sheriff told the *Gazette* reporter?"

Morales looked at Tommy. It seemed I'd struck a personal chord. He said quietly, "That's Tommy's dad."

Tommy said nothing. He was probably leery of me because I was a journalist. I would have changed the subject if it were solely a personal issue. The thousand people gathered around us was proof that it was a public matter. I poked at it a little more.

"I've heard people say the two sentences your dad uttered to the reporter forced the administration's hand.[9] It implied the undeclared suspects are in his jail. It's the reason Washington went on TV."

Jones shook his head. "I don't know."

"He really doesn't," Morales said.

---

[9] "We have a transparent booking process that was established when this was still Kansas and the law was the law. So you can ask me about anyone who's been legally admitted to this jail."

Conversations around us hushed as a group of robed singers from the counterprotest began singing nearby. Their faces were lit in the shadows of the trees. A deep voice established the key and the other singers followed. "*My country, tis of thee....*"

Jones groaned. "Once was enough, wasn't it? Let freedom ring? I thought I'd never have to listen to those corny anthems that people in the U.S. dote on. They act like Jesús was descending from heaven."

"Hey buddy," a man grumbled from nearby. "Can you lower it a notch?"

MACK FORD

The next day, Washington's chief of staff, Mack Ford, spoke to reporters in the Presidential Hall media room. It was broadcast live on Channel 7's News Noon Update. Ford had the bearing of a military man, with a crewcut and stern demeanor. He was flanked on one side by Major Krug, who was wearing ceremonial regalia: a cavalry hat with the Independence insignia—wheat chaff crossed with a rifle—and a navy wool jacket with roomy sleeves, a yellow trim lapel, and large silver buttons. With his enormous glasses, he looked like a cross between Curtis Lemay and Kim Jong-Il. On the other side was Attorney General Mitch Black. The sharp corners of his mouth were accentuated by smoker's wrinkles and his hair was oiled back.

Ford spoke with unbendable self-assurance, as if everything he had ever said and would say could be chiseled in stone as natural law. "The threats we face today are external and internal," he began. "There are people in this world who hate our love of freedom and self-reliance. We must not forget there are also people inside our country who can't seem to grasp our ideals. Within our own media, there are individuals trying to undermine our fight against the evildoers who've crossed the borders and are preparing to unleash a reign of terror.

"These media types have accused this administration and the Justice Department of needlessly withholding information from the public and operating in secrecy. I hope most people here understand that we can't share details about terroristic elements that oppose our very existence. What you know, they know. Our national security is at stake. You get that, right? There is much we don't know. There is much we do know. What we know and don't know is not for them to know. We know who they are and we know their intentions.

"NIA agents apprehended key players in their criminal network. Wherever they're being held, jail facilitators and the community are at risk. This is why they've been moved to undisclosed locations. The enemy wants nothing more than to free them. If these criminals were to make it back, their reception would be glorious. They would be nothing less than the embodiment of god-heroes. Just escaping would add to their legacy. We cannot allow that.

"We're not dealing with sympathetic human beings. These criminal organizations have been terrorizing their own people for decades. They've ruined a country forty times bigger than ours. They've murdered tens of thousands in cold blood. They will cut down scores of innocent people to save one of their own or to simply make a point. They are actively spreading lies and propaganda in our communities, our media, and wherever they can. Be careful. Some people are not who they say they are. Some people are not who others say they are. You now know about the underground pipeline that's funneled mercenaries into the country. But don't forget, many of them managed to get through legally.

"Regarding the detainees: We're still trying to work out procedural issues. They will be charged in a civilian court, not a military tribunal, when the time is right. They are being treated humanely and fairly. Codifying every piece of our nation's laws takes time. Attorney General Black's office is working with Congress to expedite the relevant codes and statutes."

A correspondent in the front row interrupted. "Shouldn't the suspects be charged using existing laws? It sounds as though they're being customized for these cases."

Ford's jaw agitated as he glared at the reporter. "After the colonial delegates drafted the Declaration of Independence, it was another thirteen years before they had a constitution and their first government. It was a mess. There was more strife and despair than we could ever imagine. You don't just sit down and draw up an ideal government. It takes time. It takes blood, sweat, tears, and a lot of improvising. It takes sacrifice. It hurts more than anyone would willingly suffer if they knew it would be like that. That's where we are. And you're with us or against us. That's all I have time for. Thank you."

LIBERAL…NOT SO LIBERAL

On Wednesday afternoon, I caught the Independence Arrow out of Capital City. It was a straight shot to Liberal, forty miles northeast of Las Agoras, and where I was staying for the night. Liberal had a pre-secession population of twenty thousand people but shrunk to half that. As with most other towns on the Plains, everything was so spread out you could see the prairie growing between lots. Even along the main drag, the low buildings knuckled under the immense sky. At a deserted shopping center, old promotions on signs and windows were cruel reminders: three-packs of razors $9.99; Store brand lotion $1.99; Burger, fries, and drink $2.99.

I was told no place was as anti-secession as Liberal. They fought desperately against the movement, but in the end, they were stuck in the center of the thirty-six counties. I wanted to see if the sentiment persisted.

After checking in at a sleepy motel on Pancake Boulevard, I found an open diner, Barb's Good Food, on a block of empty stores. It was still early. The only other customer was a large bearded man sitting at a corner table with his back against the wall and his thumbs hooked in his camouflage vest. He returned my greeting with a simple nod.

"You know what you'd like?" the waitress asked before I'd settled into the booth. She gestured to the menu written on a chalkboard behind the counter. It was standard diner fare with one wrinkle: it was mostly vegetarian. Independence was a hair's breadth from being vegetarian. You could find beef and poultry in restaurants but it cost more. For example, a burger (V) at Barb's was $3.99, while a burger (M) was $8.99. The priciest item on the menu was Meat and Potatoes for $14.99. I ordered a Sloppy Barb (tempeh based).

When I asked the waitress if she could recommend some social spots around town, she laughed. "*Social* spots?" I suppose that was an odd way to phrase it.

From across the room, the other diner chimed in. "How 'bout The Red, White, and Blue Saloon. Good place to socialize, if you ask me."

"Where are you from?" the waitress asked me.

I told her I was from California and she reacted with surprise I'd already come to expect. Visitors were a rare breed in Independence. Foreign journalists even more so.

"Hey, Barb," she called back to the kitchen. A woman wearing a pink paisley do-rag poked her head out of the service window. "This guy's writing about places to visit around the country. You better make his food good."

Barb looked at me for a moment and shrugged, "You like it or you don't."

"This is the best food in town, if you ask me," the man in the corner said as he leaned over his plate with utensils in hand. Steam rose from brown gravy ladled over a pile of mashed potatoes. He stuck his fork into an indiscernible slice of meat and sawed at with his steak knife. "They'll treat you right over at Blue Saloon." He cut a piece off, plunged it into the potatoes, and said nothing more.

The saloon he recommended was in an otherwise empty strip mall down the street. There were six pool tables at the front of the room. The bar was in the back, where all but one stool was occupied.

"Is anyone sitting here?" I asked.

A woman next to the empty seat told me it was available. "Haven't seen you here before," she said as I squeezed in.

"I came down from Capital City today."

"You from there?" the man on my right asked with suspicion.

"Nope," I said bluntly. After I had situated myself, I added, "California. I'm writing a story about Independence." I told them this, not to elicit reactions, but in hopes they would be more forthcoming with their opinions.

"You mean for a U.S. magazine?" the woman asked.

I nodded. "Have both of you lived here long?"

"Forty years," the woman replied.

"Most of my life," the man said. "No place like home." He raised his hand eye level to shake mine. "Phil's the name."

"I'm Peg," said the lady. "What exactly are you writing?"

"I'm calling it 'The Spirit of Independence,'" I said with inflated reverence.

"That's not a word people around here care for," Peg muttered.

"Spirit?" I asked, tongue-in-cheek.

"Independence," Phil said, unamused. With his elbow on the bar, he pointed to a U.S. flag mounted on the back wall. "That's where we belong."

"Then why'd you stay?"

"This is my home, man!" Phil snapped. "I couldn't leave my people behind."

Peg wanted to know how long I'd been in the country and where I'd been. When I told her it was the first time I'd left Capital City, she nodded as if it explained my ignorance. "You gotta get out of there," she said. "They probably still think this was a brilliant idea. Anyone with sense can see this socialist back-to-land experiment was just plain stupid."

"Make no mistake, sir," Phil said. "Our town is called Liberal but we're no liberals. Neither was Meade or Ulysses or any of those other places." He was referring to notable towns of the Flatland Revolution. "They didn't have as much to lose as we did."

"Like what?" I asked.

"Like baseball. We had one of the best minor league teams in the country. We also lost our agriculture. The packing plants shut down. Our tourism died."

"Above all, we lost our trucking," Peg added. "Me and my old man were long-haulers for twenty-five years. Just like that"—she clapped her hands—"it was over. All those years we got along just fine. Now we're penned up in a cage and hate each other."

"We lost it all and couldn't do a thing about it when this was forced on us," Phil said.

"What tourism you talking about?" the bartender asked Phil.

Phil counted on his fingers. "The Air Museum. The Land of Oz. The Pancake Race."

Unimpressed, the bartender waved his towel at Phil and walked away.

"How come so many people from Liberal were against secession?" I asked.

"Because it was stupid," Peg said.

"But why was it so prevalent here? Are you just smarter than everyone else?"

"We loved our country," Phil said. "The greatest country in the history of the world and some people would rather have this piece of crap. You can quote me on that."

A man sitting on the other side of Peg leaned forward so he could see me. "To answer your question, it didn't happen overnight. Those small-town demonstrations, like Meade, were more about getting rid of the tax-and-spend welfare policies that were bringing the country down. We were fine with that. We knew a bloated government was about as un-American as you could get. It's when it started getting secession-oriented that we took a step back and were like, 'Whoa, hold on now.' You all remember the Sunday paper they devoted to the pros and cons of secession?" he asked Peg and Phil. "The entire issue. We should be thankful we had a good paper. Other towns didn't do their due diligence like we did."

"We didn't gain any freedom. We lost it all," Phil said despondently. "Freedom to travel, freedom of choice, you name it."

"Freedom of choice?" I asked.

"Having money and being able to drive down to the grocery store or the mall."

"Did you ever listen to Chuck Gannon on 1270?" the other man asked Peg and Phil. "He hated the secession craziness. Early on, he sniffed out where it was going. He would go off on the 'seditionists,' as he called them."

"You all listened to Maude Grese, yet?" Peg asked. "Boy, she's a pistol. Tells it like it is." She explained how Independence Broadcast System recently bought the radio station in Liberal. Now they could listen to popular Southern shows at a higher quality.

"Bill Tyson might be the one who's gonna get us through all this," the other man said.

"Yep," Phil and Peg both agreed.

Bill Tyson was the owner of the IBS media conglomerate. He was also the man behind a desperately needed ethanol plant in the works. During the Transition, the U.S. dismantled a handful of small-scale refineries in the region. The Independence government gave what was left of those refineries to Tyson, who was using those parts to build a switchgrass refinery near Dalhart.

Tyson was also involved in the early effort to build a pipeline through Texas. His great-uncle founded the Corpus Christi contracting company that was consulting the delegation in Mexico. The U.S. took issue with this even though Tyson didn't have any financial ties to the company. Besides this, there wasn't much known about the man people hoped would end the national fuel nightmare.

"I just thought of something," Phil said, gazing through everyone with a stupefied look. "Why don't *we* secede from Independence? They gonna fight us about it and say they're the only ones who get to secede?" He tapped the bar top with his finger as he articulated a complicated thought. "By seceding, they have acknowledged not only their own right to secede but all counties' rights to secede."

"You're slower than a slug," Peg said. "You just might be the very last person in this town to think of that."

"We'd be a bubble inside a bubble," the other man added. "Double insulated, double trapped."

"At least we wouldn't have to put up with their B.S.," Phil whined.

"You've lost too many brain cells," said the bartender.

"Give him a shot of hooch," said Peg. "On me."

"And lose what brain cells I got?" Phil said. "I'll pass on that."

"It's best to forget," said the other man. "It's all about what we got, not what we lost."

"Alright then, make it a double."

LAS AGORAS

A flurry of opinion pieces and political rags accused Las Agoras of being a "haven for terrorists." I quickly found out for myself how people there felt about that label. Signs of discontent were posted on light poles, windows, and storefronts. Their outrage was graffitied on corrugated metal fences, the sides of abandoned buildings, and in the middle of the road with fresh yellow paint: SECOND CLASS CITIZENS THIRD WORLD LIFE.

Juan Diego Morales had set me up with his longtime friend and Las Agoras newspaper reporter Luis Estrada, who I met at a Main Street café for lunch. Estrada grew up in Southwest Texas and attended college in Lubbock, where he met his future wife. They moved to what is now Capital City, where he worked with Morales at the *Gazette*. Ten years later, Estrada and his wife divorced and he moved south.

What interested me as much as anything when I spoke with people in Independence was why they stayed. Estrada wasn't tied to the country by marriage or family. Most of his friends left during the Transition. He could have done the same and re-established his career elsewhere. He saw a "once-in-a-lifetime opportunity." I often heard this from people like Estrada and Morales, who were drawn by the intellectual aspects of the Independence experiment.

Estrada believed the vast majority of people stayed for two reasons. They were either rooted in their communities by family, friends, home, and habit or they believed that in this new America, they would be part of an equitable society. This latter expectation was already at the root of his town's discontent before the current events occurred.

The people of Las Agoras felt disrespected. Rogue armed militias were acting with impunity, "patrolling the town in giant gas-guzzling trucks with their shotguns and arrogance." The disparagement of Velasquez and their community was hurtful but the final straw was the federal government perversely legitimizing those false accusations (in the eyes of residents) with the illegitimate covert NIA raid that only perpetuated the injustice.

"What the hell's going on up there?" Estrada asked. "Charge the suspects in court. Why is that so hard? We know who they are. Some of them were born right here, no criminal records or anything suspicious." He lowered his voice. "But I will say this: three of them probably came in illegally. We know little about them and they had a certain vibe? Maybe that's why they were all targeted."

"So you believe they're connected to criminal groups?"

"I'm just saying we don't know who they are. But the families of those we know, they're furious. They swear on their mothers' lives that those kids are nothing close to what they're being accused of."

"What about the murder?" I asked. "What are people saying?"

Estrada pressed his palm to his chest. "When you see his wife and son, it breaks your heart. He was shot by a high-caliber hunting rifle from long range while he was walking home. The militias are the only ones out there at night. So you tell me."

We walked to the park after lunch. Luis carried a handkerchief folded into a square and dabbed the sweat from his forehead and wiped the back of his neck. I noticed his clothes were a size too big. It seemed he'd lost weight since the secession but his body's cooling mechanisms hadn't adjusted.

We sat on a shaded bench. Out in the grass, a wiry Asian man was practicing tai chi. On the other side, a group of young Latino men was hanging out by a Honda Civic repainted glossy forest green and modified so that it sat just inches from the ground.

"They're always running out of gas," Estrada said. "I can't tell you how many times I've seen them pushing that car around town." His laugh gave way to a thoughtful gaze. "There was a lot of movement in this country early on. People were trying to find their place. Mostly from one town to another or the countryside into town. That meant there were people who looked different or acted differently from what residents were used to."

The town was predominantly Latino. To me everyone looked like typical Independents: a culture that shuns panache. The Cholos were an exception in their plaid shirts with only the top button fastened, bandanas, short pants, and tube socks.

In Las Agoras, cultural friction pre-dated Independence. The most contentiously fought counties in the Flatland Revolution were those with a big industry presence. Here, the fight was as bitter as anywhere. A fifth of the town worked at the pork plant. It was the foundation of the local economy. Factory execs, farmers, and feedlots owners publicly accused the pro-secessionists of trying to destroy the county in the name of dystopian ideology.

Another part of Las Agoras considered themselves the tried-and-true Oklahomans. They lived through the town's transformation and remembered the old days as being simpler and purer. Several years earlier, when a presidential candidate had run under the slogan "Restore America," they vigorously embraced his campaign. The candidate faded from the race but the Restore America bumper stickers and flags never lost meaning. Years later, the secession movements gave their ideology a new vision: If America is too far gone, why not restore a small piece?

This time around, they recruited workers from the hog factory and feedlots. These were mostly immigrants who would have felt diminished by the earlier Restore America rhetoric. It climaxed when two thousand shift workers didn't show up one day. They shut down the factory and all its ancillary business connections for a week.

The demonstration was a wake-up call for many in the movement. They didn't like what they saw as an economic attack on the county. Secessionism suddenly wasn't to their liking. They attempted to change the movement's language and pull people off the bandwagon but it was too late. So they bailed. It was told the founders of the local Restore movement were nowhere to be found in Independence.

In an article in the *Liberal Post*, the author writes, "The people of Las Agoras are very aware they sacrificed everything and got nothing in return." The meat processors shut down, feedlots shut down, the hog farmers left, and the money left. "Even immigrants from rural Mexico must endure conditions far worse than where they came. Underfunded schools, crumbling infrastructure, collapsed farming…." The author surmised it should come as no surprise that Las Agoras could become a hotbed for insurrection.

A community rally was originally supposed to take place in the park where Luis Estrada and I were talking. When the organizers realized the space wasn't big enough for the expected turnout, they moved it to a shopping center parking lot. By 6:30PM, the entire town was on the move. Thousands of people congregated outside a shuttered box store. Near the entrance was a flatbed trailer with two large speakers.

Luis and I worked our way around until we found a suitable spot where he could photograph the stage. It took a while. He must have stopped to chat with at least twenty people. It seemed he knew almost everyone there. That's saying a lot. The turnout was impressive. "The entire town is here," Luis said. "I'm not exaggerating."

The Las Agoras mayor, Marissa Lopez, was the first speaker. "It's like a ghost town out here. Look around. We gave up our security for the idea of being Independent; free of political corruption, free of tyranny, and free of inequality. We didn't stay to be treated as second class citizens without basic rights and respect."

Next was an older man with long hair pulled back in a ponytail. He appealed to his townspeople's "better angels." I don't believe his message prevailed. "We had a vision: one nation under God, indivisible, with liberty and justice for all. Now I'm having nightmares in which our communities are becoming isolated like the city-states of the ancient world where fear and distrust flourished and warring was endless. When we succumb to fear and mistrust, we close our hearts and withdraw to a primitive place where truth doesn't matter anymore. It's the dominion of the false, where values and beliefs are formed by deliberate untruths. It's a wicked place. Instead of seeking someone we can lash out against, we should search for those we can reach out to. When we are angry, we should be most cautious. Let's allow justice to take its proper course. If they are innocent, they will be free. Let truth be our saving grace."

A long queue of family members proclaimed the innocence of those arrested in the raid. "My name is Eulogia De Leon. My son was *taken* from his home in the middle of the night. He is not a terrorist or a criminal." "My name is Jose Romero. My brother was dragged from his home by a federal agency—our own government! He was born and raised here. He is an Independent citizen."

The local pastor and friends of Daniel Velasquez took the stage to memorialize him. A somber fifteen minutes ended with a funeral hymn. The emotional shift set the stage for the last speaker, who addressed the in-town militia patrols.

"These bands of lawless vigilantes and their warlords come to intimidate, dominate, conquer, and rule over us. But this is not their town. Do you hear me out there?" He pointed over the crowd to the back of the parking lot, where several dozen militiamen were leaning against their pickup trucks, watching the rally. The speaker berated them from the stage, yelling into the microphone so loudly that it was hard to tell exactly what he was saying. The meaning of his words was clear. The entire crowd turned to watch the militiamen and some began walking toward them. A moment later, the entire back portion of the gathering was on the move. As the militiamen scrambled into their trucks and drove away, the crowd erupted with applause and fierce cheering. It was a chilling moment.

The speaker continued. "The power belongs to the people! We are under attack from the tyrants in the North, media propaganda from the South, and militants from our own county. We have to protect ourselves and fight back. We are Las Agorasites. We are Independents. Let them hear us north, south, east, and west: we will not sway! We will not falter."

The roar was tremendous and the energy frightening. Even the Cholos—lingering under a tree off to the side, appearing too cool to show any interest for most of the rally—came in and blended with the crowd, shouting with fists thrust in the air.

"To those people who have called us a 'haven for terrorists,' 'vassals of the drug lords,' and 'hotbed for insurgents', it's your own hate that's the gateway to evil. To the tyrants of Independence: We are not your scapegoats and we will not back down. We'll go up there if we must and we will huff and we will puff and we will blow your castle down." A war cry ten thousand strong reverberated through the shopping center parking lot.

Ninety minutes earlier, they trudged to the rally site with the burden of existential threats and weary from an uncomfortably hot spring day. On the way back, you could see a lightness in their step. The few restaurants in town were bustling. People were out on their front porches and in the park.

"If nothing else, it lifted our spirits," Luis said.

The rally did more than that. I spent the following three days traveling the Southern Loop bus route that ran from Las Agoras thru Boise City, Dalhart, Dumas, Spearman, and Perryton. Each night I tuned into radio shows accusing Las Agoras of putting race before country and making the arrests a divisive issue.

Back in Capital City, the reaction the reaction was much different. The front page of the *Gazette*: LAS AGORAS WANTS ANSWERS. This was an understatement for anyone who was there. Secondhand accounts of the rally took on mythic proportions. There was talk of an even bigger demonstration coming to Capital City. It was as though a great army was on the move. It would be like the Siege of Malta.

On the morning of the supposed super rally, police battalions spread across the Plaza. The Sheriff's Department deputized dozens of volunteers for the event. Reporters and news teams were on hand. Local supporters came to take part in the demonstration but it was all for naught.

There was never a rally planned for that weekend. The possibility of one day staging an event in Capital City had been discussed, according to Luis Estrada, but it would take a major effort to transport that many people. The caravan that showed up at the jail was a collective feat in itself.

Part of the hearsay circulating that week leading up to the weekend suggested it was a secret operation. "They wanna take the capitol by storm." Many believed that someone spread the rumors to demoralize supporters and to make Las Agoras something to be feared.

CITIZEN OR FUGITIVE?

Eventually I got to know Tommy Jones. Through him, I met his parents, Gail and Tom. Gail was a squat and sturdy woman with short hair she curled herself. They lived a mile northeast of town on Tom's family farm. Tom didn't farm though. Neither did his father, who preceded him as the sheriff. For the past fifty years, they had been leasing out the land. When I was there, a former wheat farmer was growing biodiesel feedstock.

Gail had been a longtime school administrator but with the drastic post-secession cuts, she needed to find something new and useful to do. She grew up on a working farm, an hour southeast of Capital City, and learned to sew at an early age. Even before the embargo, she expected there would be a high demand for seamstresses who could not only repair fabric but also make clothing from found and foraged materials. So she launched her own business and had been operating out of their barn ever since.

She told me about her experience on the Monday following the non-demonstration. From the moment her employees showed up for work in the morning, she noticed they were uncharacteristically taciturn. After she went over the week's schedule with them, she asked if everything was okay. Instead of answering, they busied themselves with whatever they could. Gail didn't press but when she returned at lunchtime, the ladies were standing together, waiting for her.

"We're going home," Rosa, the head seamstress, said in an accent stronger than normal. "This is nothing personal against you."

"Say what?"

"We're going home," Rosa repeated with discomfort.

"You're quitting?" Gail asked.

"No."

"I'm so confused," Gail said.

"You'll understand later. I'm sorry."

All across the country, similar scenes were playing out. Work crews stopped at noon sharp and Latino-owned shops closed. The prominent Independence farmer, John Mayberry, laughed when his longtime employees said they were done for the day. Then he saw no one else was smiling.

"This is happening everywhere, John. We've been treated with disrespect for too long. We're not standing for it anymore."

"Hector, how have I treated you with disrespect?" Mayberry asked.

"The government, the president, the police, the NIA, the judges, the radio, the people. We were here in the beginning like everyone else. We sacrificed and struggled as much as anyone but we're still being treated as inferior."

The nationwide walkout affected food markets, shops, services, and municipal operations. I thought people in Capital City took it in stride, but in rural areas, particularly farming communities where they were still learning how to feed a hungry nation, the walkout fueled anxiety. Many farm and ranch hands were told they weren't welcome back. "Selfish" and "thankless" were often heard.

The strike only lasted two days but the national debate was just getting started. Radio listeners dialed in their judgments and diatribes while the hosts kept the fire going. It seemed as though secession and all its aftereffects, plus the tribulations of the past several weeks, had acidulated these once mild-mannered flatlanders.

There was a time when the Latin American community felt like guests in their own land. Maybe they didn't face the same overt and violent racism African Americans endured but an undercurrent of animosity was indisputable. They were called names, such as wetbacks, beaners. One woman, whose parents moved from Mexico forty-five years earlier, told me she remembered these revilements used on the playground, even though she was born in the U.S. She went home and asked her parents, "What does beaner mean?" Words used like germ warfare, sent from parent to child to child to parent. Target hit.

In the short time I'd been in the country, I witnessed more subtle disparagements in the speeches about the alleged criminal incursion. At the militia rally, Bud Keller said, "We're not talking about an invasion to take over our jobs and schools." A cruel but common jingoist sentiment. Even President Washington made the link from past to present when he said the intruders were being "harbored by families blinded by their desire to help, as they too were taken in when they came to our land."

In decades past, the Latino community would have endured these passive-aggressive tactics. But now they were empowered as original citizens of a new nation. With the strike, they lifted the bias and bigotry up from under the surface and forced their fellow countrymen to look at the monstrosity uncovered. Now we would see people's true colors.

A new radio station fortuitously launched the same week as the walkout—*1010 AM Capital City*—was part of the expanding Independence Broadcast System. People in the Northeast could finally listen to shows that had already made a mark in the South, such as the *Maude Grese Show* and *What Matters*, hosted by Davey McGraw. Featured in the 1010 launch was a brand-new program called *The Boz Flannigan Radio Roundup* premiered on Wednesday night.

"We humans, we're a suspicious lot so we don't mix well. Parents distrust their children and vice versa. Neighbors distrust neighbors, one side of town distrusts the other, rural folk distrust town folk, counties distrust counties, and races of men distrust other races. It's primitive, encoded in our DNA. You can put on yer liberal shades—yeah, I said it—and see it differently but underneath it is what it is: innate distrust. So we shouldn't be so surprised we have this racial divide. Every other country with delusional multi-racial ambitions has this problem. By ignoring the root of our conflict, we're only prolonging it.

"Now I have nothing against the Mexican people. I have plenty of friends who are Hispanic. Individuals aren't the problem. Cultures and communities are. We should look at this national crisis realistically. If we reorganized our communities with people of the same race and creed, we could eliminate the friction. Imagine distinct areas of our country where you could travel and see people living in their own unique way. The Mexican immigrants have done a lot for our country, especially pre-Independence. They came and did good work. It changed the demographics, sure, but America was forcing us to change and that's when the immigration helped. They profited from our economy, our schools, our health system. But that was back when we could take on extra weight."

Flannigan was admonished on all sides for using the L word. This was how I learned it was considered derogatory to use the word "liberal," among others, in a political context. The *Gazette* panned his show for being "cold," "arrogant," and an injection of "American-style divisiveness."

During this controversial period, a group of assemblymen announced they were co-sponsoring a citizenship bill that would require everyone in Independence to establish legal status. The Independence Constitution stated that anyone present inside the borders at the "moment of independence" automatically became a citizen. They practically copied Section 1 of the U.S. Constitution's 14th Amendment word for word.

> All persons born or naturalized in Independence, and subject to the jurisdiction thereof, are citizens of the Independence and of the county wherein they reside. No county shall make or enforce any law which shall abridge the privileges or immunities of citizens of Independence; nor shall any county deprive any person of life, liberty, or property, without due process of law; nor deny to any person within its jurisdiction the equal protection of the laws.

There were two exceptions. One, fugitives from justice. Two, a defendant charged with a felony in court. So if a man in Dodge City was arraigned but never tried before Independence became a nation, he was not granted citizenship since he had been formally charged in court. An extradition treaty was negotiated during the Transition so authorities in Independence were required to hand over fugitives if requested.

The sponsors of the citizenship bill argued that undocumented U.S. immigrants living in the thirty-six counties when the borders closed were technically fugitives. There was no legal precedence since no one had been arrested or charged for this. The amendment would clarify the ambiguity.

"If they were here illegally before the borders closed, then they were here illegally thereafter. If they're decent, law-abiding citizens, then let them stay and participate in the naturalization process. But until they're legitimate, they shouldn't be eligible for certain privileges like homesteading and voting." [10]

An op-ed from the *Dodge City Patriot*: "We believed by committing ourselves to these borders, we were all mutually born

---

[10] The Homestead Act allowed citizens to claim an abandoned house or farm. Claims were made in county court. Buyers purchasing at the appraised value were given priority.

Independent. Staying was our pledge. Citizenship was implicit. Now, after four years of hardship, are we expected to prove ourselves again?"

From the *Ulysses Mirror*: "The Mexican cartels are the greatest existential threat to Independence. Cartel operatives are here. How do we identify them? By separating them from the rest of us. How? With documentation. They are Mexican. Mexican heritage is a big part of our country. It makes it easy for them to blend in. We, as Latino Independents, must separate ourselves from our enemies. Race is an issue because this *is* about race."

No evidence or legitimate reportage proved Mexican drug cartels were meddling in Independence affairs. Yet it was becoming a matter of fact in many circles. Inaccuracies aside, for those who supported the militia movement and feared a foreign threat, the citizenship legislation was an obvious choice.

If legislators introduced the bill at any previous time in the country's existence, the soundness of having clear policies wouldn't have been as controversial. It wasn't surprising that the timing and language in the bill offended Latino Independents, not to mention the rhetoric flaring up around the debate.

Juan Diego Morales could no longer deny the racial component of the national discord. He didn't blame the militias. He believed they were victims of innate human reactivity and their fears were being inflamed by hyperbole. Southern media figures fueled the fires but Morales and others wondered if someone else was ultimately responsible. Someone who had the most to gain. The short list included Bill Tyson and Grady Washington.

CONSULATE AFFAIRS

My press visa extension was about to expire so I returned to the State Department to meet with Jon Becker again. Based on our previous conversations, I thought we had a good rapport and getting an extension wouldn't be a problem.

"Oh, Roman, I don't know," he said as he bristled in his desk chair. "These are the rules."

He finally agreed to run it by his boss. When I returned the next day, he informed me his superior wanted to meet with me. Becker's smile seemed forced, which made me uncomfortable. He led me down the hallway to a corner office and closed the door behind me.

I was left alone with the Director of Consular Affairs, Paul Gray. He was an angular man in his late sixties with thick-framed glasses and a heavy out-of-season cardigan. "Mr. Wolfe," he said in a tone both imperious and cordial. He gestured to the guest chair.

The consul sat down and opened a manila folder on his desk. After he quickly flipped through all the pages, front and back, he looked up at me. "We're familiar with the pieces you wrote about the independence movements. It didn't seem you had an agenda tying you to one position or another. You genuinely wanted to understand what was driving the movements and who the people were. That's why we felt comfortable giving you access to our country. We're hoping you'll be as even-handed as you were then. Like any nation, we need to keep track of how many foreign journalists we allow in. It would be too easy for someone, especially from the States, to portray us in a less-than-impressive light. I trust you're putting in the time to understand the supreme effort it's taken to build what we are today."

"Absolutely," I assured him.

"People believe the U.S. Congress was graceful in letting us separate. Make no mistake, they did it out of spite and to make an example of what happens when you go against the powers-that-be. Our freedom threatens them. Roman, managing relations in this small country is more complex than you might realize. If there's one thing I learned from secession, it's that when ideas—right or wrong, true or false—gain enough momentum, they can steamroll all good sense and civility and leave a mess in their wake. We believe everyone deserves the same freedom we've struggled for. We have an obligation to protect ourselves from inside, as well as outside, threats."

He paused as a new thought took form. "You said the people who demanded and fought for their independence were *not* guided by noble ideals but by something more personal? What did you mean by that? To me, it sounds like you're saying their efforts were just a waste of time."

It took me a moment to realize he was referring to the conversation I had with Jon Becker nearly two weeks earlier. "What I meant was we all have a deep urge to control our lives. It comes with a sense of desperation because we're never really in control. This causes us anxiety and the feeling of powerlessness." Another thought occurred to me. "Maybe work and career is the American way of grappling with it. Rising through the ranks gives the illusion of being in control of your destiny and sometimes even in control of others' destinies. Maybe that anxiety and feeling of impotence is the reason I write. To make sense of chaos, I find order by creating my own narrative."

Gray furrowed his brow. "Are you here to write about Independence or the powerlessness of man?"

"Self-determination. That's what secession was all about. My view is that anxiety from not being in control was at the core of the independence movements."

This was essentially what I told his assistant director. If I were being more forthcoming, I would have expanded on the idea that the secession movements were driven by a deep fear of losing control over one's own life. I had a feeling that Mr. Gray, in particular, would take offense.

"So it's about the poor, misguided, hopeless Independents who foolishly thought secession would bring happiness." Gray looked down at the top page in the folder. "This is what you mean by *The Spirit of Independence.*"

"The soul of this country and the people who define it."

He nodded pensively. "It's reminiscent of something the founding fathers would have written. He waved his hand as if visualizing a Broadway marquee. "The Spirit of Independence."

"Or the Four Chiefs."

He was not amused. "Pardon?"

"Sitting Bull, Chief Joseph, Geronimo, Red Cloud. Sometimes they're called the original founding fathers." I could see mistrust in his eyes so I tried to qualify my reference. "They fought with the U.S. You fought with the U.S. They're isolated on reservations. This country is isolated."

"What are you trying to say?"

"It was only a loose reference."

He walked over to a metal cabinet and retrieved a map he unrolled on his desk. He tapped a finger on Western Montana. "You spent time here during the Panhandle Revolution, did you not?"

"I did."

"You wrote about the Flathead Indians supporting that movement. How much time did you spend with them?"

"A day."

He slid his finger across the state to a spot east of Billings. "What contact did you have with Cheyenne tribal members?"

"I'm sorry, but where are you going with this?"

"A simple question. What contact did you have with people from the Cheyenne Indian Reservation?"

"None."

"What about the Arapahoe?"

"I honestly didn't mean anything with the Four Chiefs reference," I said.

"Then why did you say that? You know they're here."

"Who?"

"The Cheyenne and Arapahoe."

"I didn't know that. Did something happen?"

He sighed and sloughed off his aggravation. "Yes, as a matter of fact. It was an unfortunate situation but everything ended up okay. Thank you for clarifying." He let the map retract into a loose roll and sat down. Pensively tapping his cheek, he studied me. "Jon Becker has spoken on your behalf. I'm glad we had the chance to meet and clear all this up."

Gray stood, but it took a moment to realize our meeting was over. It took longer to figure out what exactly we had cleared up. Becker was waiting in the hallway. We didn't speak until we were back in his office.

"Did something happen involving members of Cheyenne or Arapahoe tribes?" I asked. "He asked me about my contact with them."

"You've had contact with them?" Becker asked with restrained exasperation I sensed would spill out if I said yes. "Have you spoken with anyone from Black Kettle?"

"I don't even know what that is."

"It's a place in the Northwest. Mostly Cheyenne and Arapahoe. They came during the Transition."

"Is that a problem?" I asked.

"A few years back, there was a dispute between Black Kettle and some local farmers. Things got a little tense. Whatever you and

Mr. Gray discussed on this matter, I have nothing to add. But I will say this: the U.S. wants us to fail and they want to humiliate us in the process. I know your intentions are good but anyone can take a story and spin it to suit their agenda." He lowered his voice. "They'll portray us as a bunch of rednecks. You know what I mean."

BLACK KETTLE

The county library was in a peaceful residential neighborhood with massive oak and locust trees. Out front was a statue of Mark Twain. He sat on a wooden bench, gazing out at something that had captured his interest. His relaxed manner and serene curiosity evoked a bygone era, before the secession and before life had become so politicized.

At first glance, it appeared the library was closed but I knew how heavily everyone relied on natural lighting. Sure enough, the doors were unlocked and all the tables in the main room were occupied. Kids were running in the aisles as their mothers chased after them, reprimanding them in Spanish. From behind the librarian's desk, a stern-looking woman with red horn-rimmed glasses and hair done up in a beehive looked on with consternation.

She showed me to the Independence Room, unlocked the door, and hurried back toward the ruckus. On the back wall, two front pages of the local newspaper were framed. U.S. CONGRESS PASSES SECESSION ACT marked the start of the stormy national debate over whether the president should or would veto the historic bill. INDEPENDENCE! commemorated the birth of the nation nine months later.

Although it was called the Independence Room, most of the collection was pre-secession local and regional history: hunting and trading on the Great Plains, life on the Santa Fe and Cimarron trails, Manifest Destiny, prairie populism in the 19th century, etc. I randomly pulled a hardback from a row of agriculture-related titles. On the dust cover was a monochrome photo of a family posing in front of a rudimentary one-room home surrounded by endless fields of dirt. It seemed as though they came from the land itself. In an instant, a gust could blow them apart—dust to dust. Somehow enough of those sodbusters persevered and cultivated this land.

Atop a low shelf was a clear acrylic case that contained the *Chronicle of Independence*. On this visit, I was looking for information about the Black Kettle affair. In Volume Five, I found an article from the *Kiowa County Sentinel* about a Colorado farmer who gave his entire ten-thousand-acre farm to the Cheyenne and Arapaho tribes. His property surrounded the Sand Creek Massacre National Historic Site. That was where, in 1864, U.S. volunteer soldiers ambushed a Native American camp that was supposed to be under the protection of the U.S. Army. It was a savage affair. Over 200 natives were killed, including 150 women, children, and the elderly. The camp was burned to the ground. The dead were mutilated. Afterward the commanding officer deliberately mischaracterized it as a valiant battle against Indian warriors when, in fact, it was an unprompted surprise attack. The following year, a congressional investigation stated that the colonel "deliberately planned and executed a foul and dastardly massacre."

The farmer offering the land thought it was the right thing to do. His offer was accepted. Six weeks later, people from the Cheyenne and Arapaho nations arrived. It was mostly scrubland with a dirt road going through it. They built a general store and administration building and spread out on the arable tracts. When the border closed, the population of the new township, Black Kettle, was 360. Only a few people lived in the town proper.

I didn't find anything else in the history chronicle until an incident two years later made news. One morning, a group of Black

Kettle men on horseback discovered a section of their land had been fenced off with NO TRESPASSING signs. It turned out that their neighbor, a rancher named Hank McLean, was claiming the land was his.

The contested property contained two small ponds that the Black Kettle community used to farm fish, millet, and watercress, among other things. McLean wanted to return the ponds to their "natural state" so he could water his cattle there. The Black Kettle men moved the new fence so the ponds were on their side again. McLean caught them in the act and, in a fit of rage, swore he would be back with an army. He returned a few hours later with about thirty armed men but the Black Kettle contingent was ready with their own armed battalion.

A standoff lasted for nine hours until the sheriff convinced everyone to back down The following day, it was determined the land once belonged to Hank McLean but he had sold it to the farmer who included it in his offer to the Cheyenne and Arapahoe.

Angry about the whole affair, McLean took out a full-page ad in the local paper claiming the "Black Kettle Tribe" had stolen his land. He argued they would continue to take over the county piece by piece if they weren't stopped. This prompted a militia call- -to-arms but many of the would-be volunteers refused to be lured into what they saw as a private squabble. McLean ended up filing a civil lawsuit that went nowhere.

LET'S BUILD A CHURCH

Juan Diego Morales invited me to a luncheon honoring the Windsor founders. I met him at his home. He lived in a small yellow house a woman had owned for fifty years, right until the day before the border closed and her kids came and took her away. The interior was pretty much as she left it, including the 1970s harvest gold kitchen appliances.

Morales pushed his Yamaha scooter into a detached garage, where he also kept a small ethanol distillery. He secured the scooter with a heavy square chain and locked the door using a solid brass padlock with a short thick shackle that was impossible to break with bolt cutters. The two most common crimes in the country were fuel and food theft. At one point, garden theft got so bad that Congress made it a Class A felony.

"Three years ago, someone stole over a hundred beet plants from my garden," Morales told me. "Pulled them right out of the ground!"

"A hundred plants? You must really like beets."

"Sugar beets, for fuel."

Adding to the gardening and farming challenges Independents already faced were drought restrictions making it illegal to irrigate from 11AM to 7PM. The country desperately needed to preserve the Ogallala aquifer, North America's largest underground reservoir. Every square foot of Independence was above the aquifer. Without its water, it was unlikely the country could survive. The entire High Plains owed its agricultural success to the Ogallala. Even with states like Kansas and Nebraska implementing conservation measures, water table levels were already low in many areas. Some say it's just a matter of time before industry collapses and the entire region returns to its natural state.

As Morales and I walked to the luncheon, we passed dozens of people tending to their gardens. "You wouldn't have seen any of this during the first spring," he told me. Everyone knew the supermarkets were about to shut down but were still weren't prepared. We had wheat, alfalfa, soybeans, and potatoes. "Lots of potatoes," Morales said to himself, quietly recalling those struggles.

We could hear lively chatter as we approached the rec center, where the luncheon was being held. There were at least 150 guests already there. Morales took me around and introduced me to congressional aides and other government types he knew from covering Plaza affairs. Being a rare bird—a foreign journalist—folks were eager to talk to me but they were interested in my take on their country rather than divulging their own insights. When I brought up current events, they tended to bristle.

A social butterfly wearing a scarlet dress and matching lipstick was hopping from one conversation to another with a plastic cup of sparkling apple cider. A martini or champagne cocktail would have suited her better. When she caught wind that I was a foreign journalist, she took me by the arm and pulled me across the room to meet her husband, a heavyset man in an ochre hand-knit sweater whose head was completely bare except for strips of closely trimmed hair above his ears. "May I present Stanley Carlton, esquire and statesman, Vice Chair of the Transitional Congress, and member of the Constitution Committee."

Carlton introduced me to Sam Russell and Wallace Fisher, members of the Transitional Congress and the Constitution Committee. No one was more forthcoming than these three men I was fortunate to meet. They were legitimate architects of Independence. For nearly a year, they worked tirelessly until the nation's first election. After that, they slipped into the background and had remained there ever since.

"Our biggest mistake was not allowing ourselves to run for office," Carlton said. The Transitional Congress banned its members from holding seats in the new legislature. "We were being such damn purists. We were so immersed in it all. To just walk away and have people step in cold was a mistake." His eyes flickered with anger as he lowered his voice and told me, "The wrong people are in Congress."

Carlton was not bashful about his views, even with members of Congress around. "All this crap with procedural laws and jurisdiction; we identified those issues four years ago. They were supposed to figure it out in the first session. Instead, what have they done? Your guess is as good as mine, Roman."

"What about the Home Defense Act?" I'd spent many hours at the library poring through newspapers for information about the programs the bill created, which included the NIA and Militia Readiness Initiative. It was big news when Washington signed the bill because Congress hadn't passed attention-grabbing legislation until that moment.

The subject made Carlton writhe with discomfort. He ran his hand back and forth over his smooth dome. I wondered if he was hiding something. He was candid, yes, but not unrestrained. I recast my question. "It was a big deal when it passed but why is it so hard to find information about its programs? The NIA especially?"

"I told you the wrong people are running this country. Now, the Homestead Act," he said, redirecting the subject. "You know about that? We created that. All the First Congress had to do was vote on it. The legislation was already written to every dotted i and crossed t."

Sam Russell and Wallace Fisher crafted an early proposal to replace the U.S. Dollar with a national currency. They wanted to invest the dollars internationally and issue government bonds on those investments. They could have used the money raised in various ways, such as providing low-interest business loans. "People were afraid of parting with that money," Fisher told me. "It was the last thread of a security blanket they couldn't let go of. Congress eventually crushed the idea."

The lunch bell interrupted our conversation. The Windsor founders, a group of congressmen and women, and Vice President Kindler sat at a long banquet table facing everyone. Morales and I were at a round table in the back with other less notable guests. As keynote speaker, Kindler's speech would end up dominating coverage of the event. It was both lauded and denounced. It befuddled most people I spoke with around the Plaza.

Kindler began with reminiscences of the Windsor construction. These were mostly humorous anecdotes that got predictable chuckles from the audience. He praised the founders for their dedication and determination to "work through obstacles unique to our country and yet symbolic of our righteous aims." It was common knowledge that the Washington administration resisted, even fought against, assisting the project. "Hotel Windsor has become an emblem of the Independent will. Our next great achievement"—he paused for dramatic effect—"will be the disbandment of the terrorists but not terror itself."

Except for frowning and stifled groaning in the back, I thought the audience showed restraint, given that the Vice President was equating the country's still dubious fugitive incursion to terrorism. In hindsight, I realize he was signaling to those people in the country who already believed in what he was saying.

"For we wrestle not against flesh and blood, but against principalities, powers, rulers of the darkness, and spiritual wickedness. What I propose today is instead of building monuments to our earthly achievements, let's build to honor He who is greater than all. Let's build a church! Let's build a church that aspires to the glory of God. A church for the ages. One that people will journey from all over the world to worship. The greatest church in the Western Hemisphere. A church that will reflect the righteousness of Independence, which is one nation under God, *for* God. The greatest error the U.S. founding fathers made, the nation's mortal sin, was separating church from state. We must never forget our purpose on Earth is to serve Him. Therefore, the purpose of our government is to serve Him."

I had a clear view of Stanley Carlton sitting at the front with his arms crossed. After this comment about the separation of church and state, he uncrossed his arms and looked up at Kindler. For a split second, I thought he was going to erupt but he kept his emotions in check. Next to him, Wallace Fisher, who had been listening with his elbow on the table and his chin resting in a thumb-to-index-finger cradle, pressed his face deeper into his hand with a vice-like grip as he stared at his empty plate as though he were trying to bore a hole through it.

To finish, Kindler opened a bible. "'Give ear to my prayer, O God, and hide not thyself from my supplication. Attend unto me, and hear me. I mourn in my complaint, and make a noise. Because of the voice of the enemy, because of the oppression of the wicked, for they cast iniquity upon me, and in wrath they hate me. My heart is sore, pained within me, and the terrors of death are fallen upon me. Fearfulness and trembling are come upon me and horror hath overwhelmed me.'"

On our way out, we bumped into *Gazette* editor Colm O'Brien. While we were talking, a newspaper staffer came running up in a tizzy and told O'Brien that a convoy of law enforcement vehicles had left the Plaza earlier for Holcomb.

O'Brien looked at Morales. "Can you get there right now?"

"Yes," Morales answered without hesitation.

Talk about opportunity landing in one's lap. I asked if I could come along and without further delay, we ran back to his house. More accurately, we jogged for one block and power-walked the rest of the way. Despite being in a rush, Morales locked up the garage and double-checked it was secure.

UNWELCOME STRANGERS

I rode on the back of the scooter. Within minutes, we were on a local highway west of town. A barricade of flashing lights far ahead forced us to reroute north to Old U.S. 50. When we arrived in the small town of Holcomb, dozens of scattered residents were all walking in the same direction. A crowd was amassing at an intersection where a squad car had blocked the street. This was as far as we could go. Sheriff units and Capital City police had sealed off the entire southeast corner of town.

It was unclear what was happening but we could see the epicenter several blocks down. On the west side of the street was a general store, a few houses, and an empty parking lot. On the opposite side, the block was undeveloped. Nothing but grass and weeds. Two pickups were parked there. We were told four men had taken cover behind those trucks after an altercation in the store.

"That's gotta mean someone drew a gun," a man beside me said.

"Why stop there if that's the case?" I asked.

It was because the men hiding behind the vehicles were armed. It looked like a scene out of a classic Western. I couldn't help but imagine inside the general store were cowboys standing beside the windows with their backs to the wall and heavy six-shooters in hand. It felt like a performance, with us, the audience, gawking at the scene from several blocks away.

Fruitless commentary and questions bubbled around us. "I see a boot behind the back tire." "Looks like Dirk's truck." "No, his tailgate's all rusted." "Didn't know there were that many police cars in the whole country."

Someone lent Morales a pair of binoculars. The closest truck was parked at a slight angle so he couldn't see whoever was behind it. While he was describing a cowboy hat lying on its crown in the middle of the street, a head appeared over the truck bed for a split second. Then a few others poked their heads up like a whack-a-mole.

"They got Bill Martin in there!" a man yelled as he jogged up behind us. Martin was the owner of the general store. "Holding him hostage!"

"Who's got him?"

"Cartels, gangbangers. We don't know for sure."

This caused a great deal of distress. The messenger told everyone that townspeople were meeting a few blocks away. Morales and I followed people to a flat white building with MOVIES BINGO CARDS painted on the façade. The place was already packed, standing-room-only, except for older folks who were sitting at the cafeteria tables.

It wasn't easy with everyone talking at once but I gathered that three Latino men had arrived in town about an hour earlier. Those who saw these men described them as urban, gang, or cartel types. They parked on Main Street across from the school and walked all the way to the general store. This was emphatically repeated because if those three men had come to "shop peacefully" at the store, they wouldn't have parked so far away.

They were inside for less than ten minutes—doing what, nobody could say—when the two pickups came tearing down the street. Four men or boys, depending on who was telling the story, jumped out and ran inside. They came running back out a minute later, nearly tripping over one another. They hid behind their trucks and grabbed rifles from the gun racks. The most common theory was they confronted the villains inside the store. The cowards inside drew weapons but the young men escaped and took up arms, pinning the bastards inside.

The gathering at the community center was around seventy percent Caucasian, which reflected the town's population. Latinos and whites alike were referring to the three strangers as cartel and gangbangers. I spoke with a man who kept referring to "those fucking Mexicans" A sense of urgency and the need to take action possessed him but I could also see fear in his eyes. But I didn't sense any meanness in him directed toward Latinos or his fellow townspeople. He believed without a doubt the cartels were coming and he was terrified. The entire room was awash in fear.

Morales got caught up in the discourse. "We know nothing about them!" he repeated to anyone who would listen. "All we know for sure is they walked to the store and they're still there. We don't know what happened. We don't know the history between the two groups. We don't know who provoked who."

His voice was a whisper in a windstorm as the discussion turned into a red-faced, vein-bulging argument about whether to bust the storekeeper out. Men on both sides emphasized their indignation by jabbing a forefinger toward the floor, as if they were shaking the truth from their fingertips. Those who thought charging the store would be a disaster won the hour with help from a few elderly ladies who reasoned with the would-be-combatants.

When we returned to the intersection with the view, police were moving everyone back. "This is an armed standoff," an officer said. "We don't want anyone getting hit by a stray bullet."

As this was going on, a dozen men in cowboy boots and trucker hats came running up behind us. They pushed through the crowd and urgently studied the scene at the general store. "That's them," one of them shouted, pointing at the pickups. "They're totally exposed! We gotta go!"

With a rebel yell, they sprinted off. They ran past the first line of lawmen, who ordered them to stop. Behind the last lone squad car, a deputy (the first officer on the scene) waved his arms, signaling them to turn back. At the last second, the mob changed course and dropped down beside him. A half dozen cops in pursuit were closing in, so five of the men, still trying to catch their breath, made a break for it. The deputy held his head, bracing for the worst as they scrambled across thirty yards of open space between the squad car and the pickups.

They ran with desperation. Hip and boob flab thrashed under-shirt, creating a flurry of movement, perhaps an optical illusion of sorts. The first two rolled onto the sidewalk and the others tumbled in behind them. Hootin' and hollerin' abounded as the newcomers pulled out various pistols, food, and supplies from their backpacks.

That was the end of the excitement for the day. It was a stagnant standoff, at least at the epicenter. Extra law enforcement flowed in from nearby towns and counties. They primarily worked to strengthen the perimeter. Every few hours, Capital City Police Chief Buzz McCoy updated reporters at a media center set up in the school cafeteria. Negotiations between the sides were ongoing but he wouldn't disclose who was inside the store, what they wanted, or what set it all in motion.

During a radio interview, Holcomb mayor Lew Blatt said the men in the County General came to frighten and intimidate residents. "We don't know why they're here but we know they're either from a violent street gang or they're straight-up cartel." He didn't substantiate those claims.

By evening, truckloads of militiamen were arriving at road-blocks surrounding the town. They left their vehicles on the side of the road and hiked in with backpacks and loaded wheelbarrows. At least a dozen unaffiliated militia groups staked camp in parks and front yards. The next day, buses arrived with spectators who came for the show. Confrontations between homeowners and trespassers were common. Residents would chase away encroachers only to have someone else take their place.

Latino groups were quick to mobilize. They hiked, biked, or pooled their fuel and loaded into pickups. The largest camp was at the municipal baseball field where dozens of tents and makeshift shelters were spread across the grass.

By the time Juan Diego and I left town that night, officials still hadn't presented an account of what was going on. All we knew for sure was there were armed men outside in plain sight and armed men inside who had possibly taken the store owner hostage. On the nightly call-in show, *Talk of Independence*, host Dennis Knight interviewed two people from Holcomb who witnessed the Latino men walking through town.

GUEST ONE: They wore bandanas round their heads, jeans sagging past their underwear, struttin' like the cartels already won the war and they owned the town.

KNIGHT: I haven't heard anything about jeans sagging.

GUEST ONE: Oh yeah! They came to intimidate and offend.

KNIGHT: I'd like to see photos of these guys. Surely somebody took pictures.

GUEST ONE (disgusted): No one wants to see that.

KNIGHT: What I don't understand is how three boys—three!—could be so threatening to an entire town. It's the mouse in a herd of elephants.

GUEST TWO (with nasally Midwest cadence): Everything about them was threatening. They were saying, "Hey, we're cartel and we're here to F you up. La viva loco."

KNIGHT: They actually said that?

GUEST TWO: Through their actions! How is acting like murderous terrorists not threatening?

KNIGHT: They were so frightening, yet no one called the police until whatever happened inside the County General went down?

GUEST TWO: We don't have police in town anymore. Don't forget that! People didn't know what to do.

GUEST ONE: And stop calling them boys. You make it sound like they was a group of grade-schoolers. They're grown men.

At 11PM, breaking news came out of Lakin, a small town seventeen miles west of Holcomb. This statement was read live on the radio.

"My name is Modesto Mendez. My son is Jorge Mendez. He is one of the three men inside the County General."

Mendez spoke with a pronounced accent as he read from a script. His voice trembled with nervousness.

"He called me earlier to tell me he was there. I want to be clear he's not a member of the cartel or gang and never has been. He and his friends are good kids. They went to school and got diplomas. Jorge didn't have to stay here after secession but he wanted to—they all did—because they believed in this country. It's broken their hearts to see Latino Independents disrespected in our media and to see our leaders refuse to address the hateful talk. This is why my son dressed up en el estilo Chicano.

"In California, back in the 1960s, Mexican Americans came together to protest inequality and prejudice. They called themselves Chicanos, a racist name given to children born to Mexican migrants. The Chicanos were seen as villains when all they were doing was fighting for fairness and respect.

"Jorge and the others walked through Holcomb dressed in the Chicano style. They didn't threaten anyone like people are saying. They build computers. The store there has computer parts. While they were shopping, those four men who are outside told my son and his friends they have to leave. They called them 'cartel scum'.

"This is what Jorge is demonstrating against. It's the whole point they're making. The way a person looks does not define who he is. Being Latino does not mean you're Mexican. Being Mexican does not make you a member of a cartel. Being Chicano does not make you criminal. Being criminal does not make you cartel. My son and his friends have done nothing wrong."

On a Capital City radio show, one caller theorized that Mendez and his buddies chose Holcomb for their supposed demonstration because their mayor had said anyone who opposed the citizenship legislation was an "imbecile or traitor." It didn't take long for sound clips from the mayor interview to go viral on regional radio. "*We need a way to separate the wheat from the chaff like the rest of the modern world.*"

On day two, they released the names of everyone involved in the standoff. They built it up on the radio all morning. It was becoming a national spectacle. There might as well have been an emcee on site.

*Ladies and gentlemen…*drum roll…*from inside the County General, hailing from Lakin, give it up for twenty-two-year-old Jorge Mendez; twenty-one-year-old Benji Ornelas; and twenty-one-year-old Briiiaaan Lopez! Across the street, hiding behind two magnificent pickup trucks, we have Brice and Nathan Pride, sixteen and eighteen years old, from the town of Deerfield; and with them, from Ulysses, it's Dickie Jenkins, seventeen, and Chad McLouth, eighteen!*

A more complete narrative unfolded. Jenkins and McLouth, who lived forty-five miles south of Holcomb, were on their way back from picking up a load of perlite (a type of volcanic glass used in agriculture) east of town.[11] They happened to pass through when Mendez and friends were taking their much-ballyhooed stroll.

Like others, when they saw the Latino men, they saw gangbangers, which they immediately associated with Mexican cartels. They drove to a payphone where Jenkins called his two cousins who lived nearby in Deerfield. The cousins immediately jumped into their parents' truck without asking and sped to Holcomb. Together, these four confronted the Lakin men inside the County General.

---

[11] It was no small expense to travel long distances so farmers would pool their gas for pick-ups.

Nothing happened in the standoff on day two. Police Chief McCoy told reporters, "We want everyone involved to walk away. That's what we're working on." This brings up another curious aspect of the event. On *Channel 7 News*, they showed a wide-angle camera view, revealing the open space behind the boys hunkered down outside. The big empty lot with spotty grass and weeds left them exposed. On the other side were law enforcement vehicles. I know very little about police tactics but it seemed nothing prevented them from going in and taking the suspects down. Once they were out of the picture, dealing with the men inside the store would have been easier.

Experts and former policemen speculated day and night about what could and should happen. To me, that open space suggested the standoff was being allowed to continue. The group outside obviously knew law enforcement wouldn't bother them because in a photograph taken overnight, they were all asleep in their trucks or right on the sidewalk.

Juan Diego was tipped off about a commission meeting in Holcomb to resolve the dispute. He woke me at 5AM and picked me up a half hour later. Daybreak was clear and cold. From afar, we could see smoke rising from camps around town.

At 6:30PM, the first of many black government Suburbans arrived. Passengers were escorted inside. At 7:30PM sharp, nine members of what was being called the Council of Peace emerged. Presidential Hall Chief of Staff Mack Ford led them outside to where reporters and news cameras were waiting. A sizable crowd gathered behind the media.

Ford introduced the members: Albert Gonzalez, the three-term pre-secession Capital City mayor; Holcomb mayor Lew Blatt; Modesto Mendez, father of Jorge; Duane Emmett, a prominent rancher and landowner from Grant County (Ulysses) who was selected to represent the boys on the sidewalk; Pastor Victor Estrada of Las Agoras; B.B. Dixon, co-captain of the Texas County Rangers (the militia where Las Agoras is located); Police Chief Buzz McCoy; Judge Dinkens, member of the Constitution Committee and retired Independence High Court judge; and the only woman on the council, Samantha Cruz from Dodge City, whose father was the current state representative for Kansas House District 37.

Mack Ford talked about the character and ideals of Independence. He spoke of an epidemic blighting the fiber that bound the people and about an evil presence that had crept in from faraway lands. "Lightness will conquer darkness. Believe in yourselves. Believe in our country. Believe in them, our sons," he said, pointing toward the County General. To the council members, he said, "Each one of you is here today because your communities respect and believe in you. Many of the issues that'll come up could be debated for a generation. You get a day. The president and all Independents wish you the best of luck."

The nine council members turned and walked inside without further ceremony, except for Duane Emmett, a country man with broad shoulders, long arms, and a protuberant pot belly. He gave a thumbs-up to a rowdy section near the back of the crowd. This fired them up even more and got them yelping and whistling. I learned they were part of a Grant County militia called the Freedom Fighters.

While the Peace Council deliberated inside, Jill Nguyen of Channel 7 News moderated a rotating panel out front.[12] This was part of the station's "Standoff Special." Public discourse was shifting from the actions and intentions of those involved to the related discord in the country. I thought this exchange (edited for brevity)

---

[12] Ms. Nguyen was born and raised in Capital City. Her parents came from Vietnam to work at the slaughterhouse. There was still a significant Vietnamese population in town but they somehow stayed under the radar during these conflicts.

between two of her guests illustrated the conflicting viewpoints. Marcus Herrera was the founder of the Civil Liberties Union. Burt Thomas was a member of The Krug's Guardsmen during the Flatland Revolution.

HERRERA: Everything went haywire after the arrests in Las Agoras. The suspects should have been arraigned right away. Due process can't be for some of us but not for others or for some crimes and not the rest. We deserve better.

THOMAS: What if nobody knew about the NIA? Say Congress made it in secret and those agents went in, apprehended them, and left without a trace. That would be the kind of secrecy they're being blamed for. But that didn't happen. We know we have the NIA. We know what they do. They're trying to stop the bad guys. They arrested them and then announced why. All the sudden, it's become this big racial issue.

HERRERA: They did not announce why. Have charges been filed? No. What we're seeing right now in this town is a fight over government secrecy, the eradication of civil liberties, and whether or not Independence will be a free society.

THOMAS: Don't lecture me about freedom. I put my freedom on the line when I fought for this country. I went to jail for five months with my brothers. If Independence had never been born, I'd be in Leavenworth right now, rotting in a cell. Do you really think I'm about to give up my freedom?

HERRERA: I respect you for that but the rest of us gave up a lot too. We stayed to be part of a just nation. But let me say this: when some people talk about freedom, they mean having the license to do what they want regardless of others.

THOMAS: You're talking about suspects who were arrested for their connection to a terrorist network that wants to destroy our country. I don't understand what reality you're living in.

At sunset, the east-facing doors of Town Hall opened and the nine council members emerged, resembling a jury coming to deliver their verdict. Albert Gonzalez stood before the microphone as the others formed a row behind him. Camera bulbs flashed while he delivered the Peace Council Accord.

"Jorge Mendez, Benji Ornelas, and Brian Lopez came here to protest against defamatory rhetoric they believe is plaguing our national dialogue and dividing our country. The young men who confronted them—Brice and Nathan Pride, Dickie Jenkins, and Chad McLouth—didn't see it as a political statement. They saw a threat and it conjured up their worst fears. The resulting standoff reflects us as a nation right now: angry, afraid, and lashing out against one another.

"We depend on one another. All of us share the values and sanctity of Independence. But without each other, we are half a nation with half the potential. These past few days have shown us how impassioned our youth are. They are self-empowered and prepared to stand up for their country. They are the future of Independence. But we must secure the path for them because there are powerful entities who want us to fail as an independent and democratic society. The only way we can withstand those forces is to be united. Divided, we are weak but together we are strong.

"Independence is a nation where the democratic ideals set forth by the influential thinkers of Western civilization and moral beliefs taught by Jesus Christ are celebrated and exalted. Here, we can say with conviction what they can only recite across the border. We are one nation, under God, indivisible, with liberty and justice *for all*.

"Tonight, those seven young men are going to walk away from an unfortunate tangle that created a remarkable opportunity for us to come together and face our differences. For that, we should thank them. We need to work together and listen to each other."

Et cetera, et cetera. The accord was packed full of lofty rhetoric and short on specifics. It wasn't as much an accord as a closing speech. The finale was a yawner, literally. When the attention turned to the County General, one boy from Deerfield, stretched out on the sidewalk with a backpack under his head, was caught yawning.

The Council of Peace paraded to the south end of town with the rest of us in tow. The members split up and spoke to the seven young men. Police detectives debriefed the store owner, Bill Martin, who had already said he wouldn't press charges. The militias and other camps packed up. Reporters and news teams left. Residents began cleaning up after everyone. And that was that.

Regarding the gunshot, Martin said that when the four men ran out of his store, they threw the screen door open so hard it sprung back and slammed shut. That's what someone mistook for a gunshot. Regardless, when the Lakin guys inside the store saw the guys arming themselves outside, they panicked and locked the front door. While Martin called the police, they broke into the gun case. That was how the standoff began.

The unofficial and unconfirmed story was one of the Latino men drew an unloaded pistol when they were first confronted. This would explain why the country boys desperately fled. Brandishing a weapon was a felony aggravated assault. This would make it difficult to dismiss. For this reason, it made sense if the standoff participants agreed to keep it to themselves. It allowed them to walk away, exactly as Police Chief Buzz McCoy envisioned.

TREPHINATION

The national media featured the Council of Peace in their follow-up coverage. The council members had nothing but positive things to say, although they wouldn't discuss details. Duane Emmett told the *Ulysses Mirror*, "Once you get people together in the same room, they're gonna fight it out or work it out. No one came out bruised or bloodied."

Have you ever smashed a finger and had the blood get trapped under the nail? This is called a subungual hematoma. If there's enough blood, it can cause unremitting pain. But once you trephinate the nail, say with an electrocautery unit, it releases the pressure on the nerve bed by draining the blood. The instant relief can make your eyes roll back in your head.

Independence had slammed its fingers in the car door (perhaps from the frustration of running out of gas). A few days after the standoff, *Channel 7 News* reported that congressmen behind the citizenship proposal would table their bill for the time being. On the same day, the Justice Department announced they would soon begin arraigning the Las Agoras detainees. All of this had the effect of releasing pressure that had built up under a nerve bed.

It felt like order had been restored. Even the most acrid talk show hosts lauded the handling of the standoff. The county attorney, Jim Sheridan, tainted the goodwill by announcing he was bringing charges against those seven young men. In the press release, he stated it was not a *choice* he made. "Since the law dictates it, as the county attorney, I am beholden to uphold the law."

On the day of the arraignment, I was at CJ's Saloon having lunch. "News at Noon" opened with live coverage in front of the courthouse. Unexpectedly, Mack Ford was standing there with the county attorney. They spoke to the gathered reporters.

"I came here to meet with Mr. Sheridan," Ford said. "I informed him the president plans to pardon any and all men involved in the Holcomb standoff."

"In light of this," Sheridan said, "my office is dropping all charges."

The lunch crowd inside the saloon erupted in applause but not because they backed one side or the other. It was the magnanimous spirit of the moment. I could sense the good vibes around town and on the radio. The political environment had caused so much angst.

I didn't believe all the mistrust and divisiveness suddenly dissipated. In my view, the Council of Peace was a bust. The underlying issues. The contentious issues. That is what the Peace Council was supposed to undertake. At least, this is what we were led to believe. Independents were going to face what they had become (or had always been). In the end, no one had to face anything unpleasant about themselves because the council delivered a dud. The fluffy rhetoric was laughable. I expected it to backfire on the Washington administration. It didn't.

THE DISAPPEARANCE OF TOM JONES

After the Holcomb standoff and all its ancillary dramas had settled, Washington supporters around the Plaza and on the radio were still touting the president's visionary leadership. A few weeks later, a story in the *Las Agoras Post,* reprinted in the *Gazette,* broke up the honeymoon. It was titled "The Mysterious Disappearance of Sheriff Jones."

I mentioned earlier how the sheriff's silence in the aftermath of the NIA arrests seemed peculiar since he oversaw the jail. The *Post* story wasn't the most impressive reportage, and the title reflected its dearth of details, but it was still an important piece because it brought to light Tom Jones's absence, which had yet to be addressed publicly.

The seed for the article was planted when the Las Agoras families gathered outside the jail. Everyone remembers they broke through security that first morning. It happened again a few days later but got little coverage. At the break of dawn, as two overnight employees were being let out through the front entrance, three men sitting near the doors, pretending to be asleep, breached the foyer and disarmed the lone policeman. About twenty others stormed in behind them. Marissa Gomez, the Las Agoras reporter who wrote the Jones story, was with them.

The group made it up to the jail before being stopped by a dozen lawmen with guns drawn. As the families demanded to see the inmates, the officers shouted for them to stand down. In the mayhem, Gomez witnessed an exchange between the undersheriff and two of the family members. They had one demand only: to let them speak with the sheriff. Then everyone would leave. The undersheriff told them there was no longer a sheriff. "I'm in charge here."

Gomez followed up on this but couldn't get anyone in the Sheriff's Department to speak with her. This included the sheriff himself. She even drove out to his home but on each occasion was told by his wife, Gail, he wasn't there. This was untrue. From a discreet distance, Gomez spotted him with her binoculars. Over the course of a week, she noted he no longer used his squad car and rarely drove into town.

The gist of the news piece was that Sheriff Jones, who'd been a fixture in the department for twenty-seven years, suddenly wasn't there and nobody would say why. The article caused enough of a stir to prompt County Attorney Jim Sheridan to address it. In a non-televised briefing, he told reporters that Jones had initially taken a leave of absence but afterward decided he was stepping down as Finney County Sheriff.

Three days later, an explosive piece ran in the *Gazette*, in which a confidential source from the Sheriff's Department claimed that Attorney General Mitch Black fired the sheriff the day after he was quoted on the Radio Hour. ("We have a transparent booking process that was established when this was still Kansas and the law was the law. So you can ask me about anyone who's been legally admitted to this jail.") The source alleged that on the night of the Las Agoras raid, the seven suspects were brought into the jail handcuffed and hooded. At that point, nobody knew NIA agents existed. The agents refused to follow standard booking procedures—fingerprints, photos, identification, warrants, paperwork—and insisted on using an unused jail block. Sheriff Jones was called in and immediately clashed with the agents. They didn't budge so he called Jim Sheridan, who told him they were within their legal parameters. The CA's office confirmed this.

The next day, Jones went to see a federal judge named Lorne Marcum. He had been the district attorney during Jones's first term so they'd known each other for years. When asked about this meeting for the news piece, Marcum said the sheriff "didn't understand the application of the Defense Act laws."

Immediately after this meeting took place, *Gazette* reporter Meg Miller approached the sheriff outside the Law Enforcement Center. Jones was not in a good mood. What little he said was enough to infuriate Mitch Black. The rumor going around was that made the feds publicly address both the arrests and the sudden appearance of the NIA.

Mitch Black met with the media two days after the story broke. Reporters crammed into the tiny press room in the basement of the Federal Building. Black's hair was slicked back with pomade so the ends curled up behind his neck and he wore a blazer with suede front yokes and a generous lapel.[13] A characteristic he shared with Mack Ford was their borderline hostility toward reporters. Black looked pissed about being there.

"I am here to set the record straight on Sheriff Tom Jones. The speculation about his departure has been disproportionate to the facts. I guess the media isn't interested in truth. I'll make this clear: Sheriff Jones did not get fired. End of story."

For a moment, it seemed this really was all he had to say. He glared at the reporters for a few moments before he continued.

"The Home Defense Act initiated the need for structural changes to law enforcement. We've been operating with an archaic system based on old municipal governance for a long time. We need a more streamlined organization. Independence is being divided into eight districts, each with a constable in charge. Sheriff and police departments are merging. Our nation's protective and peacemaking operations will be integrated and more prepared for the dangers we face.

"Finney County is the first to begin this transition. This was done out of respect for the Jones legacy. It seemed fitting he be first or last. If we'd known the media was gonna warp the facts so much, we would've approached it differently. Instead, we ended up with a lot of confusion and misunderstanding."

The Finney County commissioners publicly expressed their vexation. They had appointed Jones and didn't believe Black had the authority to dismiss a county level employee. A federal official firing a county sheriff seemed incongruous with localized power the nation

---

[13] Mitch Black came from Dodge City, where he did well representing packing plants and corporate clients in the region. His experience with big business was the primary reason he was picked to be the nation's first A.G. Grady Washington got a lot of pushback on his corporate appointees. There were numerous conflicts of interest between his administration and the nascent Independent fuel industry. In both instances, he argued he appointed the men because of their experience in the industry. "They're doin' what they love to do."

loved to tout. The commissioners and others demanded an investigation but nothing ever came of it. I think a lot of that had to do with Tom Jones remaining silent throughout the affair. If he had corroborated the *Gazette* story, it might have ended differently,

The public was impotent in the face of these missteps and apparent governmental abuses. It's not farfetched to think if the NIA sting had gone off without a hitch, an elite police force would still be operating secretly in the country. The narrative about the missing Las Agoras residents might have been spun as the type of kidnapping prevalent in Mexico and parts of Central America. As it stood, a federal agency had tried to disappear its own citizens.

HOME DEFENSE ACT

Every official, reporter, and conscientious citizen I spoke to about the NIA and Home Defense Act (HDA) complained about the dearth of information available. Juan Diego Morales suggested I speak with Colm O'Brien, the *Gazette* editor. We met after work one evening.

I waited for him outside the *Gazette* office. When he came out, he shook my hand and then reached into his pocket and pulled out a wrapped candy cane. You'd hear stories of farmers having the foresight to invest in non-sterile seeds, carpenters stocking up on nails and sandpaper, and so forth. O'Brien? He bought six cases of candy.

"Your timing is impeccable," he said before he put the hooked end in his mouth. "You might be the only foreign journalist in the country. The entire English-speaking world will go through you to get the story of our failings."

"You know Independence is under-reported in the U.S.?"

"Of course," he said. "They don't want people reading anything good about us. They certainly don't want reporting that would make them look bad. Like, say, engineering a blockade that nearly starved us."

His house was ten minutes away. When we walked inside, three small kids with matching bright red hair came charging from different directions and launched into him. The "little monkeys," as he referred to them, played on the living room furniture while we had dinner with his wife, Regan. Afterward, he and I went down to his basement study.

The HDA had its roots in a bill introduced years earlier called the Wartime Powers Bill. The wholly unpopular legislation included a clause that gave the president supreme power during a state of emergency, i.e., carte blanche over the militia, law enforcement, and civil law. If that doesn't sound bad enough, the power to declare an emergency would have been in the hands of…yes, the president.

The controversial legislation was scrapped but taken up the following year under the new name, Home Defense Bill. The presidential wartime powers were basically the same, except Congress made a big deal about changing it so only they could declare a state of emergency. In O'Brien's view, if they had started with what they ended up with, nobody would have gone for it. It was only after they offered something completely unacceptable that it became palatable.

They did the same thing with a War Preparedness Tax included in the HDA. "People here hate taxes like you wouldn't believe. It's why our schools and healthcare are among the worst in the world." To make it more copacetic, Congress replaced it with a lesser tax they called the Homeland Security Tax, which again, if proposed in the first place, wouldn't have gone over well.

Surprisingly, when the HDA passed and was signed into law, it was done with little fanfare. O'Brien thought this was deliberate. It allowed the Home Defense programs to remain completely off the radar. When administration or cabinet members were asked about them, the answer was the same: it's in the works and no progress to report.

O'Brien tasked his top reporter to find out what was going on. He wouldn't tell me his name so I'll call him Max. They came up with a strategy that focused on the program's funding mechanism, the Homeland Security Tax. Freedom of information laws gave citizens access to government information. It wasn't a straightforward task.

Max had to fill out dozens of request forms for specific information and then meet with the department employees. Invariably they asked him to fill out additional applications that took weeks or months to process and he was frequently sent to other departments that required appointments weeks out. Long story short, they didn't make it easy for him but after six months he put together a flow chart, albeit stunted, of how the tax funds were being used by the NSD.

More than half of the money was going to the NIA. But what exactly the agency was doing with the money was, of course, classified. That was a dead end. There were other programs and provisions in the bill, such as Border Surveillance, which included equipment, contractors, and construction costs; and Ports of Entry Modernization that involved adding temporary holding facilities, aka jails. Max was told the construction projects were slow to develop because of supply problems. There were rehabs and upgrades being done, but calling it "modernization" was a stretch.

The Militia Readiness Initiative, part of the HDA created to kickstart county militias, was first proposed as a standalone bill. It didn't go over well with the public. If border security was the issue, it made more sense to find a way to hire more patrolmen. People also took issue with the basic idea of financing militias. If they were federally funded, they wouldn't be the people's militias. It would be a government military.

Congress agreed on nominal funding but it was insignificant. Max barely gave it any thought. Through a chance encounter, he found a crack in the wall of financial secrecy. He had been reporting on the militia movement since the early days of the volunteer border patrol. While attending a meeting for new militiamen, he overheard someone say, "If we tap into that money they're getting down south, we go full-time."

When Max questioned the captain about this, he was told established militia companies had access to more robust funding. It turned out private organizations were providing support more substantial than what the NIA provided. "Once we show we're worth a hoot," the captain said, "we'll qualify for proper backing."

The names of the organizations were disingenuous: Humane Immigration, Rural Fuel Assistance, Rita Blanca Hunger Project, Fuel For Farmers. They existed solely to channel money to militias. One husband-wife team oversaw all these nonprofits, or at least the distribution of their funds, from an office in Dalhart.

Max visited them at their spare downtown space, formerly a vacuum repair shop. When they had spoken on the phone two days earlier, they sounded thrilled about the prospect of being featured in a major Independence newspaper. By the time Max arrived, they had cooled to the idea. Their donors didn't want the publicity. The couple said the generosity was for a good cause but, "They're anonymous because they wanna be anonymous."

"Why don't the donors give the money directly to the militias?" I asked O'Brien.

Those donors did not solely fund the nonprofits. Most of the money was coming from a Capital City organization called Independence Integrity and Freedom Fund. Unbeknownst to the husband-and-wife team, this was a funnel for Critical Citizen Support

Financing, an HDA amendment provision. The government was covertly funding militias.

O'Brien and Max spent weeks trying to set up interviews with relevant government officials but no one would speak on or off record. So, they decided to go to print. The evening before the piece was to appear, O'Brien received a call from the *Gazette* owners who told him not to run the story. They said there were national security complications and it could jeopardize the paper's reputation. O'Brien was furious and regretted giving them a heads-up (in anticipation of the blowback he expected).

Not long after this, Max defected. "Left everything he owned and got the hell out of here." As O'Brien told me this, his gaze bored into an empty corner of the basement. He clearly hadn't moved on from the affair.

What I found extraordinary about all of this was the effort that went into bolstering the militias with misappropriated funds while neglecting established law enforcement and border patrol. Even though the Home Defense Act had allocated money for border improvements, there was little evidence it was being used.

Some argue the NIA bolstered nationwide law enforcement, which justified not spending money on local departments. But it didn't negate the fact that an experienced police force was being spurned in favor of amateurs. It wasn't as if the militias were composed of former police and military. Lawmen abhorred the militias. They saw them as sloppy, dangerous, and embarrassing.

If border crossers were an existential threat, it's fair to believe officials top-to-bottom would dump all the resources necessary on the problem. One congressional staffer told me that when they were negotiating the defense bill, they didn't see the border as a point of crisis. The *NY Times* story was alarming but not panic-inducing.

The biggest impact the *NYT* article had was that it galvanized the border militias by validating their existence. Many months later, militiamen and rescue house workers clashed in Dumas. For Juan Diego Morales, this was the big bang moment. From the eruption came an energized, if not frenzied, militia drive. Their cause gave talk show hosts material they could really sink their teeth into. Voices of fear and anger paved the way for the national militia campaign.

The second explosive event was the NIA's debut in Las Agoras. Even if the political climate was brimming with the joys of spring, the egregiously sloppy affair would still have been incendiary. In its aftermath, the Washington administration not only failed to rectify the NIA's glaring missteps, but through Mack Ford, it arrogantly defied criticism. The operation was fodder for the fire and particular congressmen dumped fuel on it with the citizenship bill.

From your perspective—assuming you're somewhere outside of Independence—does it not seem like upheaval and divisiveness was exactly what someone wanted? On the other hand, considering the small government principles that helped fuel the Flatland Revolution, one could argue it was necessary indifference, not purposeful negligence. In this case, it would have been extreme aversion to government interference. Still, it's not out of the question.

Neither Congress nor Presidential Hall showed interest in quelling national discord. Not until the standoff. That was a strange affair that was obviously engineered after the initial clash. Experts reiterated what I suspected; law enforcement could have easily neutralized the group outside of the store.

I heard people say it would've been unfair if police had gone after them first. It implied they were in the wrong (legally and morally). Regardless of how one views either party involved in the standoff, it's a relevant point when looking at it from a political perspective. Once they got involved, Presidential Hall was careful to not show bias for or against either side. The real question was whether the president acted benevolently or was exploiting an opportunity.

It's worth noting the national elections were less than six months away.

* * *

"Roman!" Steve shouted before the door had closed behind him. "What are you doing here? I thought you were long gone."

"How could I leave you guys now?" I answered.

"Get this," said Gus. "Roman's thinking about staying."

"Staying—what!" Steve exclaimed with exaggerated confoundment. "There's gotta be a woman involved."

Gus lifted his root beer to toast. "Here's to Independence, the romance." He took a sip and sucked the foam off his mustache with his bottom lip. "Watch out. Stay too long and you might never leave."

Colm O'Brien said my timing was impeccable. I'd say it was tremendously fortuitous. The country was undergoing metamorphic changes. The Holcomb standoff highlighted the deepening rift and growing hostility. Two armed and angry parties were within shouting distance but couldn't come together to hash it out. The upheaval had settled, at least for the moment. I wanted to see how long it would last.

I had accumulated a lot of material but there was still more to learn and more connections to be made before I could lay it all out on a canvas. The elections on the horizon would likely be a defining moment in the future of Independence. My U.S. and Independence papers were expiring but how could I just up and leave at that moment? Oh, and Steve wasn't off the mark when he said there must be a woman involved.

INTERLUDE & DISCLOSURE

Exploring the new republic wasn't the only reason I journeyed to Independence. Her name was Kat Taylor. In part two of this book, she's inextricably intertwined with my experiences. So, she needs a proper introduction.

After covering the Texas Republican Convention during the secession movements, I drove down to La Serena, a resort south of San Antonio. [14] I was burned out and desperately in need of a recharge. That's when I met Kat. The moment I first saw her is still so vivid in my memory. The doorman opened the handcrafted lignum door just as she was passing through the lobby. She wore a chiffon cover-up over her two-piece swimsuit. Her hair was clipped back under a wide-brimmed hat decorated with a band of sterling and turquoise. She barely glanced at me but it was enough. I was smitten at first sight.

I assumed she was there with her husband or lover. Still, I couldn't stop thinking about her. The force of my attraction to her

---

[14] The world was watching the convention to see if state leaders would declare their intent to withdraw from The Union. When party leaders quickly tabled secession talk, it sucked the air out of the entire national movement. If it had gone the other way, the U.S. might have fractured into at least three big pieces.

was something I'd never experienced before. It was more than sexual desire. It felt like I already knew her. Until that moment, I never gave credence to the idea of soulmates, which to me was a candied apotheosis of infatuation. In a single weekend, my notions of love and attraction were turned upside down.

That evening, I found her dining alone on the patio. Without hesitation, I asked to be seated outside. The hostess led me to a table near hers. I minded my own business and avoided looking at her but there was never a moment I was not aware of her. She appeared engrossed in thought, savoring each bite. After she finished her main course, she remained at the table, sipping her white wine and looking around at the resort grounds, as if she were basking in its *serenidad*.

I was almost done with my entrée when she caught the server's attention with a polite wave. Looking at the dessert menu, she said she couldn't decide between a twisted churro dipped in white chocolate and covered with a matcha crunch or cornhusk meringue, which the server described as a custardy puree of white corn, mascarpone, and vanilla pastry cream inside a crusted meringue made from the white corn husks. She chose the latter.

"Good choice," I said to her.

"You've had it?" she asked.

"Well, no. I don't have a sweet tooth but it sounds so fascinating."

The server overhead me as he was walking away and turned back. "Should I make it two?"

I declined but ordered an Armagnac.

"I rarely have desert, alone," Kat said. "But it's such a beautiful night." Meaning she wanted to prolong the evening.

Fifty feet beyond the patio was a glowing swimming pool surrounded by thick, velvety bluegrass. From there, lamplit paths wound through landscaped trees and out to low, shadowed hills.

"The resort lives up to its name," I said.

She raised her eyebrows in agreement. "That's why I drive four hours to get here."

"From where?"

"Dallas."

An older woman nearby overheard this and said she was also from Dallas. They chatted until her dessert arrived. The merengue looked like a crusted mound cracked in half and squeezed around the custard.

"How is it?" I asked.

"Mmm," she murmured. "You want to try?"

This was unexpected. Of course I accepted. The crusted merengue was made with roasted and ground cornhusk, giving it its name and distinct character. The dessert was rich, not too sweet, and had a savory hint of smokiness. It made such an impression that I made note of it later. I mean, it wouldn't have been appropriate to write in my work journal about a woman I was infatuated with. I wanted to sing.

We sat at her table until she paid her bill and said goodnight. The next day, I invited her to dinner. Except for her spa treatments and my work obligations, we were together night and day for the rest of the getaway. She was supposed to leave on Sunday afternoon and I had a Monday flight. We ended up leaving together on Friday morning.

As we sat in her car outside the airport terminal, we leaned across the console and kissed farewell. "Until next time," I said.

"Until next time."

I was certain we'd reunite sooner than later. It took four years. The night I arrived in Capital City. I didn't hear from her at all for six months after we parted ways. She wouldn't return my calls or answer text messages. A week after Independence seceded, I received a voicemail from an international number. It was Kat. She called from a payphone to tell me she had moved there. That was a shocker. At La Serena, she turned her nose up at the secession movements. She disliked politics in general. For her, the climate around that time was unpalatable. So we didn't talk about it, which was fine with me.

Kat grew up in Lakin, a small town thirty miles west of Capital City. Her mother was the sister of Gail Jones. That meant Tommy, who'd I'd become friendly with through Juan Diego, was her cousin. When we met, she had been living in Dallas for ten years, where she was the top administrator of the largest animal hospital in the state. Her bygone career would become a point of pride and longing.

Among the people I met who moved to Independence, Kat's story was possibly the most unlikely. After graduating high school early, she moved to Colorado to live with her father. She said she was desperate to get out of the "claustrophobic" town she grew up in. If not for her mother, she would have never returned to Kansas.

Kat was in Lakin during the congressional secession debates. Her mother was in the hospital with pneumonia. Kat vacillated between awe and anguish when she described that week. Wherever she went—nurses' stations, gas stations, convenience stores, restaurants—people were glued to CSPAN. When the Secession Act passed, people were in tears. Sure, there were others celebrating but it was traumatic for tens of thousands of residents who lived in the thirty-six counties.

Her mother was even more scornful of the independence movements than Kat. She wanted no part of secession. Kat encouraged her mother to move to Missouri, where Kat's aunt lived. This was toward the end of the Transition. Kat didn't like to talk about this "dark time." Banks were repossessing cars, tractors, and whatever else they could transport. Construction projects stopped and the contractors left with the materials. Businesses were shutting down daily and people were moving away in droves. Kat was there when the last food shipments came and the gas stations refueled for the last time.

"All the media attention they lavished on us turned to nastiness," she recalled. "People in the States called us traitors, communists, anti-Americans, anything they could say to break people's hearts." Yet inexplicably, days before the border closed, Kat uprooted herself from the cosmopolitan life she adored and moved back to the childhood home she had escaped years earlier. She told me Independence was a rare opportunity to build something unique and personal.

The U.S.-Independence border kept us apart but we stayed in touch, mostly by handwritten letters.[15] What I appreciated about our written correspondence was that I could spend hours pondering a single idea or feeling before putting pen to paper. Her letters I read like poetry, going over them line by line, weighing the meanings of words and searching for unconscious links in her longing, despair, and childhood dreams. That's not to say we didn't write about our daily lives; events, crises, and successes. Kat's letters were a private window into Independence and her heart.

I hatched a plan to visit Independence on its first birthday but the U.S. and Independence State Departments denied my applications. It took three more tries (and a commission from a major magazine) to get approved. Independence allowed very few foreign journalists in the country. I mistakenly believed my resume would make me a shoo-in.

The moment finally came. As I walked down the stairs at the Windsor, I noted the iron sconces and restored crown molding and paused more than once to study the old photographs on the walls. But all the while, I held a vision of Kat in her wide-brimmed

[15] Internet and cell services were severely lacking. Copper landlines were available in areas with functioning telephone exchanges.

fedora she wore at La Serena. It had been years since I saw her but this image felt so familiar.

I expected a tremendous gravitational force would exist between us. I expected her to be nervous, even hesitant, but the impact of reuniting would shake her loose. I expected her to be waiting in the lounge, watching the entrance. I expected too much. She was forty-five minutes late and later admitted she almost didn't show up at all.

The spacious hotel lounge was furnished with leather sofas and club chairs grouped around cocktail tables. Skylights and picture windows provided plenty of light during the day but at night the tealights and gas lamps offered little more than ambiance to the unadjusted eye. Two musicians in the back corner were tuning their instruments mid-set. Once guitar and fiddle were in tune, diverging melodies settled into an easy swing.

Behind me, three judges were having a heated discussion about the state of Independence law. I began recording their conversation in my notebook and became so engrossed in their debate that I didn't see Kat enter. I glanced up and saw her standing just inside the entrance. The mahogany frame and orange-hue lighting brought out the subtle auburn in her long hair that fell over her shoulders in textured layers. She wore blue jeans tucked into fancy cowgirl boots that were decorated with an emerald floral design, matching the embroidery on her suede jacket. I stood and waved. She started toward me with quick steps but quickly recovered her composure.

"Wow," she exhaled. "It's busy in here. I guess Congress is back in session tomorrow."

"It's so good to see you," I said. "You look great."

She daintily patted my back as I embraced her. As I write this, I'm struck by how that moment exemplified our future together. I'm not sure if her desire ever matched mine. Her inner life was rife with conflict—uncertainty, fear, despair, longing for something else, somewhere else, or someone else.

She was first-date nervous, uncertain where to stand or whether to sit. I was practically shaking with trepidation but I played it cool. When we sat down, she ordered a glass of mead. It took a few minutes of awkward small talk before she could settle in and relax.

"So," she said as she crossed her legs and fine-tuned where her hands rested. "You're here for two weeks and then back to the simple life."

A year earlier, I had moved from San Francisco to a town thirty miles east of the city. I left *The Atlantic* and was desperately trying to cut expenses. A friend of a friend was leaving the country for two years and needed to rent her house. It was a fortuitous opportunity. I told Kat I'd be living a simpler life. But her point was that I would only be there for two weeks. We hadn't discussed the possibility (a certainty in my mind) of staying longer. It was heavily implied in my letters. How could it be any other way?

"I reserved the room for two weeks," I clarified. "I decide how long I stay."

She considered my answer and then casually asked, "What happened to the woman you were living with in San Francisco? Do you keep in touch?" She acted as though she already knew the answer was yes.

"No." It wasn't a secret we had split up two years earlier. "Why are you asking me this?"

"It's strange you were living with her while—in your letters, you were so—" She laughed to conceal her embarrassment. "You were so madly in love with me."

Her mocking tone didn't sit well with me but I didn't let it dissuade me. "I was traveling. I was busy. I didn't have time to deal with that." It was true. Secession work for the magazine didn't end with Independence. I continued to follow secession movements across multiple continents.

"You lived with her for another two years." She said this as if it had been tormenting her for ages.

"That might seem like a long time—"

"It is a long time!" she said with a laugh.

"Not as long as those first six months! I was ready to fly to Texas at the drop of a hat. I heard nothing from you. Nothing."

"I had a lot going on in my life," she said severely.

"Kat, why are you bringing this up now?" I said calmly, with a smile, hoping to reset the mood. "I finally made it here and this is what you want to talk about?"

"Did she see my letters?"

"Of course not!"

"You somehow managed to get the mail every day even while you were *traveling*," in air quotes.

"Maybe if you had decorated your envelopes with hearts and kisses, she would have been suspicious." I smiled. "I had my mail forwarded to the office. We didn't technically live together. I mean she stayed there. It was my apartment." I stopped myself as I tripped over my words. "Listen, the weekend at La Serena shook up my life. On my way to Quebec," where I flew from Texas to cover the huge demonstrations, "all I could think about was you. That's when I realized my work had consumed my life. I never wanted a career for the sake of a career. It was supposed to be a way to experience this existence, to suck the marrow out of life. Yeah, I continued to cover secession but a revolution was going on inside of me. It just took a while before I could say enough is enough and fight for my own independence." She rolled her eyes. "That weekend was brief but it's not an exaggeration to say it altered the course of my life. It would have been tragic if we had never found each other again. For the rest of our lives, we would've wondered what if."

"Well, we can't go back to that moment," Kat said as her eyes flashed with anger. "We can't live in the past. I live here. This is my life."

"I'm here to move forward," I said.

My words were missing their target but my visible anguish might have softened her defiance because she sighed and leaned back in the sofa. "You just got here. Slow down."

There was little I said up to this point that I hadn't told her before. Her distrust, though, was new to me. Of course we had talked about my previous relationship. By the time Kat and I met, it had already run its course. I admit, in an ideal world, I would've ended it much sooner, if not right away. But from San Antonio, I went to Quebec City, Montreal, New York City, Quebec again, the Michigan U.P., Vancouver, Florida, and finally back home to San Francisco. Over six weeks had passed, much had happened, and I was burned out.

"I swear if you weren't so far away and completely silent, I would've acted sooner," I said. "The border has kept us apart but it's allowed us to evolve in a way almost unheard of in this day and age. Our feelings, desires, hopes, and fears, handwritten. Our relationship isn't conventional. It doesn't have to be. We can be revolutionary. Instead of hiding behind walls of distrust, let's tear them down and open ourselves to one another. No doubts, no games, no expectations. We have to trust the moment. Trust each other."

The room fell away and voices around us melded in stochastic babble. How long this space prevailed is hard to say. I watched the emotions cycle through her like a wheel of fortune, by which our fate would be determined by a lifetime of emotional impressions that had formed her will.

After the guitar and fiddle duo finished their set, men in business suits began to lumber out. Kat and I decided to go for a walk. As we stepped outside, a woman on a Dutch granny bike rode past in the middle of the street. Kat explained why I had seen so many of those bikes. Holland donated thousands of them years ago. Technically, it was Russia. Because of the embargo, Holland sent them to Russia to be flown over on a giant cargo plane.

"Does Russia support Independence like they did Cuba?" I asked.

"Watch it," she warned, and not idly.

We walked through the intersection. Kat's car, a red Mercedes GL350 she brought from Texas, was parked under the drooping branches of locust trees lining the adjacent park block.

"You need to know something," she said in a solemn tone that made my stomach sink. "When I look back on that weekend, I remember it as a dream. It fades a little more every day. Thinking about that period of my life brings back terrible memories."

"It was a time of change for me too."

"You went back to the same job, same home, same girlfriend."

"That's where my belongings were but not my heart."

She didn't dispute this. We walked through the park without speaking. Redbud and cottonwood blossoms had settled in the grass around the walkway. At the center, a single gas lamp illuminated the bottom of the trees.

"How do clients get ahold of you if you don't have a phone?" I asked.

"My pager."

"They still make those?" Then it occurred to me, "Hey, why don't I have that number?"

She didn't answer. Her boots evenly struck the pavement as we passed through the far corner of the park. I repeated my question on the backstreet but she shushed me before I could finish. Straight ahead was a dim figure on a front porch, lit by the intermittent red glow of a pipe. Without speaking, we maneuvered across shadowy bulges in the sidewalk where tree roots were pushing up the concrete.

"Has something changed?" I asked when we were past the rough patches and the gaze of the man on the porch. "I feel you're not as sure about this as I am."

"A life in letters isn't the same as flesh and blood," Kat answered. "You're much more than words. It's more complicated. Every choice we make here has consequences."

I didn't know what else to say. Neither did she, judging by her silence. We turned onto a block unusually well-lit because of the hospital on the other side. The emergency sign illuminated the hollow north wing that had been abandoned mid-construction. The concrete skeleton was another monument to remind people of what they gave up.

I buoyed my spirits by telling myself she just needed time. She said as much herself. With hands in my pockets, I strolled next to her. She buttoned her jacket against the light chill and hooked her arm inside mine. We continued around the block arm-in-arm until we reached her car.

"I should get home," she said. "I have to get up early."

"Will I see you again?" I asked in all seriousness.

"Of course," she said. "Come on. Don't be so dramatic. I told you this is all so sudden."

"So, I should email you and wait two weeks for your response," I said sarcastically. "Or send a letter?"

"Let's meet for lunch," she said without specifying when or how it would be arranged. "Don't worry, I'll see you soon."

A minute later, she was gone and I was alone on the sidewalk. The Windsor lounge and restaurant windows were dark. The street was darker. It felt as though I had traveled across oceans and continents and was still uncertain where I was.

We never met for lunch. She left messages at the front desk, each saying urgent work matters were keeping her away. A week after arriving, I saw her again. She picked me up at the hotel and we drove out to her grandparents' farm.

We didn't encounter another car or even a bend in the highway before we turned west onto another straight empty road. Without halogen lights to mark farmhouses and country stores, nothing but darkness existed beyond the edges of the cropland. Kat shot through intersections without bothering with stop signs. Twenty minutes later, we turned onto a gravel road where decaying wheat fields pressed close to the narrow lane.

A house appeared with black windows, a sagging carport, and twisted trees that gave it a most unwelcoming and eerie character. God, what if the car broke down right now, I thought. A moment later, Kat pulled into the driveway and parked under a half-dead cottonwood tree.

Nobody had lived there since her grandmother passed away ten years earlier. It was a regular clapboard farmhouse. In the shadows of the trees were grain bins, rickety sheds, and various farm implements overgrown with grass and weeds.

Ever-so-gently, I shut the car door so as not to disturb the airy euphony. Kat incautiously closed her door with a muted thud. The night remained undisturbed. She went to open the house, leaving me turning in circles, gaping at the clear and starry sky.

On our way out there, she told me about spending a night there a few years earlier. "Used to be you could see lights from other farms and the glow from the nearby town," she said. With bulbs difficult to come by, turning on a porch light wasn't a common practice anymore. It was heavily overcast that night, making it "pitch black like the lights went off in the world."

Kat returned with a blanket that we unfolded on the best patch of crabgrass we could find. We sat facing the open flatland.

The quietness peeled back and the trill of crickets and buzzing katydids scored the scene.

"What kind of people would we be if we didn't have stars?" I mused as I gazed upward at the clear sky. "Self-centered and small-minded, I would think. The Earth would be our entire universe."

"Is that supposed to mean us?" Kat asked as if she had been expecting a diminishment from me all along.

By "us," she meant Independence. This reflected an underlying inferiority complex that was widespread in the country. The cruel rhetoric, aimed at the soon-to-be Independents before the border closed, planted those seeds of this insecurity. All I meant was the stars give structure to our perception of space. Without them, we'd look up and see nothingness. The Earth would be everything—the universe, our domain. Instead, we're just a speck in existence.

The edge of the universe is (or was) forty billion light years away. A mere forty light years is close to 240 trillion miles. The closest star is twenty-five trillion miles away. I find it deeply frustrating the universe is so utterly inaccessible. It makes sense we create mythologies to explain what's beyond our comprehension.

I reclined and rested my head on my hands. The stars were more vivid than I could ever remember seeing. I let celestial fingers reach down and pull my thoughts up and away from the worldly convulsions of hope and despair. It felt like the uncertainty that had troubled the space between Kat and me was settling.

A patch of cool air wafted over us. Kat rolled down her sleeves. When she put her arm down, her wrist bumped my ribs. "Sorry," she whispered, resting her arm on the same spot. Before long, I couldn't feel it anymore, as if her arm had fused to me.

Unfortunately, our story wasn't the happily-ever-after sort. While returning from my trip to Las Agoras, the bus to Liberal was delayed, causing me to miss my connection back to Capital City. The next morning, Kat showed up at the Wheat Lands Motel. We were supposed to go to a barbecue her friend was hosting. Not only was I stuck in Dumas until the next day, but I'd also left her pager number in my room. When I finally made it back, she wouldn't return my calls.

Her cousin Tommy tried to intervene on my behalf but Kat was unforgiving. In no uncertain terms, she told him she wanted nothing to do with me ever again. I didn't see her for the rest of my authorized visit, including the extensions. I was certain it was just a matter of time before I'd see her again.

A few weeks after my press visa expired, I came home to find her waiting out front. I was renting a room at a retired barber's home. At half the cost of the motel, it was mostly a financial move but I admit I was also worried Immigration and Customs would show up at Wheat Lands looking for me.

Kat and I sat on the porch swing talking long after the sun went down. She admitted she had been conflicted since the outset. I admitted it was naïve of me to believe she could go all in, heart and soul, especially when I was technically supposed to leave after a few weeks.

"I'm not leaving anytime soon," I told her. *Soon* was left undefined. Nobody knew if Independence border agents would let me through if I tried. If they did, since I violated my special passport, I figured jail would be in store for me on the other side.

We spent as much time together as her schedule allowed. She lived in a small cottage on Gail and Tom's property. Technically, it was a trailer home embellished with a pitched roof, white siding, and flower boxes. I stayed there a few times but it made Kat uncomfortable. It made her feel like she was in high school, with her aunt taking the role of her mother. If Gail disapproved of me being there, she didn't share it with Kat or me.

My room at Johnny the barber's house was big enough to fit a twin bed and a dresser. When Kat visited, his wife always reminded us (with an obligatory laugh) to keep the door open. This wasn't sustainable but we were stuck in limbo. We talked about getting a house through the Homestead Act but the courts were backed up so it took forever. Besides, Kat thought all the good places were taken.

She was one of the few veterinarians in the country who practiced solely herbal medicine. Each day and all day, she worked in her garden and kept busy making poultices, powders, extracts, and oils. She even made her own activated charcoal. Nothing about this new career came naturally to her. Although she'd been an animal hospital administrator for fifteen years, she wasn't a veterinarian. Even gardening was new to her. She'd never grown more than a few houseplants.

When Kat first moved to Independence, she tried to mobilize veterinarians to start an animal hospital. While recruiting at a job fair, she met John Mayberry, a prominent farmer. He introduced her to herbal animal care and mentored her. Mayberry inherited a cattle ranch he converted to a fruit and vegetable farm after secession. He sold most of his livestock and invested in work horses and sheep (for the wool). Since pharmaceuticals were in short supply, he began experimenting with nutritional, sustainable pasture plantings. This soon expanded to medicinal herbs.

I've never known anyone who worked as diligently and with laser focus as Kat. Since she wasn't a trained veterinarian, she couldn't join the Independence Vet Alliance. This meant she couldn't receive the medicine and supplies flown in two to three times a year by international nonprofits. To compete, she made rural house calls since all the vet clinics were in town.

Her challenges didn't end there. She was on the futile side of a perceived value bias. Herbs were viewed as an inferior alternative to pharmaceuticals. She struggled to get clients to agree to cash payment. Everyone wanted to haggle and barter. Since she desperately needed clients, she usually agreed to their demands. Fuel was the one non-cash payment she accepted and often required.

One day in late spring, Kat stopped by my place unannounced. She cut straight to the chase and asked if I wanted to move out to her grandparents' farmhouse. The area was underserved by vets so the idea was to set up her own clinic. I didn't see the business opportunity. There weren't many people out there. But for me, I'd have a quiet space and plenty of time to write.

The farmhouse was ten miles from Ulysses, where the population had shrunk from six thousand to under two thousand. There were a couple of food markets, a few restaurants, a library, and the county's only school. Besides an old dairy farm down the road, there wasn't another operational farm within five miles of us. Kat was determined to make it work.

A few weeks later, we made the move. We transplanted as much of her garden as we could. She harvested the rest and immediately began drying the plants and collecting seeds. We converted her grandmother's sewing room at the front of the house to a visiting office. A corner upstairs bedroom with windows overlooking the farm became my office.

With lumber and paint we found in the barn, we made a business sign and staked it by the gravel road: KAT'S DOGS AND HORSES. Business was sparse from the get-go. She may have overestimated business potential and I completely underestimated the isolation. I had imagined spending time with Kat on beautiful summer evenings while our dogs ran around. In reality, we didn't have a dog and she worked late into the night until she was too tired to work or do anything else. Because of fuel restrictions, we rarely went to town.

For the first few months, it didn't bother me too much. I finished my magazine piece in August and sent it to the editor, using the internet station at the Ulysses Library. Afterward, Kat and I had dinner at the café in town. A rare treat. Although she didn't say it, it was clear she was looking forward to the financial boost. The magazine commissioned my trip to Independence but that didn't guarantee they'd publish it and pay for the resulting essay. I didn't tell Kat. The mistake would come back to bite me.

PART TWO

Whose Independence?

LINGERING FRICTION

The post-standoff calm lasted through the summer, although there were still rumblings coming up from Las Agoras. The Peace Accord had done little to ease friction between militiamen and townspeople. The mayor banned armed groups from city limits, only to have the county commission overrule him a day later. This reversal by the three rural commissioners (the vote split three-two) predictably sparked outrage in town.

NIA detainees were still being held at an undisclosed location. Congress was blamed for the delay because they still hadn't finished ratifying and/or modifying over two thousand criminal statutes and administrative rules pertaining to court proceedings. At last, they completed the ratification in late spring. The following week, charges were at last filed in federal court but only against two of the suspects. In the Southern District, they were charged with affiliation with a terrorist organization, pornography, obscenity, drug trafficking, and tax evasion.

One detainee was to be extradited to the U.S. The four others were sent to Las Agoras to be arraigned in Texas County Court. They were released within a week. The county attorney said the "spattering of evidence paled compared to the governmental abuse they endured."

The Justice Department immediately released a statement saying this was a "major letdown for justice and a blow to our intelligence agents," but they respected the county's sovereignty. Many believed the Justice Department, which oversaw the NIA, didn't want to admit fault in the arrests and/or procedures. Sending the suspects to Las Agoras was a way out.

And there was the Daniel Velasquez case. The Texas County sheriff was at the center of this controversy. He was accused of conspiring, or at the very least, siding with militiamen. In his own defense, he pointed out he didn't have an investigator. It was only him, one deputy, and a few part-time administrative assistants. Pre-secession, he could have asked the state Bureau of Investigations for help. He asked the Justice Department to send an investigator from Capital City. Six months passed before his request was granted.

ELECTIONS

There was no time for political disputations and distractions during the late spring and summer months. Farmers were busy from dawn to dusk and so were everyday gardeners and homeowners. That was pretty much every capable citizen in the country. Winter food security depended on seasonal crop yields.

The six-week national election season opened on the second Monday of September. Media outlets were swamped with ads. Television stations expanded broadcast hours. Radio stations shorted shows to make space. During the first ten days, most of the spots were candidacy announcements, e.g. "My name is Jane Doe and I'm running for Independence Assembly." There were a handful of third-party endorsements and attack ads. Most notably, Todd Leiker and

Carey Dobbs spearheaded a full-scale national campaign against President Washington.

Before opening day, federal law strictly prohibited campaigning and advertising. Campaign financing was restrictive but simple. Individuals could donate a maximum of 250 dollars to any one candidate. PAC and special interest contributions were prohibited altogether. Contributions were made through the National Election Commission.

Anyone could be on the ballot for a fee that wasn't due until after the second week. There were a lot of candidates testing the waters. Juan Diego Morales's *Weekly Independent* did excellent work covering every local and federal election.

Morales and others believed the right candidate could challenge President Washington. They thought his popularity was superficial, based on name recognition. The targeted third-party campaigns against him were robust. But with very few candidates generating much of a buzz, it seemed Washington merely needed to survive the offensive.

The owner of the nation's largest dairy facilities, Herm Whitehead, emerged in the South as someone who might give the president a run for his money. Two weeks in, another potential challenger emerged. Council of Peace participant Albert Gonzalez dropped his name in the hat and good fortune plucked it out. Being a recognizable figure and former mayor of the nation's largest town helped garner media attention. He was well-dressed and charismatic. Young people liked him, women liked him, and plenty of others liked him enough to make him an overnight contender.

He got a boost from being a member of the Council of Peace but I saw him as the messenger who delivered the stunningly inadequate resolution. Maybe that shows how initial impressions form our perceptions and expectations. It turned out I may have been wrong about him. Rumor had it there were deep divisions within the council and Gonzalez was unhappy with the entire process. In the end, they said he had to swallow a bitter pill in the name of cooperation.

There was another event he was involved with while mayor that came up frequently during his campaign. A few years before the secession, the county was planning a major hospital expansion. While varying proposals were being debated, Gonzalez called for the project to be localized. Echoing local advocates, he didn't want big contractors and companies from Denver or Oklahoma City, for example, taking millions of dollars away from the community.

It went against the national trend of corporate consolidation and privatization of public works. His opponents argued it would drive up costs or shrink the expansion. Gonzalez and his allies had the public's support but in the end, city and county leaders voted to outsource the project. Countless people I spoke with in Capital City remembered his position on the issue. If it wasn't an American ideal, it certainly was valued in Independence.

His campaign grew and so did his opposition. As his opposition grew, so did his popularity. In a biodiesel-solar-powered motorhome, he wound his way through northern Independence, calling for citizens to unite against the consolidation of the nation's resources. In Dodge City, the last stop on this tour, over three thousand people showed up at his rally.

"Our president and Congress gave our most essential resource to a small group of people. Soon, if they're successful, the only major ethanol plant in the country will be operated by a single company owned by a single man. A handful of individuals, many who are part of the president's circle, have bought the best land for growing feedstock near his proposed refinery site. We are on the brink of losing our country. There's no money coming in from the outside. None. Zero. So how long will it take until the small consortium of energy companies has all the money? Do you think they'll stick around or will they hop on their private jets and fly away with all the money of Independence? We need a new plan, a democratic plan. If we don't control our land and resources, then this dream of independence is hopeless [....] This election is about whether we want a free society. When your voice and your vote no longer matter and this country is owned and operated by a few organizations, it'll be too late."

Grady Washington was the spitting image of the typical Midwestern politician. He spoke in a deferential tone of a regular guy doing the people's bidding. In his speeches, he always hit certain catchwords—taxes, family, freedom, God—and played them against welfare, socialism, big brother, etc.

As president, he fought against any and all semblances of social welfare. Despite dubious taxes associated with the Home Defense Act, taxation was still minimal. They privatized all utilities. Schools were optional and funding was community-based.[16] But his brand of governance—austerity and privatization—wasn't a shared vision of what Independents aspired to, nor did it reflect Flatland Revolution principles. There never was a unified vision for Independence and the array of presidential candidates reflected this.

A congressman from Independence City, who was running for president, advocated for his town's vision of a nation composed of city-states, in which county lines would be reconfigured around certain townships. In this system, the federal government would be a barebones structure that exists to facilitate cooperation between provinces and interact with the international community.

A former long hauler from Liberal ran on a sort of Pro-U. S./anti-Independence platform. "We're never gonna change *who* we are. We can't change *where* we are. But we can change what we are.

---

[16] Washington avoided talking about hospitals, which were operating at around ten percent capacity. They were mostly volunteer-based and dependent on international donations. There were three clinics located inside hospitals that were run by foreign nonprofits.

Let's restore American values to Independence." He believed "all our resources and all our brainpower" should zero in on fueling the nation. "Washington failed so now it's someone else's turn."

A woman from Dumas, who founded a rescue center near the border for refugees, wanted to "soften the artificial separation" of church and state. She believed faith should be central to all governing decisions, yet somehow she wasn't seen as a religious hardliner. That honor belonged to Vice President Kindler, who many people believed was going to run as the "Minister of God" candidate after Washington's theoretical second term.

The most intriguing candidate to me was Lorena Jimenez, a Las Agoras woman who was the daughter of Guatemalan immigrants. Her candidacy was a self-declared referendum on Independence power. She proposed to dilute authority by abolishing the presidency (she would be the last), merging the two congressional houses into one unicameral legislative body she called the National Assembly, and appointing ten new judges to the High Court, making it a thirteen-member body. A council of thirteen congressmen and women voted in by their colleagues every two years would replace the presidency. They would create a governing cabinet—state department, commerce, energy, foreign affairs, etc.—that would be subject to an oversight and reform committee made up of elected citizens.

Jimenez could be a firebrand. She described the presidency as a remnant of totalitarianism. "Some of you just love power and bowing to those who rule over you. Have some self-respect! A king doesn't give a damn about his peasants. He only wants your allegiance." Her style upset many people. "She's so full of herself!" "The mouth on that lady!"

Nobody energized their supporters as much as Albert Gonzalez. He was gaining momentum. The Washington campaign began responding to the Todd Leiker-sponsored ads, branding them as "despicable," "outrageous," and "immoral" attacks on the president. During a press conference, Mack Ford said "such blatant lies" should be criminalized and he called for stronger libel laws. The president stayed positive and focused more on general ambitions and values than achievements. The one exception was the Council of Peace, which he claimed united the country.

More than any other single issue, the failed gas pipeline haunted Washington. During a rally in Hugoton, he blamed the U.S. (always an easy target), saying an extraction cap was why the talks fell through. Independence was forced to accept buyout terms for existing natural gas facilities and power plants. They agreed to limit how much natural gas could be extracted annually. The pipeline proposal depended on Independence being able to export natural gas in exchange for petroleum. The U.S. wouldn't budge during talks.

Gonzalez saw the privatization of the energy sector as the nation's fall from grace. It was the moment the country lost hope for real independence. For him, the future of the country was inextricably bound to reclaiming the natural resources. In his own defense, Washington claimed the yearly payments would have been an unsustainable burden for the people. The energy companies took on heavy debt and daunting responsibilities in a time of limited supplies. "They know this stuff better than anyone we got. It's what they do. We need them and I thank them."

After two weeks, candidates had to commit to remaining in their races. Presidential hopefuls paid 15,000 dollars to stay in, 3000 dollars for Congress. Unspent contributions were returned to their respective counties and used like tax revenue. Herm Whitehead and Albert Gonzalez both held rallies to announce they were staying in the race. Lorena Jimenez was the last to declare either way. Shortly before the midnight deadline, she announced she was dropping out. In her speech, she endorsed Gonzalez, calling him "our only hope."

The ballot was set: Grady Washington, Herm Whitehead, and Albert Gonzalez. Three days later, the Southern dairyman dropped out. At a televised Dalhart rally, he went all in for Washington. "Make no mistake, Grady Washington is the best man for the job, period. Without him, Major Krug, and the NIA, there'd be no one between you and the violent organizations of Latin America. If we lose Presidential Hall, we could lose all the work we've done fighting this network, especially down here near the border. You must vote for Grady Washington if you care about your safety, our values, and this country. Grady Washington is our only hope."

Heading into the last week, Washington seemed to be everywhere at once, with his wife and kids and Major Krug frequently in tow. Until this point, his campaign and administration had kept his personal ten-passenger turboprop out of the media. Now they did little to hide the jet excursions. There were even rallies staged at municipal airports.[17]

The public and the press were curious about the plane. Where was the fuel coming from? This agitated Mack Ford. "There isn't another head of state in the entire world who doesn't have access to proper transportation. The president has a full schedule. The only way he can get out to see people is by flying. This is a critical moment in our history." He told reporters the plane used sustainable biofuel but when pressed for details, he became even more agitated. "It's not my job to know where they fill up with gas, just like I don't know who washes the windows or mops the floors."

Campaigning ended at midnight on October 20th. The next day, voting booths were open from 7AM to 7PM. IBS's national coverage began at 8PM. The network's new production facilities debuted for the election. The slick stage design, video resolution,

---

[17] There were rumors that Washington, certain cabinet members, gas execs, and Bill Tyson were rarely seen in public because they used their private planes to leave the country.

and sound fidelity were a cut above the rest of Independence television.

Kat and I watched together. I suppose I felt compelled to supplement it with my take. I wanted her to be interested in something other than work. At least that's what I thought at the time. In hindsight, I wanted her to be interested in me.

The first update came with thirty-two percent of polling stations reporting, representing less than twenty-five percent of all registered voters. Those early tallies were thought to be from the least populated districts so it was the rural vote Washington was expected to carry. That's as far as Kat made it. She was asleep when Gonzalez closed the gap.

With eighty percent of precincts in, he led by ten percentage points. Supporters at Gonzalez headquarters were jumping up and down, shouting, hugging, and high-fiving. At 11:30PM, they revealed the final results from election commission headquarters. Gonzalez won in a landslide.

Exuberant supporters were calling the win "the rebirth of Independence." I envisioned the celebrations happening around the country when I walked outside. Perhaps I was expecting to hear distant neighbors blowing party horns and launching bottle rockets. There was only the familiar song of insects and nocturnal creatures in the theater of silence.

INDEPENDENCE DAY

The day after the elections was Independence Day, already renowned for early fall barbecues, softball in the park, and local parades. Kat and I drove thirty miles to Lakin to attend a party her friend was throwing. She was nervous. Before moving back from Dallas, she hadn't talked to friends she grew up with for twenty years. She'd only seen her friend Tonya, who was throwing the party, a few times since then.

Two ladies smoking herbal cigarettes on the front porch welcomed us. "Happy Independence Day!"

Tonya's mother, a round jolly lady, was the first person we ran into when we walked inside. "Katherine! Oh my goodness, how are you? Where have you been? Charlie!" she cried to her husband a few feet away. "Charlie, come here. You remember Katherine Taylor? Maeve Schafer's daughter."

Tonya was a younger replica of her mother and therefore easy to recognize. Her eyes lit up when she spotted Kat. Curled bangs bounced on her forehead as she crossed the room. She seemed like someone for whom smiling came easily.

"Oh, Kath, it's so good to see you!" she squealed as she opened her arms and patted Kat on the back. "Oh my gosh, you look amazing!" She shook her head in astonishment as she looked Kat up and down.

"How are you?" Kat asked with excitement that tried to match Tonya's. "It's so good to see you."

"I'm good. I just can't believe you're living in Lakin again."

"Closer to Ulysses."

"That's almost next door, considering everywhere you've been!"

It turned out Kat knew more people at the party than she first realized. Tonya took her around and re-introduced her to old schoolmates. Upon hearing their names, Kat appeared surprised to recall their teenage or sometimes prepubescent faces underneath decades of flesh, wrinkles, and facial hair.

Tonya led her to the dining room, where her husband and his buddies were yelling over one another. "James," she interrupted. "This is Katherine." She said this with a certain reverence, like he should know exactly who she was. "One of my best friends from school," she added for Kat's benefit.

"Katherine," he said, not with the enthusiasm one might expect from someone meeting a significant person in their spouse's life, but with a note of apprehension, perhaps because Kat hadn't been there as a friend and missed the significant moments of her life. He was still courteous, at least. "Nice to meet you," he said and turned back to his friends.

I took the bottle of a bitter liqueur we brought to the kitchen. It was Tommy's attempt at an Italian-inspired aperitivo. Another guest brought gin so naturally we tried to figure out how to make a negroni.

The aspiring mixologists and I were discussing how to replicate vermouth when Kat and Tonya returned. Tonya marched straight toward me and raised her hand to shake mine. "We haven't had the pleasure," she said.

Kat's face was the color of the red liqueur. Apparently, they'd been talking about me. Tonya proceeded to give me a summary of their friendship that began in the first grade. Then she questioned me about why I stayed in Independence, what I was writing, where I grew up, and so forth. When the opportunity arose, Kat moved in and hooked my elbow and pulled me away.

"Your friend knows more about me now than you."

For the rest of the party, Kat kept me close. It was unusual, albeit welcome. It called attention to how much we had deprived ourselves of physical intimacy since moving out to the farmhouse. If Kat wasn't seeing clients, she was in the garden or utility shed. If she wasn't working on her herbal program, she was in her office reading about pigment variation in feline irides or learning about parasitology or any number of subjects in the voluminous reference books she'd acquired. She worked until she was too tired to continue and then checked out for the night. If she didn't go straight to bed, she would lie on the sofa reading a mindless mystery or romance while I sat in the armchair with my own books and newspapers. Occasionally we would watch a movie on our VHS player. Right after we moved there, we watched the entire *Lonesome Dove* series over the course of the week. We hadn't done anything like it since.

Kat took my hand as we left the party. We could hear sporadic firecrackers from other parts of the small town. Down the block was another party where a lively group stood on the front porch. When we reached her car, she turned me around and pulled me close.

"Thanks for coming," Kat whispered as she leaned in and kissed me. It wasn't just a sweet, appreciative smooch. She engorged me. A soft but cool gust of wind rustled the autumn leaves. She gently bit my bottom lip. "Let's go home."

The first thing she did when we got home was check the answering machine for client calls. I was pouring a glass of beer in the kitchen when she came up behind me, wrapped her arms around my waist, and pressed her lips against my neck. When I shimmied around, she pinned me against the counter.

Between kisses, I asked, "What are we going to do about our contraception problem?"

"Let's just have a bunch of kids," she said as she softly bit my chin. "That's what you do if you live on a farm."

I chuckled.

"Why are you laughing at me?" she asked, rubbing her nose against mine.

I suddenly wondered if she wasn't joking. I tilted my head back to get a better look at her. "You're not serious."

When she looked up at me, she seemed startled, as though she hadn't realized what she said.

"About the kids," I clarified. But it came out more serious than I intended. She wiggled out of my arms. I tried to pull her back in. "Come on, what's wrong?"

"Nothing," she said, gripping her forehead. "The drink I had at the party…."

"Are you mad at me now?"

"I'm not mad," she said with a pained look.

"Sorry, the kids comment made me panic. I didn't mean it to come out that way."

"It doesn't matter," she said, but clearly it did. "I'll make some tea."

Neither of us knew how to move forward. That was one of the few occasions she lowered her guard since La Serena. For a moment, it seemed she was ready to let me in. I suppose we had an accident.

INTERNATIONAL CALLS

A few days later, I found out the magazine would not publish my story. The editor emailed me on Independence Day. It's hard to believe that was coincidental. The only reason she gave was that Independence was "out of fashion." I bristled at the prospect of breaking the news to Kat but I did it anyway. She said nothing. Her silence was heavy.

The feelings she bottled up burst the next day. I was in my office and heard her coming up the stairs. The door swung open and Kat entered with a vengeance.

"Who were you just talking to?" she demanded.

"Juan Diego," I answered.

"Oh, really?" she asked sarcastically.

"What's going on?"

"What if a client was trying to get through and it was urgent?"

"I thought you were gone. Am I not supposed to use the phone?"

Even in her disputatious state, she couldn't suggest this. She dropped an open notebook on my desk and pointed to nine circled California phone numbers. "I called to find out why the bill was so much. Look what I discovered! Who is this?"

"It's my bank."

"Oh, please! Nobody calls their bank every other day!"

"It's not every other day. And how could it be this much? They were brief calls."

"Those are international calls, Roman."

"I didn't think about that."

"Why were you calling your bank?" she asked with distrust. When I hesitated, she jumped on me. "You weren't calling your bank, were you?"

"Yes!" I snapped defensively. "I was trying to figure out where money was going so I could stop the payments."

"You told me you didn't have any money."

"Now I don't," I said, getting flustered.

"You are totally contradicting yourself."

"I had money in the bank," I said. "It was being used for utilities, subscriptions—whatever. I paid rent for the year and stopped everything else."

"You paid rent for the *year*!"

"Of course I did! All of my belongings are there. I have a lease. You know that."

"So while I've paid for everything here, you've had money in California?"

"Money I have no access to. You know this, Kat. We've talked about it. I told you how difficult it was to get a money transfer. I'm sorry. It's not my fault."

"Yes it is. You could have—you should have transferred money before your visa ran out. Why didn't you?"

"Because it would have looked suspicious wiring in a stack of cash when I was supposed to leave."

"Roman, no." She gripped her head with her hands. "There are a thousand reasons you could have come up with. What were you thinking? Were you assuming we'd get back together and you could live off me?"

"I didn't think it through. What do you want me to do? Stop writing and get a job at the dump digging for plastic and metal? What do they pay, twenty dollars a day?"

"You could get there on the bike," she said in all seriousness.

"Oh, Kat!"

"Just forget it!" She grabbed her notebook and left in a squall.

"Come back here!" I yelled after her and then barreled down the stairs, nearly falling. "Hold on," I demanded as I marched through the kitchen. I was hot. This was the first time she had ever seen me this angry. I'm sure it wasn't attractive. "Listen to me. Writing is what I do. I don't know what you thought I'd turn into when we moved here but I want to make this very clear—"

"I know what you do," she interrupted. "You write. That's all you do. Write and listen to the radio all day."

"If this is about money, then we should think about what we're doing out here."

"It was about the phone bill. We talked about it. Now let's move on."

"You barged into my office to show me the calls—"

167

"I've had a long day, alright!" She was close to tears. "I paid for things I shouldn't have. I took a loss. You know, I'm trying to succeed at what I'm doing and it's hard."

"I know that," I said in a less confrontational tone. "You work harder than anyone. But making me feel bad about what I'm doing doesn't help either of us."

"I was simply asking about the phone bill!"

"Well I'm glad we had that chat."

PORTENTS

The next morning, Kat asked if I wanted to take her car to get groceries and run an errand for her. At first I was distrustful. I thought she was trying to get me out of the house. Because of the fuel shortage, we didn't take casual trips anywhere for anything. Only when Kat had to drive through town for appointments. That's how I got to the library. She'd drop me off on her way out and pick me up on the way home. I realized this was a peace offering. It would be the first car trip I'd taken alone since we moved out there.

Frozen grass crunched underfoot as I walked around the expansive garden to the car. Per her instructions to save fuel, I scraped the windshield before starting the car. As I backed out of the driveway, I tuned in to the radio show I'd been listening to upstairs.

"Is anyone surprised we have a food shortage? What happened right in the middle of our prime growing season? Half the population decided to go on strike! I hate to say I told you so, but I did. I know people say that's behind us, let's not dredge up old bygones, but it's gotta be acknowledged. How many thousands of pounds of produce was left unpicked or unused?"

Ever since election day, the discontent on IBS was growing. This was the first time I'd heard the discord from the previous spring being directly referenced in this way. It was also the first time I heard anyone declare outright that there was a food shortage. This had been an unfortunate fact of life in previous winters but the major issue this year seemed to be less about supply and more about access. Food was still plentiful at the markets. It suggested the problem was a lack of income.

A substantial portion of the population had little or no money coming in. It was up to communities to provide for those in need. Early on, there had been a major campaign to teach people how to preserve food—curing, canning, pickling, freezing, etc.—but the nation lacked systems that governments normally facilitate.

After the dustup over the phone bill and finances, this struck a chord. I was completely broke. Kat had given me twenty-five dollars to buy food. When I returned home, she would ask for the change. It made me feel like a child.

After the market, I drove to the library to exchange books, read the newspapers, and check my email. Last stop was the feed store, located a mile east of town. A cat that Kat had treated was sleeping on a pillow against the wall. A small makeshift diner with a plywood counter and seven seats was at the back of the store. The farmers who frequented the eatery were always gabbing about who was doing what and were eager to opine about everything and anything. The regulars felt pretty good about themselves. A man who could eat out three or four times a week was doing alright. Showing few signs of the hard times, they were robust, like the big diesel workhorses they drove. When I had money, I would ride over on a bike I found in the barn.

I chatted with the farmers while I waited for the owner. As we were talking, the front door opened and a waft of cold air blew through. I was surprised when I recognized the man who entered.

It was Tom Jones, the former sheriff, and Kat's uncle. I'd met him a few times when I visited Kat at her cottage.

Tom had been hired by a group of well-to-do ranchers. The most prominent among them, Duane Emmett, was a member of the Council of Peace, who representing the young men who confronted the group inside the store. He and other area ranchers wanted a professional to look after their property so they called on a private security company owned by a law enforcement friend of Tom's.

Over the summer, there was a spate of rural thefts down south. It mostly involved fuel and food but one case of cattle rustling near Dalhart made the news up north. Concerns about theft becoming more prevalent were most likely sparked by the fear of border-crossing criminals. That controversial issue had remained dormant over the summer but picked up again during the elections.

"Hey there, Roman. I thought that was Kat's car outside," he said as he looked around for her.

"She's at home," I said.

"How's life out on the farm? I've been meaning to stop by."

"I'm still getting used to it, to tell you the truth. It's quiet." Solitary confinement was what it felt like at times but I kept that to myself.

The owner came out from the kitchen wearing a chicken-print apron. "This way," she said, interrupting us. I followed her out to the back of the store, where she presented a small dead tree. "Here you go."

"What am I supposed to do with that?"

"Chop it up and take it to your wife," she answered. "She wants to make activated charcoal and my customers are asking for it. So here you go."

She offered me an axe from the storage shed and left me alone with the tree. The species—Birch, I think—was supposedly good for activated charcoal but not common in that region. I stood there shaking my head. The nerve of Kat.

"Fine, I'll chop up a tree," I mumbled.

First, I went back inside to finish my conversation with Tom. He was in the back talking to the farmers.

"You said livestock?" one of them asked him.

"I've heard of cattle and horses stolen down south," Tom said. The color drained from the questioner's face. "I'm just saying be careful."

"Cattle rustling's been around since the frontier days," one of the other farmers quipped.

"Maybe they should help themselves to your grain!" the worried man snapped. "You got plenty of it."

"Calm down, Hal. I'm not saying it's okay."

After Tom gave them his satellite phone number, we left them anxiously discussing how they were going to protect their property.

"Should Kat and I be concerned?" I asked when we were outside.

Tom shrugged. "Best to be prepared. Don't advertise valuables and don't give thieves opportunities.

He stopped next to a lime-colored hybrid vehicle. The juxtaposition of Tom, a full-sized man, next to the tiny economy car was striking. "Company car," he grumbled.

The farmhouse was built atop a small rise that was barely noticeable even though it might have been the highest point around. A row of cedars protected the house from northern winds and gangly locust trees gave shade in the summer. Most of the farm buildings were rotting or rusting and served no purpose artifacts of a bygone era. Dead and decaying farms were as much a part of this land as the soil and sky.

The gravel road hadn't been graded for years. The washboarding had become so bad that I was certain Kat's car would eventually begin falling apart from the rattling. The best section was alongside Earl McCrary's dairy farm. He used an implement on the back of his tractor to grade the half-mile stretch contiguous to his land.

As I was passing McCrary's farm, I noticed a pickup truck leaving our house. When I mentioned it to Kat, she told me someone had brought in their sick beagle. I found out much later it was Gail Jones. She grew up on the farm but rarely had a reason to make the hour drive. I know for a fact she didn't have a beagle. Or any pets, for that matter.

I backed the Mercedes up to the barn to unload the wood. When I went inside to get Kat, she was nowhere to be found. After searching everywhere, I assumed she left in the pickup I saw. I poked my head into her office on my way back out and discovered her sitting at her desk. Heavy clouds had rolled in so the window allowed just enough light in to sculpt her form from darkness.

"I've been looking everywhere for you," I said.

Startled, she looked up at me and hastily folded a letter on her desk and put it away in the top drawer. "I'm looking over something," she said in a strange tone.

"In the dark?"

She turned on the desk lamp, revealing puffy eyes and a cheerless disposition. She still had her coat on.

"Are you okay?" I asked.

"Yeah," she said without force or conviction.

"You didn't hear me calling you?"

She shook her head.

"Well, it turns out your wood was literally a tree in the ground."

"I'll be out in a minute."

We unloaded the wood in the tractor barn, where Kat planned to cure it until it was ready to be burned and turned into charcoal. She came out of her malaise and was high-spirited, almost giddy. When we finished, she wrapped her arms around me and thanked me for "being a man and chopping down the big tree" for her. But by dinner, her preoccupation weighed on her again. I gave up on small talk and gave into silence, giving her time and space to share what was on her mind.

Her detachment lasted into the evening. She tucked into the sofa with a mystery I checked out from the library for her. This is how we spent our evenings when she wasn't working. But on this night, she was more reticent than normal. Hollow clicks from the radiator accentuated the silence. On several occasions, I caught her gazing off into her own thoughts.

My mind was flitting through potential provocations that might have caused this bout of aloofness. When I was young, my mother married a Bay Area art dealer, which enabled her to hire an *au pair*. Her name was Alma and she took care of me from the age of five to fourteen. Every winter, her brother Daniel, who came from Colombia with her when they were teenagers, would visit for a few days. I remember him watching me throughout my angsty pubescent years. With an amused grin, he would say something like, "What's eating at you, my friend? Surely not Alma asking you to clean up."

His curiosity and patience were boundless. I wished I could be like Daniel and ask Kat what was eating at her. But often, his probing stirred up deep-seated anger and I feared what it might stir up in Kat.

In a fit of frustration, I slapped the newspaper I was reading down on the table. "These windows are terrible! I can feel the draft all the way over here. No one should have to wear a hat in their home." I yanked the wool beanie off my head and threw it on the floor.

In the upstairs closet, there were two wool army blankets. I took both of them and fetched a hammer and nails. Maybe I just needed to release tension by beating something. Good chance I would've smashed a finger with the hammer if Kat had allowed me to proceed with my DIY project.

"What are you doing?" she asked.

"Blocking the draft."

"We won't be able to see out."

"It's like closing the blinds, Kat."

"It's creepy. And tacky," she added.

I threw the blanket all the way to the kitchen and then marched in and snatched it off the floor. Kat sat up to watch me. When I finished putting everything away, she closed her book and went up to bed.

This is how we transitioned into a winter of discontent.

THE HOLIDAYS

Popcorn balls and candied apples made a strong return to Halloween after a forty-year absence. I heard Ulysses was crawling with little ghosts and hand-me-down costumes. Pilgrims and Indians no longer symbolized Thanksgiving in Independence. Instead, the country celebrated the "bounty of the land and the industrious spirit of its inhabitants." The outgoing administration irked many people by announcing a food supply alert that week and cautioning people against over-indulging during the holidays. They just had to put a damper on the holiday spirit.

Santas, snowmen, and nativity scenes were abundant. In the countryside, holiday decorations masked the bleakness of bare trees, brown fields, and flat light. The nights were suddenly long and the cold temps came earlier than I expected.

On Christmas morning, we picked up Tommy in Independence City and drove to his parents' house. The day was uneventful and relaxing for everyone but Gail, who spent the entire day in the kitchen. I read through the pile of newspapers and chatted about inconsequential matters with Tom. Kat helped in the kitchen while Tommy and his younger brother Chance watched the original Superman movie on DVD.

Chance was twenty years younger than his older brother. When he was born, Tommy had already moved out of the house. In a way, they each grew up as only children.

"How can they breathe up there?" Chance asked as Superman and Lois flew into the stratosphere.

I laughed but Tommy took the question seriously. He considered different ways Superman could exist without oxygen, but Lois, the only way she could survive was if Superman shared his breath with her. No one knew if that was even possible. For me, the thought of being carried into the sky was nauseating.

From the kitchen, Kat interrupted my horrific vision of wrenching air sickness. "Roman, can you come in here?"

We added a leaf to the table and covered it with a tablecloth that had been passed down from her great-grandmother. Gail had all six burners going. Her cheeks were rosy and her forehead was beaded with sweat.

"Is there anything I can help with?" I asked her.

She pointed to a cupboard. "You can get serving bowls and plates. Do you know how to properly set a table?"

"I believe I do," I said. "Forks on the left, knife and spoon on the right."

"Two forks, a bread plate, and no soup spoon. Thank you, Roman."

Kat slipped away to the cottage as I arranged the settings. Gail didn't seem like the type who cared too much about etiquette. During dinner, I saw her put her elbow on the table more than once to make a point between bites. My mother would glare at an offending elbow as if she could crack bone by will alone. Perhaps another example of my mother's lifelong effort to escape her rural upbringing.

"So how are you taking to country life?" Gail asked.

"Turns out it actually is good for writing."

"I just don't see how it could be good for business. Does she actually have clients?"

"She sees animals almost every day," I said reassuringly. "People come from all over the county."

"That's nice to hear," she said, pleasantly surprised. A skeptical gaze lingered on me before she turned back to the stove. She lifted the lid from a stockpot but immediately put it back and turned toward me. "Can I ask you something? Back in October, I dropped off a letter for Kat. When she saw who it was from—a law firm in Dallas—her face turned whiter than Grandma Greum's tablecloth. She refused to talk about it! I was afraid she was being sued or something worse. I looked it up when I got home. It was from a matrimonial lawyer." Gail put her hands on her hips as if I were the one withholding information. "Is her divorce finally happening?" Her eyes widened when she saw my confused reaction. "She didn't tell you about it, did she?"

"When did you drop it off?" I asked casually, trying to mask my emotions. Gail tried to pinpoint the day but I already knew. The letter Kat was reading in her office that day was connected to her marriage, which she hid from me for four years.

A few days before I missed the bus after the Las Agoras rally, Kat and I were out with Tommy and Juan Diego. We were discussing my magazine piece. They both wanted to know how I planned to describe or personify the "Spirit of Independence." The answer was simple: real people. I used Kat as an example. "She comes from a cosmopolitan city, successful career, but gives it all up to come here."

"Just upped and walked out on a brain surgeon husband, a big house and pool, a stable of horses," Tommy exclaimed with his crazy grin. "Take that, American Dream!"

"How do you divorce through an embargo?" Juan Diego pondered.

That's how I found out she was married. The blunt force of their unintended revelation rung my bell. He immediately noticed something was amiss with Kat and me.

"So many people are desperate to change their lives but they don't know how or they're too afraid," Tommy said. "You did and you're happier for it, right?"

I'm not sure if she answered. We left a few minutes later and walked to her car without speaking. When we got in, Kat took a deep breath. "Listen—"

"I don't even know who you are," I interrupted. "Kat? Is that really your name?"

"Stop it."

"Stop it? You hid the fact that you're married and you tell *me* to stop it?"

"So what! It's in the past! My past, my life." Her anger went from a two to ten in a flash. I thought she was going to snap. "You don't get to walk into my life and take anything you want. It's my fucking life!"

Wasn't I the one who should've been most upset? I was careful not to match her emotion and intensity. "How could you hide this from me?"

"You lived with your girlfriend for years!" she shot back. "The whole time you were writing to me, you were living with her.

You were sleeping with her," she said with disgust. "Would you sneak downstairs after having sex and write love letters to me?"

"Oh, stop it. Our sex life was dead long before you and I—"

"Ew! Don't talk to me about that."

"We were rarely ever home together," I said. "She worked long hours and traveled for work. I was gone all the time. You know this."

"I think we're even. Very even."

"You think we're even!" I could tell by the way she was looking at me that now I was the one who looked crazy. "We're not even."

"You're not the grand decider," she declared and turned on the car and sped off without checking for bikes or pedestrians.

We drove straight to my motel without speaking and parted ways without saying goodbye. When I fell into bed, it felt like I'd unscrewed a plug in my spine and drained my spirit. The tail-end of the night replayed over and over in my mind. Although I didn't begrudge myself the shock of learning she was married, the way I reacted embarrassed me. I failed to live up to qualities I expected of myself. When I tried to extricate myself from the shame by making it a teaching moment and imagining how I could have reacted differently, nothing changed because I was bound by a familiar, debilitating, childlike feeling of being abandoned.

A knock on a neighbor's door distracted me from my anguish. After a couple more knocks, I realized it was my door. When I opened it, I saw the night's emotional fallout in Kat's face.

"I don't want to leave on that note," she said.

"Sometimes a musical piece will end on a chord that was only suggested before," I said. Kat took an agitated breath but before she could let it out, I added, "But I don't want to end on that note either."

"Who wants to talk about their failures? 'Hey, let me tell you about how I suck.' You need to believe me when I say it's in the past, okay?"

I didn't want to disturb this resolution even if it was irregular to my ear so I agreed.

"Do you want to go to a barbecue this Saturday?" she asked. "It's out near my grandparents' house."

On the bus ride to Liberal the next day, I thought about how hard it must have been to keep her secret locked inside all those years. I was looking forward to a reconciliation with her. Since I missed the return bus, it didn't happen as I imagined.

When she showed up at my rental a month later, she apologized for not telling me about her marriage. "But you have to understand, the past is the past. I was unhappy in my marriage, okay? It ended. So why should I continue to live through it in my mind if it no longer exists in my life?"

Her vulnerabilities remained guarded while she explained her past was off-limits. I wanted to find a way into that mysterious realm but I also feared tromping through dark places. If she had experienced trauma, there would be painful memories I wasn't sure I could face.

In hindsight, her marriage was always present in our relationship. It was like a black hole my thoughts were pulled into. I didn't have puritanical beliefs about marriage. Her secrecy, the antithesis of intimacy, is what filled me with doubt. It was a denial of our relationship and me.

When Gail told me about the letter, it wasn't a gut punch like before but it still stirred up bad feelings. "She doesn't like to talk about it," I said.

"I heard how you found out about it," Gail said as she removed a heavy iron braiser from the oven. "Tommy felt bad. But later, he took an earful for you." She was referring to Tommy being my liaison to Kat after I missed the bus. Tommy took the brunt of her anger. "Once in a blue moon, something erupts in her," Gail said. "Her mother never could understand how her own daughter got such a crazy streak."

"You're talking about Kat?" I asked skeptically.

"In her youth, you wouldn't have recognized her. She dressed head-to-toe in black with black lipstick, black eyeliner, hair dyed black."

"Wow," I said, genuinely wowed.

"Her dad left when she was young. Did she tell you about that? One day he came home all in a tizzy and dug into Maeve (Kat's mother). Accused her of everything in the book. She went right back at him. Bad things were said and Kat heard it all. Next day he was gone. Never came back. That'll affect any kid."

This glimpse into a transformational moment in Kat's past wasn't revealed to me by Gail. It was Kat who first told me about this episode. It was the night we sat on Johnny the barber's porch, discussing how things had gone awry between us.

"When I was nine, my parents split up. My dad came home late for supper and my mom was upset about it. She refused to let us eat until he showed up. When he came home, my mom started yelling at him and he got mad at her for being mad at him. No one spoke during supper. And they wouldn't look at each other.

"The Hamburger Helper had been sitting on the stove for two hours. I couldn't stomach it. My dad was the only one who ate. With each bite, he'd hit the plate with his fork like he was trying to crack it. After I'd gone to bed, it went off the rails. They started yelling at each other and it kept getting worse and worse. It was the longest night of my life."

"All because he was late for dinner?"

"Of course not." The truth: there was another woman. Her father insisted she was a colleague and nothing more. Whether it was true was inconsequential. The deep resentment toward one another is what harrowed Kat. When she came home from school the next day, her father had moved out. A month later, he moved away for good.

"I haven't seen a feast like this in ages!" Tommy exclaimed as he sat down at the dining table.

"We're not being greedy," Gail said defensively. "There will be plenty of leftovers. Would anyone like to say grace?" No one spoke up so she did. "Lord, we thank you for blessing us on this Christmas day by bringing us together. We thank you for a plentiful but modest supper and a warm house. We thank you for our health after such a hard year. We thank you for seeing us through our struggle as this nation tries to get back on its feet. Bloodied and battered, we continue on. So we ask that you continue to look our way in the days ahead. We pray you will bless us with prosperity appropriate to this land and its people. Food, water, and health are all we could ever expect, but a sip of good life from time to time would go a long way in sustaining us on this long journey…."

The briefest of pauses allowed Tom to interrupt. "Amen."

Tommy seconded the interruption and then added before his mother could continue, "Creamed corn, black-eyed peas…."

"Will you pass the potatoes?" Tom asked.

Gail offered me a platter of shredded pheasant. "Here you go, Roman. The man who farms this land dropped it off for us this morning."

"He doesn't eat meat," said Kat.

"I'll have some of the trout," I said. "Thank you."

"Me and my dad caught it this summer," Chance said.

"You know, Kat was a vegetarian when she was younger," Gail mused.

"I'm surprised you remember that," said Kat.

"It's ingrained in my head because your mom talked about it all the time. You turned out fine, though. As long as kids don't do too much harm to themselves, they usually come out okay."

"Are you really a vegetarian?" Chance asked me.

"I'm a pescatarian. Don't hold it against me."

"Why would I do that?"

"Some people get upset about it."

"I didn't get upset," Tommy blurted out. "I just said no one would trust you if they knew. This is the Beef Empire, man."

"Not anymore," said Tom.

"Okay, it's a fallen empire. The point is that to be a vegetarian here is like being an atheist in the Vatican."

"We don't eat meat but a couple times a week," said Tom. "I guess down in Utopia City, everyone lives like royalty."

Tom was referring to Independence City. Pre-secession, it was a typical small farming town with a single store that was part of the gas station. During the Transition, a group of residents persuaded townspeople that if they were going to stay, they would have to reimagine their lives. They envisioned a new community in which every resident would have to contribute to its well-being. The land around town was converted into food and fuel crops. The grain co-op became the biodiesel co-op. Its residents loved to tout their home-town pride. They believed it was a model for what Independence could be.

"We have more gardens and vegetable crops per capita than anyplace else in the country," Tommy said in the didactic tone he always used when speaking about Indie City. "And we do a better job at drying, freezing, pickling, and preserving."

"So what you're saying," said Tom, "is you're basically vegetarian."

"I don't go around saying that! People would start calling us a commune if they knew."

"I thought you had cows," Chance said.

"Raising cattle takes too much water," Tommy said. "The Ogallala's drying up."

"Roman, whatever happened to your magazine article?" Gail asked, apparently trying to keep the conversation focused on me.

She caught me with a mouthful of chewy greens. Everyone was looking at me. Why is it when you're asked a question while eating, it takes longer to chew and swallow? I washed it down and told them the magazine had decided not to publish it. "I guess they had other pieces more pressing."

"But somebody else would buy it if he took the time to send it out," Kat said.

"That requires being online," I replied.

"There's a library in Ulysses."

"It's hard to get anything done in fifteen-minute increments."

"You can spend an entire day at the library," Kat said.

"The internet's too slow."

"You're more than welcome to use our computer anytime," Tom offered.

"I doubt if it's any faster," Gail said. "We all use the same satellite."

"It's a slow process," I said. "It's just a matter of time."

Underneath the homegrown Christmas tree were bundles of hats, scarves, and gloves tied with twine. Tommy wrapped his presents in thin Weekly Independent newsprint. All day long, Chance made a show of how underwhelmed and unexcited he was about opening presents but when the time came, he was eager to distribute the gifts.

The first one he picked up was a small balsa box with a string and button closure. He read the paper tag tucked into the seam. "For Kat, from Roman."

Kat winced with surprise. "Oh…I'll be right back."

As one would expect, Chance had the biggest haul. First, he untied a stack of vinyl 45s I found at a garage sale in Ulysses. They were all in their original sleeves and bound with twine.

"I don't know what your musical tastes are," I said, "but these are classics and they're in great condition."

He flipped through the records. All the names were unfamiliar to him. Bill Haley, Dean Martin, Smokey Robinson & The Miracles, Linda Ronstadt, Marvin Gaye, and Merle Haggard. Tommy looked distressed, as if they should have been for him.

"You don't have a record player," he said to Chance.

"Oh, yes we do," Tom said as he pointed at the television cabinet.

Gail might have noticed Tommy's mild dismay because she told him to open a large bundle that was wrapped in a sheet of canvas and tied with a ribbon. It looked like a blanket. It was a blanket. A quilt, to be exact.

She helped him spread it out so he could see it in its entirety. The colorful medley was made up of different geometrical shapes inside the blocks, as well as traditional patterned squares. Interspersed among these were pieces Gail spent at least ten minutes describing. A sunflower, pheasant, and a stalk of wheat represented the land. Fragments from a quilt that belonged to Tommy's great grandmother, cuts from a baby blanket he didn't remember, and an old plaid shirt linked his ancestral past to the present. There were blocks for places he had lived (Central Nevada, Olympic Peninsula, Alaska, Southern New Mexico).

On each corner the imagery was specific to their former statehood: The Kansas State Seal, Stars and Stripes, the Liberty Bell, and Ad Astra Statue (a Kansa warrior shooting an arrow). At the center were the thirty-six counties that made up Independence. It was indicative of how self-aware Independents were of their nationality, similar to how exiles and expats might feel.

It was a work of art. Tommy was moved. As he hugged his mom, I think I saw a tear.

"She's been working on that since last year," Tom said.

A chilly breeze preceded Kat when she returned. "I left this in the cottage," she said before she handed me a small bundle wrapped in a paisley handkerchief.

I insisted she open hers first. From the wood box, she lifted a silver and brass bracelet with detailed floral etching. This also came from a Ulysses yard sale. Garage sale-ing isn't my thing. I don't even like casual shopping. Ads for the sales were posted on the library community board one day and it gave me something to do while I waited for Kat. Who knows, maybe it's in my DNA because it's the sort of thing my mother lives for. Although she's more of the art auction and Rodeo Drive type.

"This is beautiful," Kat said and seemed to mean it. She ran her thumb over the etched design. "Thank you."

With uneasiness (I thought) she watched me untie the handkerchief. Inside was a multi-purpose utility knife that looked exactly like the one she kept in her car. "Ah," I said with as much excitement as I could muster.

The most doted over present of the night was an antique German doll Kat gave to Gail. The two-foot blonde doll was dressed in a white nineteenth-century dress with blue flowers and a lacey bonnet. Its fixed gaze and tight lips created an expression of one determined to maintain order. A woman who brought her obese cocker spaniel into the clinic several times wanted Kat to have it because she was concerned about what would happen to it after she was gone. Once upon a time, Gail collected these types of fancy dolls. She got emotional when she unwrapped the present. So did Kat. As doll-collecting was more of a pre-secession hobby, the gift released a myriad of emotions they both related and responded to.

FAMILY AFFAIRS

Gail turned on a Christmas special on a local radio station. After everyone played with their new toys for a bit, we moved to the kitchen to play Hearts. A phone call interrupted our game. Gail took it in the front room. A few minutes later, we lost another player when she called for Kat.

I followed her to the living room to get the scarf given to me by Gail and Tom. Like most households, they set their thermostat at the lowest bearable temperature. For the holiday, they dialed it up a few notches. I was still chilly.

"Here's Kat," I heard Gail announce. She was sitting at a rolltop desk with the phone on speaker. "It's your mom and Aunt Colleen."

Curious to hear her mother's voice, I eavesdropped on their conversation.

"Merry Christmas, Kat!" her Aunt Colleen (the third sister) shouted over kids and commotion in the background.

"Merry Christmas," Kat said. "Mom, are you there?"

"I'm here," her mother said dryly. Kat once mentioned she could maintain a surly tone, no matter the occasion.

"How are you?" Kat asked. "Sounds like a full house."

"Oh, it is. All of Colleen's grandkids are here."

"That must be fun," said Kat.

"It's nice having them around but they're wearing me out just watching them."

"Maeve, it sounds like you're having a wonderful Christmas," Gail exclaimed with extra cheerfulness.

"We had the most amazing Christmas dinner you've ever seen," Kat's mother bragged. I caught a peek of Kat's head tilt back as she rolled her eyes. "There was turkey and ham, stuffing, mashed potatoes with two kinds of gravy, maple carrots, cranberry sauce—"

"We had quite a feast ourselves," Gail interrupted.

"—macaroni salad, corn and cheese casserole, candied sweet potatoes, pumpkin pie, chocolate pudding."

"Tommy came up with Kat and her friend this morning. We got Grandma Greum's table setting out. 1240 puts on a nice Christmas show with live choristers and readings."

"And we went to the most amazing light show you've ever seen in your entire life," Kat's mother continued. "You won't see anything like it there, I can tell you that."

On our way home the next morning, Kat told me her mom never failed to point out ways life was better outside Independence. She frowned as if her mother's low opinion of the country was really a critique of her. "She's had a hard life," she sighed. After reflecting on this, she corrected herself. "A disappointing life. My grandma was hard on her. More than her sisters. She was a daydreamer when she was young and my grandma resented that. She wouldn't accept her wanting anything other than farm life. She was just a child."

Maybe it was a form of rejection that disabled her grandmother's ability to nurture her own daughter's ambitions. It sounded like she did everything she could to stifle the girl's imagination and eventually succeeded. When Maeve was old enough to break free from those parental constraints, she continued to live at home as her mother required. She took an entry-level secretarial job at the county hospital in Lakin, where she met a young intern, Dr. Taylor.

Marriage was a way out for her but their breakup led to *him* leaving while she remained in circumstances arguably dictated by her mother. He landed a residency in Colorado Springs and then took a permanent position in Ft. Collins. The foothills of the Rockies, a mile above sea level, is the geographical opposite of the Kansas flatlands. She probably hated him for that.

Many months later, I asked Gail about growing up on the farm. She told me their Great Grandma Greum, whose handmade tablecloth we dined on, was the most severe human being she had ever known. She immigrated to America from Scotland when she was a teenager. Along with other European settlers, her family made their way to the Great Plains. Twenty-five years later, she returned to her native land after losing both of her parents, two of her own young children, and her husband. Her daughter married young and farmed the land where Kat and I were living. For Great Grandma Greum, life in America was a perpetual struggle. She despised the land that took nearly everyone she loved.

"She visited every three or four years to point out what was wrong with all of us," Gail said. "Her only living daughter bore the brunt of her disparagements. I told you about Kat being a rebellious teenager? Her mother and I weren't allowed to rebel in any way, shape, or form or to be anything other than what our mom wanted us to be. I don't think she knew what that was."

Kat's mother finally got another opportunity to rebel. It came in the form of Independence. This time, she didn't fail.

THE COB HOUSE

Tonya invited us to her New Year's Eve party but Kat didn't feel up to another reunion. The mere thought of it visibly pained her. So we had our own low-key New Year's. We checked out VHS movies at the library and bought popcorn at the market. I know, movies and popcorn, ho-hum. You might take it for granted, as I once did.

While Kat was finishing up work in her office, I watched the evening news on *Channel 4*. They were running a story about a Ulysses family whose gardening ambitions fell short of their needs. With a news team in tow, community members showed up on Christmas with boxes of food and presents for the kids.

It was supposed to be a feel-good story about the community coming together to help the family. But for some, it was a painful reminder of yet another winter of food shortages ahead. Local pantries had done their best to stock up on bulk grains and flour but they were still appealing to the public for "desperately needed" food.

"Why do they have to show this tonight?" Kat asked, walking out of her office. "This is how they want us to end the year? I'm sure they've gone through all that food and are sitting around hungry while the kids play with their used toys. Everyone has problems. Everyone is struggling. We don't need to see that."

"*Authorities are reporting an uptick in thefts this month and are urging people to lock doors, windows, garages, sheds, and anything with fuel, food, or other valuables.*"

"Oh my god!" Kat moaned. "I can't watch this." She turned the television off and looked at me like I was responsible.

"I was watching that."

"Never—I never want to see that on when I'm here," she said.

I couldn't help from laughing. "The news?"

"I'm serious," she said with pursed lips. This emotional facial feature would become a staple in our household.

"You know they make everything sound more serious than it actually is," I said.

"More reason not to watch it."

"Well, I enjoy watching the news and I can decide for myself what to watch or read or listen to—"

"I'm asking you to do this for me," she snapped.

"Kat, seriously. It's the local news. You're wound way too tight. What's going on with you?" I asked this with a specific idea in mind that had been gnawing at me since Christmas.

"Don't turn this on me."

"Is it the letter?" I asked.

"What are you talking about?" she asked.

"Kat, I know about the letter."

She looked like a deer caught in headlights. For a second, I thought she was going to deny it.

"Gail told you!" she exploded.

"She assumed you told me about it."

"Goddammit, Gail! Goddammit!"

"Whoa, calm down. Don't blame her."

"I can't believe she would stab me in the back like that. Why would she do that? It's none of her business." Kat fell onto the sofa, moaning, "I can't live like this."

"Live like what?"

"With you people scrutinizing everything I do. With you and my aunt—my own aunt!—talking behind my back."

"This is stupid," I said against my better judgment. But once it was out, I couldn't stop. "*You* can't live like this? What do you think it's like living with someone who's secretive, wants to be alone all the time, and doesn't care about anything except work? The air in here is thick with dissatisfaction. Fuck this!"

I jumped up and marched to the door, grabbed my coat, and stormed out. When I was outside, I wasn't sure what to do since it was cold and dark. I considered plugging in the heater in Kat's work shed but the key was in her office. Since I was already wearing my warmest socks and a sweater, I retrieved my jacket and shoes from inside and headed out.

Right after we moved out there, I found a three-speed bicycle in the barn that nobody had used in decades. It had a slanted top bar, white tire walls, cruiser handlebars, a small basket in the front, a rack in the back, and big wheel fenders. I overcame my limited mechanical skills to make it ridable.[18]

The bitter cold and wind didn't stop me from riding to a little roadside tavern five miles away. The Cob House was a one-room shack that looked decrepit and unsafe from the outside. Like so many Western homesteads, it was left to decompose, perhaps a memorial to the trailblazers of Manifest Destiny. More recently, the structure had been reinforced and the interior walls were built up with dirt cob.

When I entered, I looked like I'd come off the Santa Fe Trail. My face and ears were alarmingly red and I couldn't move my fingers, which were curled from the handlebars. Alrik, the owner, was sitting on a stool behind the bar. He looked like a frontiersman himself, with his big beard and rawhide coat. "What happened to you?" he asked with concern. "You have a breakdown?"

"You could say that." I rubbed my hands together and looked longingly at the fireplace where three cowhands were seated. A black-and-white shepherd dog was stretched out near the fire. Oh, how I envied that dog. The cowboys were the only other patrons there. They sat quietly, gazing off into their own thoughts as the wind wheezed through the hull and wood crackled in the fireplace.

After surveying the twelve bottles under the gas lantern, I ordered a whiskey. I took off my coat and hung it on the back of a

_____

[18] I rode it to Ulysses to attend a *Wizard of Oz* screening in the high school gym. As I was locking it up, someone pointed out it looked like Miss Almira Gulch's bicycle. A small crowd gathered around what they thought was a replica.

chair. One cowboy near the fire was watching me. I nodded to him, noting his impressive Fu Manchu.

"You look like you rode a ways," he said.

"Five miles on my bike."

The other two looked over at me.

"Whad'ya do out here, if you don't mind me asking?" the man with the Fu Manchu asked.

It must have been obvious I wasn't a farmer. "I'm a writer."

"A writer? What kind of writing?"

"Working on a novel of sorts."

"Is there even a printing press in this country?" Alrik asked from the bar.

"Not for novels," I said.

"Did they have books before paper?" one cowhand asked.

"I guess they used stone tablets," his buddy answered.

"Not good for reading in bed," I said.

The man with the Fu Manchu laughed and then tilted his head back to let the last drops trickle from his glass. "Well, we should probably head back."

Alrik waved to the men as they shuffled out. "Thanks for stopping by."

"Good luck with your book," Fu Manchu said and then whistled at the dog. "Come on, Sheeba."

I finished my whiskey and took the empty glass to the bar for another. "You staying open til the new year?" I asked.

"I don't know," Alrik said. "It's still early. I wasn't even planning to open up tonight. Got bored."

"I'm glad you did."

"Me too. They would've found you frozen by the road."

Outside, deep-toned exhaust gurgled as the cowboys' truck warmed up. A minute later, the idle slackened and the vehicle pulled onto the highway.

A live broadcast of President-Elect Gonzalez was playing on the radio. The next day he was being be sworn in. His New Year's Eve speech was later named "A Vision of Independence."

"As a nation, we are still so young. We have suffered the pains of infancy and struggled with who we are as much as what we are. We are a people bound together by our independence. Togetherness is the key to our success. Tomorrow we turn the page to the next chapter and move forward, together, for the good of all, for the good of our nation. This is my vision of Independence. A kinder and gentler way forward."

"You hear that?" Alrik asked as he turned the radio down and tilted his head.

I heard nothing except what the wind composed.

"An electric car," he whispered.

After a few moments, I heard the whirr of tires. The car seemed to slow down as it came closer. Alrik listened intently. Pebbles and frozen mud crunched under-tire as the vehicle pulled off the road.

"Another customer!" Alrik announced, pleased by this development.

The door opened a minute later and a man in a bulky coat with a faux-fur hood ruff entered. He closed the door and stamped his black shoes on the doormat. When he removed his hood, his dark hair stood up from static and his glasses were fogged over.

"Evening," Alrik said.

"Good evening," the stranger said in a clear, warm voice. "I'm stopping in for a nightcap if that's okay."

"Come on in."

He hung his coat on a peg by the door. When he turned around, I could see he was wearing a clerical collar. He rubbed his hands together as he approached the bar.

"Ah, gin," he said. "You wouldn't have any mixers, would you?"

"I have one bottle of ginger ale," said Alrik.

"Works for me." The minister took his drink to the fireside table.

"What brings you out tonight?"

The churchman's first sip was an inch from his lips when he paused. His pleasant mood was blown away by a gust of wind that shook the window. He took a small drink and pensively tilted his glass, studying the gin's viscosity or his thoughts, perhaps. "I was visiting a family south of here," he said with what sounded like a note of defeat. "They learned the hard way how difficult it is to be self-sustaining when you're cut off from the modern world."

"Farmers?" Alrik asked.

The churchman nodded. "They received some land in the homestead allocation."

"It's difficult if you don't know what you're doing," said Alrik.

"Are they calling it quits?" I asked, sensing there was more to this story.

The minister glanced at me. "Yes. The man's aunt is in my church." He pronounced aunt as *ont* instead of the local *ant*. "She came to see me because she was worried." He seemed reluctant to continue but when he looked up, he saw Alrik and me waiting to hear more. After another pause, he sighed and continued. "Their land is out on the back roads. A barren place. No winter seedlings or cover crops. Wind blowing dirt around the farmyard. Windows boarded up and covered with blankets. Chicken coops empty. Weeds growing all over. That just about sums it up."

"And someone's living there?" I asked.

"I suppose you could say that."

"Uh-oh," Alrik said. "What happened?"

"I'd rather not talk about it. I hope you understand."

The wood sizzled, and after a pop, quieted down. The wind whistled in the chimney. Alrik took a tobacco pouch from his coat that was hanging on the wall. I caught a whiff of dried herbs, more tobacco-like than most blends I smelled in the country. Alrik kept his rolling paper hidden behind the pouch. He was probably using paper from a bible, popular because of its thinness.

"Why did the woman come to you?" I asked the minister. "You'd think she would go out there herself or—"

"She did go," he interrupted. "She asked me to find help. If you really want to know, they're starving out there. Her nephew is too proud or…I don't know." He stared into the flames.

"You just left them?" Alrik asked with dismay.

"No." The minister said nothing more. He clearly didn't want to be bothered anymore so Alrik and I obliged him.

The churchman had one more drink before he left. I had several and would've stayed longer but no one else showed up and Alrik was ready to get home. He loaned me a scarf and gloves but the ride back was still painfully cold. I made it home without incident. Thankfully, the door was unlocked. I took off my coat and boots and curled up on the couch under the throw blanket. It never felt that warm in the house before or after.

I woke up in the middle of the night. Heavy-boned, chilled, and still intoxicated, I toddled up the stairs. My clothes ended up strewn across the floor as I slipped under the blankets.

Kat turned over. "Where have you been?"

"The Cob House," I mumbled.

She sighed and moved closer. "You smell like tobacco," was the last thing I heard.

NEW YEAR, OLD SORROWS

Pellets of sleet ticked against the bedroom window. The frosted glass diffused the morning light. Whiskey had blurred my vision so I couldn't read the clock on Kat's side. She stretched her legs and felt my side of the bed with the back of her hand.

"What time is it?" I asked.

"It's New Year's," she said before she turned over and faced me. "You rode all the way out to the Cob House and back?" she asked with concern.

It seemed unthinkable from under the covers on a chilly morning, hungover.

"I should've told you about the letter," Kat said. "Divorce papers. That's all it was."

I didn't dare move an inch or bat an eye for fear of disrupting this rare confession.

"It's just a formality," she said. "I signed the documents and mailed them the next day and that was that. I knew if I said anything, it would only upset you."

"I don't hold your marriage against you," I said in a croaky voice and cleared my throat. "I reacted poorly when I first found out but I still don't understand why you're so secretive about it."

"It's not a secret."

"You haven't told me anything about your marriage."

"Why would you want to know? I don't want to hear about your past relationships."

"It's like you're running from it but you can't escape. It's looming over us."

"Oh, I escaped," she said.

"Do you feel guilty about something that happened? Or are you ashamed?"

"You've obviously never been married. You don't know what it's like to have someone around all the time, watching everything you do, how you hold your fork, if you wear makeup or not, how high your shirt is buttoned. If you want to be alone, too bad."

"You must hate your life here," I said. "I'm home all the time. All the time. We're both in this same little house—"

"Being stuck with a person you don't want to be with is completely different."

This relieved some of the angst building inside me. "Why didn't you tell me at La Serena you were married?"

"Are you serious? The last thing I wanted to do was to spend the weekend talking about my marriage."

"He must be terrible."

"He wasn't deliberately cruel. At first, I thought he was everything I wanted in a man, but when the newness wore off, so did my desire for him. That's why you can never trust your feelings. We don't know how we're going to change. One moment you want to be together no matter what. Then later you might regret it more than anything."

"That's a depressing thought," I said.

"It's just the way it is."

"What finally drove you away?"

"His distrust. His jealousy. His prying."

This last imputation was laced with spite. She looked past me, into unpleasant memories. Something in her eye made me suspect she wasn't so innocent.

"Prying?"

Her eyes glazed over as they always did when she spoke of personal conflict. She shook her head but didn't elaborate right away. Finally, she swallowed and said, "He accused me of having an affair."

"He found out about us."

"No," she replied with disdain. "I had lunch with someone at the stables where I kept my horse. He found out and made a big deal about it."

"Lunch?" I asked. "Who was it?"

"Just someone I always saw there."

"When did this lunch occur?"

"It was just lunch," Kat answered curtly.

I fell back onto my pillow and stared at the ceiling. This subject was quickly growing tiresome. What began as a mystery that might reveal an essential truth about Kat had quickly transformed into something unpleasant.

"Did he tell you to leave?" I asked.

"I left him," Kat said. "He was at a conference in Phoenix…." Her voice trailed off.

"You told him on the phone?"

"I left a note."

"Oh," is what I said but *wow* is what I thought.

"'Oh?' Thanks a lot."

"I didn't mean it that way."

"If you want to judge me for what I did—"

"I'm not judging you. It's surprising. Not many people break up a marriage that way. I know how you feel."

"How could you possibly know how I feel?"

"It's life," I said. "I get it." In truth, I didn't get it.

A gust of wind blew sleet against the window and whined in the roof turbine. We lay quietly with our own thoughts.

"We can do better than this," I said after a long silence.

Without missing a beat, she answered, "This is as good as it gets."

"You're such a downer."

"If we're going to do better, as you put it, then we need to talk about practical matters and not about things in the past we can't change."

"Practical matters, such as?"

"Finances."

I groaned and turned away. That didn't dissuade her.

"My average revenue is less than 300 dollars a week," she said. "Minus business expenses, minus living expenses, it leaves very little. The margins are razor thin. If something happens, if my business goes under, we'll have nothing. No food, electricity, gas. And it's all on me."

I didn't know if she was deliberately trying to emasculate me or guilt-trip me into submissiveness or shame. It left me feeling worthless and regretful as hell for moving out there. Happy fucking New Year.

"Why wouldn't they print your article?" she asked with no trace of resentment or blame. "The truth. Was it because of your new style?"

She was referring to what I called my professional renaissance: the reinvention of my writing approach, my career, and life. It's why I moved out of San Francisco—to lessen the financial burdens so I could study and write without economic pressure. The new style is what you see here on these pages. I freed myself from journalistic conventions. This has meant revealing how I subjectively experience the world I'm writing about. Perhaps I've taken the concept to the extreme in the second part of this book. Even though I've become front and center, along with Kat, it's still about Independence (with a capital and small i).

"You read it," I reminded her. "There was nothing radical about it."

She pushed off the blankets and walked to the bathroom.

"Do you remember the Independence Day party?" I asked.

"What about it?"

"Something changed between us after that night."

"First it was the letter and now it's the party?"

"Not the party. When we got home."

I saw a flicker of recognition in her eyes. Suddenly—irrationally—I thought she was going to tell me she meant what she said that night; that we should have kids and make this a family affair. "I'm just searching for a way to make things better between us."

"It's not us, it's this place," she said as she pulled on her jeans and walked out.

Albert Gonzalez took the oath of office. Unfortunately, another foul affair in rural farmland tainted the day. An unidentified Latino man in his forties was discovered dead on a farmer's property. Once again, it was a single shot from a high-caliber rifle. It happened overnight about twenty miles southwest as a crow flies. It was all the talk on the radio and *Channel 4 News* spent a half hour of their pre-inauguration special reporting on circumstances that were eerily similar to the homicide near Las Agoras.

The Stevens County sheriff didn't address the media until the afternoon (during the inauguration) so it didn't air until later in the evening. He was a cantankerous man with a fleshy countenance imprinted with a sour disposition. From his desk, Sheriff Howell summarized the day's events in a whiny, agitated voice.

Around 2AM a farmer and his wife were woken by screeching tires so loud it "sounded like the vehicle was about to crash through the wall." In reality, the pickup was about a hundred feet from the bedroom window. The couple didn't have time to blink before a gunshot rang out. The farmer jumped out of bed and rushed outside but the pickup truck was already two hundred yards down the road.

The strong scent of burned rubber filled the air. He didn't spot the body near the detached garage until daybreak.

Days later, the murder victim was identified as Jesús Criollo. His car was found broken down three miles away on the north-south highway that connected Ulysses to Hugoton. He was from Liberal, forty-five minutes southeast of the crime scene or a twenty-five-mile straight shot. It was unclear why he was driving out there in the middle of the night. It made less sense to walk thirty miles home with temperatures in the twenties, especially since Hugoton was only ten miles away.

Sheriff Howell's department shared little about the case, which allowed for endless speculation. Some speculated that Criollo was hunted down and killed because of criminal connections. Others thought he was looking for a place to keep warm when militiamen ambushed him.

The leader of the county militia insisted they weren't responsible. He claimed none of his people were within ten miles of the site that night. If they were, according to him, they would've never shot an unarmed man and driven away. He also brought up a valid point: Criollo was unarmed. It had become a matter of fact among groups of armchair investigators that the farmer and his wife were in danger.

Stripped bare of all the conjecturing, at the heart of this was the fact that a man was murdered—shot in the back with a hunting rifle—out in the countryside. Farming is the backbone of rural life, the soil its essence. Now it was stained with the blood of Jesús Criollo.

POTLUCK

We decided to host a dinner party. This may sound farfetched, considering we were a million miles from civilization. At least, that's how it felt. It just so happened that Tommy, Juan Diego, and Colm O'Brien were coming through for a media conference in Hugoton. Kat invited Tonya and her friend John Mayberry, who lived fifteen miles away, and we called it a party.

Kat's mother and Gail took most of the tablecloths years ago so we were left with a checkered piece that barely covered the table with the leaf inserted. While she set the table with mismatched place settings, I monitored the cooking. We had a magnum of blackberry wine a client had given her and I was eager to sample it.

"Shouldn't we open this now to let it breathe?" I asked from the kitchen.

"Wait until everyone's here. People like to hear the cork pop."

John Mayberry was the first guest to arrive at 5:30PM sharp. I met him at the Hotel Windsor on my first night in the country. He was there meeting with agricultural officials. On his way out, he spotted Kat and stopped to say hi. Although he was cordial to me, a suspicious glint in his eye made me suspect he had a romantic interest in her. He seemed to genuinely care for Kat and her well-being.

"Good to see you again, Roman," he said with no discernible distrust. A scar on his upper lip gave him a rough complexion but his benign country voice softened the impression. He looked down at my feet. "What happened to those fancy shoes you had?"

At the Windsor I wore a pair of stylish winklepickers that were more suited for San Francisco. From looking at my shoes, he guessed I was a foreign traveler. "I traded those in a long time ago," I told him.

He opened the cardboard box he'd brought and removed a meringue-topped pie. "My first ever strawberry cream pie."

"Oh my gosh, it looks amazing!" Kat exclaimed.

"I'm surprised it turned out this good, to tell you the truth."

Juan Diego arrived on his scooter with Tommy on the back. He brought a Tupperware container with *chilaquiles* ready to bake. Tommy contributed a bottle of gin and a bag of candied pecans. Tonya and her husband James showed up in a big pickup truck with dual exhaust pipes and a CNG tank mounted in the back. Tonya handed over a platter of homemade crackers, whipped cheese, and smoked fish. Colm was the last guest to arrive. Like the others, he stopped to admire the pie.

"Real sugar," John said. "I bought a hundred pounds before the borders closed."

Mayberry was renowned for having the foresight to invest in heirloom and open-pollinated seed varietals. Since the beginning, he had been a staple at the Lakin and Ulysses farmers markets. I was told he had ten times more volume and variety than anyone around. For a year, Capital City officials provided him with fuel to visit the market there once a week. Add sugar to his triumphs.

"I hope you keep it locked up," Colm said to John. "If people knew you had sugar—if my wife knew, she'd rob you in broad daylight."

"There's hope in the sugar beet," said Juan Diego.

"We're all better off without sugar," I said, to everyone's dismay.

"Sugar I can do without," James said. "But I have not for one day stopped missing my morning coffee."

James had been a pipefitter for Great Plains Energy. Because of his experience, he got a coveted post-secession job with an

Independence gas company. He and Tonya were doing well financially but he complained privately he had nothing to spend his money on.

He was more approachable than he was at the Independence Day party. I'm guessing he was coached by Tonya. He made a concerted effort to engage Kat in particular. He asked her about growing up in Lakin and about her life after she moved away. When he asked why she moved back, Kat gave him her standard response about coming here to care for her mother and later helping her move. Somehow, she always skirted around exactly why she became and Independent. I had a feeling Independence was an escape from her marriage.

I mixed cocktails in the kitchen, and before long, it sounded like a party. After one drink, Kat was feeling merry. So I made her another. Tommy repositioned the radio near a window and tuned into *The Benny Goodman Hour* on a U.S. station. Varying static added to the nostalgic vibe.

Everyone eventually sat down at the dining table. During her second drink, Kat slipped into a Texas vernacular. "For our main course, we'll be having Texas-style chili. Git some fire in ya!"

I ladled and she served. Each dish was presented with oohs and ahs. Honey-glazed carrots, fresh sour cream, garlic pesto bread and Juan Diego's *chilaquiles.* "Just the way my mother makes them," he said.

"You've sure outdone yourself," John said to Kat.

"I didn't know you could cook," Tommy said.

"Well, *bone appeteet*," she said with her Texas inflection.

"One more," I said as I brought in one last dish.

"He's made something *special*," Kat said, then whispered, "You don't have to eat it."

"I heard that," I said. "At least try it. Crispy tofu *à la shakshuka.*" I set the cast-iron skillet on a crochet pot holder and poured a tomato, pepper, and onion sauce over slices of tofu, creating a smoky and sizzling display.

Tonya and James had the best table manners of the group. They waited with their hands in their laps until everyone was served. Their polite etiquette didn't hide their distrust of the tofu. Tonya tried it right away and commented on the "interesting" flavors. I'm no chef but I thought I did a decent job.

When I opened the bottle of wine, I made sure I pulled the cork so it audibly popped. I'm not sure anyone noticed. Kat raised her glass to make a toast.

"Thank you all for coming," she said. "It's probably illegal asking people to drive all this way for a supper party, especially with our new president."

James and Tonya were the only ones who laughed. I felt compelled to explain that Gonzalez said the fuel situation would get worse before it got better. Kat didn't like me annotating her speech.

"I don't know about ya'll," she continued, "but I haven't done a thing all winter but work and sleep. Here's to getting together with friends and having a good time."

"Cheers."

After we cleared the table, we served John's strawberry pie along with a pecan pie Kat bought in town. James stepped away to stretch his legs and perhaps to get away from us for a minute. "Looks like we have another guest," he said from the living room as he looked out the front window. "I think it's the sheriff."

"Must be a noise complaint," I said. No one appreciated my humor.

A sheriff's deputy's car had pulled in behind James's truck. The officer stepped out and shined his flashlight on the vehicles in the driveway. Kat opened the front door as he was walking up the porch steps.

"Evening," the deputy said. "Sorry to disturb you."

"What's going on?" Kat asked right away.

The deputy looked surprised to see so many people at the door and window. "You having a party?"

"A supper party," Kat answered.

"I see. Well, there was an attempted burglary nearby. Did you or anyone see or hear anything?" he asked as the rest of us gathered behind Kat. "I should tell you there were shots fired."

We all groaned or gasped simultaneously.

"We're lucky nobody was hurt," said the lawman. "Do you all live nearby?"

"We live in Lakin," James answered.

"My farm is twelve miles northwest," said John.

"I live in Garden City," said Juan Diego.

"Long ways to drive for a party, isn't it?" the deputy asked Juan Diego.

"It's not too far to see friends," John interjected. "I grow my own feedstock, make my own fuel. Look me up if you want. It's John Mayberry. Mayberry Ranch and Farm."

"What you do with your resources is your own business. You don't see a lot of gatherings like this out here."

"Who fired at who?" Colm asked.

"The homeowner spotted someone breaking into a farm building and came out with his shotgun. The perpetrator fired back and put a hole in the window about four feet from his head."

"Where did this happen?" asked John.

"About a mile west of here at a dairy farm."

"The McCrary's?" Kat said. "They've been there for over fifty years."

After asking for permission, the deputy looked around the property with a flashlight while we watched from inside.

"I guess rural crime is for real," I said.

"Oh, it's real," said John. "Somebody was on my property a couple weeks ago. You remember the morning we had that heavy fog? It was quiet as can be, like all the insects and critters were sleeping in. I put the kettle on and was standing there looking out the kitchen window, half-asleep. I could barely make out the chicken coops, the fog was so thick. I noticed one horse out in the pasture. Didn't think much of it at first 'cause sometimes I leave the stable open. He was just standing there like he was basking in the fog. Then I realized he had a rider and it wasn't my horse. It looked like the rider was staring right at me. It sent a chill through my bones. My heart was in my throat. When I got my wits about me, I swung open the front door and ran out. He kinda jumped. The horse startled. They turned and—" With a whistle and his pointing finger, he indicated they swiftly fled.

"Disappeared into the brume," I said.

"That's creepy, John," said Kat.

"A lot of gall coming out in the daylight," said James.

"I have my dad's rifles somewhere," John said. "I've thought about getting them out but look at what just happened. I don't need anyone shooting at me."

After the Holcomb standoff, there was widespread pushback against the notion that criminal networks were expanding like invasive vines. Then the cattle heist opened the door for militias, media, and political figures to argue drug syndicates, once dormant, were alive and well.

Tonya and James manifested this media influence. "I've heard the Southern burglaries were coordinated," Tonya said. "Those weren't petty thefts. Horses, cattle, grain, fuel…."

"The cartels," James added.

"The cartels don't come quietly and steal your cows," Juan Diego snapped. "They come in the daylight and take what they want and murder anybody who tries to stop them or even glance at them the wrong way. You think if the cartels were here, they'd break into a tool shed?"

"They can't behave here like they do in Mexico," James said. "They have to stay hidden. Strike here and there. Organize under the radar."

"Cartels in Independence is just a rumor, nothing else," said Juan Diego.

"John, what will you do?" Tonya asked.

"If the farmers lose, everyone loses," he said. "Everything I own is a part of my farm. Equipment, supplies, food, fuel, stock, seeds, animals, you name it."

"It's no wonder farmers are hiring their own security," said Tommy.

"Shots have now been fired," John said.

"Will people start moving their valuables inside?" I asked. "It'll be like sleeping with your food so the bears don't get it."

"That's a terrible idea!" Kat exclaimed as though I was actually planning to do that.

The deputy came back and handed out his number, handwritten on slivers of paper. We stood in the living room and watched the squad car back out of the driveway. We were left with discomfiting stillness. I turned up the radio as Jelly Roll Morton played "Hesitation Blues."

FULL REPORT?

For many, the burglary "shootout" and Criollo murder was evidence a criminal incursion was moving north. Here's Boz Flannigan on AM radio 1010:

"*This is what we know for certain: One, Jesús Criollo was driving in the middle of a bitter cold night. He was low on fuel. Nobody in their right mind would do that unless [dramatic pause] they were running from something or someone. Why leave the warmth of the car? Why not wait until morning? Why leave the main highway and walk away from town and safety?*

"*Two, county militia leaders have said they were nowhere near the crime scene and have gone to great lengths to prove it. This means someone tracked him down, gunned him down, and disappeared. Militias have been patrolling our rural areas for years. They don't do that. They don't arbitrarily execute wanderers—or anyone, for that matter—in the middle of the night or in the light of day. Their track record is perfect. Who has a horrific track record?*"

Radio hosts would go on like this for hours and the callers would complete the narrative. "Track record? In Latin America, the drug scum gun their own people down like wild animals. You think killing the Criollo man was a big deal to them?"

Unfortunately for the new president and his administration, a new television show launched that immediately became a major player in the national media. *Full Report* debuted on IBS shortly after the inauguration. The show was two hours long and aired twice a week. There were three permanent hosts: Rachel Collyer of *Channel 11 Dalhart-Dumas*; Zane Schmitt, a former assemblyman; and Maxine Severo, a self-styled Independence maverick. They each had their own sound stage for individual presentations that were five to ten minutes long and rotated for the entire show to give a "multifaceted view of every issue."

The show didn't look small-town, low budget, or amateur. Lighting, set design, and broadcast resolution were as sharp as anything you'd find in a major U.S. market. The hosts were well-coached. Their body language conveyed confidence as they kept their eyes on the correct camera. In contrast to the lo-fi public access shows that made up nearly all programming in Independence (sewing, food preservation, and DIY home repair with foraged materials were popular topics), *Full Report* popped with modern aesthetics.

In the first episode, they explained the show's format and how they would "break down the issues, examine the pieces, and get to the heart of the problem." For their very first segment, they dove into a discussion of the new Gonzalez administration. They talked about his campaign platform, what was to be expected, and gave brief descriptions of his cabinet and department appointees.

This inaugural episode also included a rotating discussion of food shortages. The segment featured a montage of up-close-and-personal news clips of regular folks describing their struggles to obtain food and their fears of what lay ahead. Food pantry volunteers pleaded for donations. Interspersed shots of children (e.g., two young siblings, wide-eyed and innocent) intensified a somber message.

Included in the montage was a clip of one farmer complaining his workers didn't care about feeding people because "They just upped and left as part of their strike." They didn't bother pointing out the strike lasted only two days. They also didn't mention that many employers wouldn't allow workers to return. Recruiting, hiring, and training new employees would have caused more disruptions than the two-day walkout.

Rachel Collyer chronicled the weather disasters that different regions had faced over the spring and summer. Heavy rains in the north led to widespread rot. Hailstorms devastated grain crops and shredded garden plantings. And a plague of grasshoppers ravaged southwest Independence.

Zane Schmitt concluded the discussion by correctly pointing out that nothing contributed more to the food crisis than the fuel crisis. He declared the situation was worsening and the nation's future was bound to the fate of the Ceres Energy plant. They didn't bother to mention Ceres was owned by Bill Tyson, who also owned their network.

The food and fuel crises brought them back to Gonzalez's campaign rhetoric, promises, and his much-ballyhooed "Vision of Independence." For this segment, Maxine Severo interviewed a second-term assemblyman from Perryton. Severo's rise to prominence got a ton of media attention in the run-up to the show's premiere. Before secession, she was a jane-of-all-trades handywoman. With no television or radio experience, she launched her own public access show in Dumas called *Fixing Independence*. It was about home repair and upkeep but she frequently went on political tangents. It was so popular that the radio station gave Severo her own two-hour talk show in the congested Southern market.

SEVERO: The president has talked about hospital care and schools and an expanded food program. Who doesn't want all that?

ASSEMBLYMAN: Things we already have. If you need a hospital, you can go. If you want to send your kids to school, there's at least one in every county. There's not enough money in this country for the government programs he's proposing. Look at every other welfare state in the world and how much trouble they're in. You think we can handle even a smidgeon of that burden? What concerns me most is his energy proposal. Make no mistake, he's talking about nationalizing our gas industry. Our gas companies do the drilling, maintenance, distribution, and everything else because that's what they do. The government's not equipped to handle any of it. This scares me, Maxine.

The bias against President Gonzalez's agenda wasn't surprising. The network's political tilt and brazenness were trademarks of IBS. *Full Report* was criticized for its "uni-faceted presentation of Bill Tyson's aspirations." It's likely the producers expected this. They were unapologetic and said they were simply presenting obvious facts. They rebuffed accusations of a conflict of interest. Ceres Energy, they said, was the sole existing organization proactively working to solve the crisis.

It's true that during his campaign, Gonzalez spoke unabashedly about reclaiming the country's natural resources. But my understanding of his energy proposal was more nuanced than how they were spinning it on *Full Report*. After pipeline talks broke down, Congress passed the Fuel Stimulus Act. This legislation exempted feedstock crop sales from being taxed and offered credits on expenses related to these crops. But to qualify for these incentives, one had to plant a minimum thousand acres of approved feedstock. Gonzalez wanted to change that.

Very few farmers in the country could plant and harvest even a hundred acres. The days of unlimited fuel, fertilizer, and combines were long gone. Gonzalez wanted to remove the cap completely so that all feedstock sales were tax deductible. He also wanted to incentivize fuel sales to encourage farmers to produce and sell ethanol or biodiesel.

A week after the new IBS debut, *Channel 7* in Capital City ran two new shows back-to-back on Thursday night. One was a half hour original sitcom and the other was an hour-and-fifteen-minute production of Thornton Wilder's *Our Town*. The comedy series revolved around a family of four and their daily travails in Independence. With a small office in the laundry room, the father worked as a financial adviser, while the mother, a real estate agent, wore stylish but worn-out designer outfits and jewelry. The parents blindly clung to their former lives but the kids saw their reality for what it really was. The mother's shortcomings in the kitchen (e.g. homemade pasta mush) and the father's home repair failings were part of the shtick. In the premiere, the father tries to replace their TV's power supply with the motor from a vacuum cleaner.

Kat loved it and I have to admit it was funny. Shot in front of a live audience, it skewed the reality of daily life so people could laugh instead of cry. It was cathartic.

NO TAXALEZ

Gonzalez minimized discussing taxation during his campaign but the feedstock incentives and other programs he was advancing needed funding. The time had come to sell the public on his desire to raise taxes on the top twenty percent earners, luxury items, and gasoline sales, to name a few revenue proposals. The president introduced his energy bill in Congress and immediately headed out on a cross-country tour to promote his "Vision of Independence."

Full Report spent half of an entire show covering his tour and policy proposals. This included the resistance he faced along the way. The further south the campaign traveled, the more concentrated protests became. NO TAXES. NO TAXALEZ. TYRANNY BY TAXATION. It reached a crescendo in Dalhart, where hecklers disrupted his speech. At one point, he stopped and addressed his adversaries.

"Why would anyone argue against affordable fuel? You're okay with roads ruined by potholes and decay? What happens if our water system erodes beyond repair? What about access to health care without the burden of lifelong debt? Who would protest against creating more jobs? To object to educating our youth is to object to human progress."

This befuddled *Full Report*'s Rachel Collyer. "What in Sam Hill is he talking about?" Her guest answered, "He's dreaming of a place where unicorns poop candy corn and rivers are flowing with chocolate milk."

The popular radio host Maude Grese appeared on the show. She would become a regular guest on Maxine Severo's segments. The two were cut from the same cloth. Both were in their late fifties, homegrown, and fiery.

SEVERO: Gonzalez did not mention or even utter the word *tax* during his campaign. Now he's talking about entitlement programs, bloated health care, brainwashing a.k.a. school, and social welfare. It all means the same thing: big government and *more taxes*.

GRESE: He's suggesting slipping government fingers into these companies' pockets and taking their money. You know what that's called? It starts with a C.

SEVERO: And ends with *ism*?

GRESE: I've said it over and over on my show. Throughout the campaign, Gonzalez reeked of despotism. That man speaks softly and carries a big beat-down stick. He's gonna continue candy-coating reality and before you know it, boom, all the sudden, we'll be paying thirty-five percent income tax on top of sales tax, firearms tax, fuel tax, and walk-out-your-door tax.

SEVERO: (Mockingly) But we'll have ho*sss*pitals and sch*ooo*ls.

GRESE: Money ain't gonna do much for our hospitals, I'll tell you that. We're screwed on that front til we have proper trade partners. We can talk about bringing in supplies when we have money coming in, not just bleeding out. Does he think we can just give our money to China for cheap medical supplies?

SEVERO: And what about schools?

GRESE: (Blows a raspberry with her tongue) We need labor. The kids wanna work.

SEVERO: We've heard reports that Gonzalez is considering a national military. Does it make sense to nationalize our militia units? The threats we face are real.

GRESE: To control a country, you have to control its energy. To maintain control, you need the military. He can't control the militias unless he makes them dependent on government funding. He can't get funding unless he taxes us. This is all being laid out right in front of our faces. Something else people aren't talking about enough is his economic secretary, who's talked about switching over to non-U.S. currency. He wants to print money and we all know how that goes: hyper-inflation and massive depression. Let's say, for instance, his new currency is backed by the U.S. dollar. When the Independent dollar crashes, who will have those U.S. dollars? The government and the banks. Another way to concentrate power. The Independence people need to wake up and look at what's happening. Albert Gonzalez and his cronies are attempting to turn us into a welfare-totalitarian state.

The president's appearance at a packed gymnasium in Hugoton was broadcast live on Ulysses television. The town was the namesake of the Hugoton gas field, one of the largest natural gas deposits in the North America. It was the foundation of Independence energy. Gonzalez didn't talk about gas or energy in his speech. Instead, he focused on schools, infrastructure, and health care and touted taxation as the most proven and relevant method of building a modern society.

"I have nothing against success. Nothing against profiting from hard work and ingenuity. You want a better life. That's why we've chosen to be here. We are independent of the establishment that champions personal greed and extravagant wealth at the expense of everyone else. We have chosen to build and participate in a society that embraces a more Christian way of life. Do unto others as you want done unto yourself. Let's work for each other so no one is left behind. Instead of thinking 'What can I get for myself,' think 'What can I gain for my community?' Then success becomes a symbol of even greater worth because the more you succeed, the more your community succeeds."

He was clearly responding to his opponents' rhetoric depicting him as a communist despot and equating his "Vision of Independence" with Mao's Great Leap Forward. The Hugoton speech was the first time he presented this moral argument against American-style capitalism. I naively thought it might neutralize his critics or at least take the edge off their attacks. No. They doubled down. A media deluge of talk show hosts, pundits, and legislators accused the president of shamelessly unleashing this bid for new taxes like a Trojan Horse that would bring down Independence.

In The *Weekly Independent*, Juan Diego printed a collage of front page headlines. From *The Dighton Bee*: THE RISE OF OUR KING. The *Independent Advocate*: TAXATION=TYRANNY. *The Southern Standard*: THE END OF INDEPENDENCE (AS WE KNOW IT). And my favorite, taken from the monthly newsletter *Prosperity and Economics*, was a parody of James Montgomery Flagg's lithograph of Uncle Sam with Gonzalez in a top hat with hammer and sickle, pointing at the viewer: I WANT YOUR MONEY.

RURAL TERROR

After the president's tour wrapped up, IBS and Southern media turned their collective eye on rural crime. The Moscow murder, McCrary shootout, incidents of cattle rustling, and sightings of mysterious riders on horseback stood as evidence of something treacherous happening in the country.

Most recently, a farmer out west had lost equipment and all of his fuel in an overnight barn fire. This prompted *Full Report's* Zane Schmitt to declare rural Independence was "in the grip of terror."

Video of the burning barn was superimposed over images of the grieving farmer and his wife. "This was done with explicit purpose. Destroying this innocent family's livelihood was meant to frighten and intimidate all of us. This is called terror."

Maude Grese laid into the Gonzalez administration for not publicly condemning rural crime, for not utilizing the NIA, and for turning a blind eye to the cartel crisis. "*Last summer, a special interest group convinced a third of our population to shut down the country. At the same exact moment we were trying to deal with the influx of foreign hostiles, this group decided it would be a good time to start a domestic war. It not only shielded the terrorists but it crippled the economy. They—helped—the—terrorists. You think they were oblivious to this? It makes you wonder if somebody inside the Hispanic leadership wanted to protect the insurgents. Why has there not been an investigation into this? There were plenty of people saying 'This ain't right!' You remember what happened? The movement leaders played the race card so anyone who dared question their motives was shot down as a racist. Enough is enough. It's time to call a spade a spade. Mr. Gonzalez, are you with us or are you against us? You're sure not acting like you give a damn about what's happening.*"

Anxiety over a criminal invasion had seized rural Independence. I saw it manifested firsthand at a rally in front of the Ulysses courthouse. Hundreds of people gathered on the lawn with improvised sheets of drywall and plywood painted with catchphrases such as SAVE INDEPENDENCE and FIGHT BACK. A flag made with bedding and metal piping was blowing in the brisk wind: YOU STEAL YOU DIE. A life-size straw dummy, dressed as someone's idea of a cartel mercenary, jounced over the crowd with a blue bandana around its forehead and a plaid long-sleeve with just the top buttoned over a white t-shirt. Red paint was splattered on its chest like a gunshot.

The bloody effigy triumphantly hoisted above the crowd was eerie. I've been to energetic protests where you could feel order and civility buckling. Invariably, there were cliques within the demonstration emanating conflict and poised to explode with rage at the slightest provocation. The men and women outside the courthouse appeared resolute in their anger but not visibly homicidal. But knowing the potential for keyed-up mobs to turn savage at the flick of a switch made the event a bit discomfiting.

This exaltation of murder made me think of the grotesque barbarity of *La Violencia* in Colombia, when neighbors and family members murdered and dismembered one another. The only distinction between them was being liberal or conservative. It wasn't unlike the artificial class and ethnic divisions between Hutus and Tutsis that left at least a half million dead. I've wondered if this potential for utter depravity is deep-seated in all of us. It's a depressing thought.

A man on the courthouse steps shouted into a bullhorn, "Sure, it's been hard. I can take it, though, 'cause I'm a survivor! When survivors band together, can't nobody get us down. All the thieves and terrorists, listen up and listen good: Not in my country. Not on my land." He wagged his finger. "You come here, we'll track you down and we will punish you. Go on back from where you came!"

As I studied the fringes of the gathering to see who was and who wasn't applauding, I spotted Tom Jones watching from the sidewalk. I waved at him.-"You here for the rally?" I asked facetiously. I don't think he got my humor. He held his cards close.

"The McCrary thing has got people riled up around here," Tom said.

"Not just here. Kat's talking about getting a gun."

I expected Tom to warn against this sort of reactionary thinking, which I could use against Kat. "The burglary wasn't as random as some people are making it sound," he said. "The perpetrator popped the lock on the outer door where the milk was stored. It tripped an alarm in the house. Someone in the know targeted his farm."

Tom's gaze fell on the same group of young men I noticed earlier. They weren't whooping and hollering with the rest of the crowd. They were too cool and exuded an aura of contempt. One of them reminded me of the hellhound I clashed with at the militia rally in Capital City.

"Right now, I'm more concerned with them," Tom said.

"Who are they?" I asked.

"Young men taking it upon themselves to settle matters that may or may not be legitimate."

While we watched the demonstration, the Grant County Sheriff pulled into a handicap spot near us. He was a tall man and his height bolstered his swagger as he walked to the edge of the grass to get a better look. Satisfied nothing illegal or too strange was going on, he put his sunglasses back on and sat on the car hood as if he were taking in the three-legged race at the kiddie fair.

Tom walked over to talk to him and I followed. "Good afternoon, Sheriff. I'm Tom Jones from Finney County. We've never had the pleasure of meeting."

"Ah," Bradley said with a grin as he shifted on the hood and unhooked his thumbs from his pockets. "I heard you were around."

"Quite a crowd," Tom said.

"I guess so."

"What's with the scarecrow?" I asked as men pulled the figure down and began beating the straw out of it.

"Gotta take their frustrations out on something," Bradley said.

"What are they frustrated about?"

"Life, I guess," he said. He looked at Tom. "I hear you're hired help for Duane Emmett and Bud Goldman."

"And Max Brennan, Walter Morgan, Tim Barkley, Guy Wells."

The sheriff raised his eyebrows apathetically. "They're free to do what they want with their money."

Close by, two men were posing for a news camera. One had painted *Freedom Fighter* on the barrel of his shotgun. The other had scrawled *Bandito Killer* on his.

"You see that kid in the camo and red hat?" Bradley nodded to the group Tom and I had been watching. "That's Clint."

The name resonated like fingernails on a chalkboard and raised the hair on the back of my neck. Indeed, it was the same brute who wanted to wreck my fine features in Capital City. At least this time I had a couple lawmen by my side but I hated he was here in Ulysses. Even worse, it turned out he lived in the area.

"And the one next to him is his brother, King. Sons of your employer, Duane Emmett. They're the youngest and most volatile of the brothers. There's about a fifty-fifty chance we'll have an altercation here. Only fifty because most people know to stay away from them. The older ones—Kenneth, Tim, Charlie—they're sensible men. You can talk to them."

"His name's King, huh?" Tom said. "What about the big guy?"

He was referring to another young man whose size and bleached white skin and hair made him stand out.

"That's Travis Kuhn," said Bradley.

"I ran into him and King in the middle of the night about ten miles south of town," Tom said. "They were patrolling the countryside."

"Don't bother with 'em. They're just trying to protect their land. Gives them something to do."

220

"They tailed me for a couple miles—I mean on my ass. I could've turned by headlights off and seen the road ahead just fine."

"Like I said, let 'em be."

Tom smirked but let it go. "You heard anything about the Moscow case? It's hard to believe the victim was trying to rob that farm. His car was three miles away. What could he take?"

"Fuel!" the sheriff exclaimed as if it were obvious.

"I went down there that morning," Tom said. "Saw where the truck skidded to a stop. It made me think the passenger had his rifle locked and loaded. The truck stopped, he leaned out the window, pop."

"You got me," Bradley said with a disinterested shrug. "It's not my business." Something caught his eye across the way and he slid off the car. "Nice talking to you both," he said before he cut through the demonstration to the other side, where two women were standing. By the way he was smiling and posturing, it looked as though there was romantic interest.

The posse of young men lost interest in the rally and dispersed. Tom watched the two brothers and the Kuhn kid as they split from the group and leave together. "Roman, nice to see you," he said. "Talk to you soon." He shook my hand and followed them.

The sentiments expressed at the rally were not confined to city limits or demonstrations. Kat mentioned signs were beginning to appear across the county. "No Trespassing, Will Shoot," "You Steal You Die," "Guns Loaded," and so on. It felt it was just a matter of time before something happened. That moment came sooner than later.

"We begin with the tragic story many of you have been following today. Last night, an unknown assailant took the life of twenty-two-year-old Rodney Cohoon five miles from his home in western Grant County.

From the kitchen where I was preparing lunch, I heard Kat's desk chair slide back and hit the wall. We arrived at the television simultaneously. According to the *Channel 4 News* story, three friends had been patrolling the area for weeks. They shared a motorcycle, working in shifts. They expected Cohoon to pass off the bike at 3AM. When he didn't show, his friend went to his house and woke up Cohoon's father.

They hastily put together a search party but it was Cohoon's friend who found him. As the sun was coming up, he spotted a bright reflection out on a large swath of grassland. He walked out and saw the motorcycle lying on its side. Rodney was lying a few feet away. He had been shot in the face at pointblank range. They found the hunting rifle that the young men kept in a scabbard near the body. The site was covered with horse tracks. They believed Cohoon spotted the rider and rode out to confront him.

The nearest inhabited home was two miles away. The elderly couple who lived there were interviewed on the news. They looked old enough to have come out on the Cimarron Trail. It seemed unlikely they would've heard a gunshot even if were outside their bedroom window. They didn't have fuel or anything worth stealing. The reason I mention this is because it illustrates how bewildering and pointless it seemed. Two armed riders crossed paths in the middle of the night on grassy lands used for pheasant hunting.

There had been legitimate theft attempts but they didn't add up to the rumors and rhetorical allegations. Obviously, the general sense of insecurity was real. Maybe people simply needed something to fill the space once occupied by jobs and entertainment and shopping. Many Independents were still going through the motions of their former lives, as parodied in the *Channel 7* sitcom.

Boredom (or the awareness of time passing, as William James put it) is wholly unpleasant. I struggled mightily with it out in the countryside. Rodney and his friends surely did as well. Protecting their land and fighting back against an incursion, real or not, was something to do and take pride in.

Ideas of heroism and glory are woven into our collective consciousness. The countless translations and interpretations of just one of our greatest hero myths, *The Iliad*, is evidence of this. But in *The Inferno*, Dante imagines Achilles in death, yearning for a simple life of farming. If Rodney was aware in his last moments he was about to die, perhaps he felt similarly. Being home with his family wouldn't have seemed so dull and purposeless. Now it was left to his family and friends to frame his life and passions.

Kat surprised me during dinner when she announced she wanted to attend the funeral. I asked if she knew the family, knowing she didn't. "I still want to show my support," she said defiantly.

"You'll just be making a spectacle of the whole thing."

"If they can make a spectacle of murdering people and tormenting us," she replied, "then we can make a spectacle of the misery it causes. I'm going."

The service was held at Bethlehem Lutheran Church in Ulysses. We sat toward the middle of the packed nave. Latecomers stood at the back and along the side aisles.

After the pallbearers placed the casket on the stand, it was draped with a black pall. A soloist, standing alone on a rear balcony, sang, "*O Lord by God, when I in awesome wonder....*" Those who knew the lyrics joined in the refrain. To my surprise, Kat sang along, using a hymnal from the pew rack.

When the hymn finished, we remained standing with eyes on the young pastor as he stepped to the pulpit in robe and stole. He looked over the congregation. I can't imagine he'd ever seen the room fuller. The somberness was weighty but you could sense the anticipation. The pastor rose to the occasion, speaking with confidence and solemnity. "In the name of the Father and of the Son and of the Holy Spirit."

"Amen," the congregation responded and sat down.

"In Holy Baptism, Rodney was clothed with the robe of Christ's righteousness that covered all his sin. St. Paul says, 'Do you not know that all of us who have been baptized into Christ Jesus were baptized into His death?'" Those around me nodded their heads. "'We were buried therefore with Him by baptism into death in order that, just as Christ was raised from the dead by the glory of the Father, we too might walk into newness of life.'"

The pastor continued but my thoughts lingered on this last verse. I was struck by the proactive acceptance of death. It's one thing to acknowledge its inevitability, but being okay with it is a whole other matter. I imagined Saul of Tarsus exclaiming this with exhilaration as if to say, "When we die it's not the end! It's not the end!" At least if you believed in Jesus. If you believed in his God.

I've never spent much time in churches. Never gave much thought to the idea of faith. I don't mean any particular strand of biblical interpretation one might believe in. I'm talking about faith as the most essential element of religiosity. Instead of going through a process of observation that might lead to proof that legitimizes belief, in Christianity, newcomers are coaxed into believing in something extraordinary and mythical without genuine evidence. In place of proof is faith, the cornerstone of religion. It flips scientific method on its head and puts the cart before the horse.

I know it's been deliberated ad infinitum but what I'm saying, what I thought that day in the church, was that looking at faith as a nonbeliever, it seems the ultimate reward of believing, and therefore religion's *raison d'être*, is to neutralize death anxiety and the corresponding drive that underscores everything we do. Faith is the linchpin and believers do whatever it takes to maintain it in order to placate death anxiety. It's not a bad idea. For me, death is completely unacceptable.

The pallbearers loaded the casket into the back of a pickup. Those with space offered rides to the cemetery. Three strangers rode with us. There were at least two dozen vehicles in the caravan, a rare sight. We drove west out of town and then another three miles on a dirt road to a tiny cemetery with an antique iron fence around its square border. The front of the procession inched around the interior loop. The back half parked on the road.

Mourners uncrated themselves from crowded vehicles. Inside the graveyard, a big dual-wheel pickup had a cargo bed loaded down with teenage boys. They were clearly from local ranching families. I watched as the boys leaped out of the back. One of them failed to stick his landing and stumbled to his knees, but with youthful verve, sprung up and dusted off his pants. Men with cowboy hats and flinty dispositions stepped out of the crew cab. Clint Emmett was with them.

After seeing him at the courthouse demonstration, I thought about what might happen if we were face-to-face. Who knows if he'd remember me? It was possible his searing rage impressed my image in my mind like a branding iron. For my safety and to avoid a scene, I kept my distance.

The people gathered around the open grave. Fittingly, the clouds hung low. When the pastor was satisfied with the mourners' quiescence, he said a few words and then nodded to a young man who stepped forward and unfolded a sheet of paper from his back pocket.

"Rodney, my friend," he began nervously, "I never thought it could end. I've been thinking about the times we spent catching carp at Derby's Pond or shooting skeet at the range. I remember when we first got our pellet guns as kids. We'd walk all over the county looking for gophers and sparrows or anything that wasn't grass or dirt."

Rodney's friend read the letter, front and back, struggling at times to keep his composure. He mostly talked about things they did together growing up. One story was about trying to join the military. They wanted to go abroad and fight terrorists. The problem was they were underage. So Rodney challenged the recruiter to a fight to prove he was worthy. "He was older and bigger but I don't doubt for a second you would've whipped him. You had the heart of a warrior and patriot."

They finally got the opportunity to fight for something they believed in (or against), even if it was on their own soil. The ancient idea of heroes as half-gods is linked to the latent desire to transcend the limitations of being a mortal human. In the end, they decided Rodney died a hero. This did nothing for him. It was for his friends and family in the same way cemeteries are for the living.

The pastor said a few words and then the pallbearers lowered the casket into the hole. Rodney's mother tossed a loose bouquet that scattered as it landed. His kid brother dropped a photo of them together. Last, one of his buddies flipped a nickel-plated rifle casing that bounced off the casket with a thump. He stood at the edge and pounded his chest twice with his fist.

People offered condolences to the family and returned quietly to their vehicles. I had almost forgotten about Clint Emmett when I saw him hoist himself onto the pickup bed and shout for everyone to hear. "Listen here. Rodney Cohoon will be avenged!"

His buddies joined him in shouting promulgations, pacing back and forth with reddened faces. The priest and others watched with dismay. The family was escorted back to their truck. As Rodney's father got into his pickup, he turned and faced them. With emotion hardening his face, he held a clenched fist high. When men saw this, they whooped and hollered and doubled down on their ardor. Skipping around the cemetery, they shouted at the cavalcade.

During the burial, Sheriff Bradley had showed up. He watched all this from the road where he was leaning against his squad car. When one man shouted, "We gonna kill the man who did this," I swear I saw a glimmer in the sheriff's eye.

SHOOT FIRST

If three murders and a rumored criminal incursion weren't enough, the emergence of masked and hooded riders added to the horror of it all. Ever since John Mayberry told us about the horseman he discovered on his property, there had been multiple reports of sightings in central Independence. Since farmers and ranchers owned nearly all the horses, some believed they were the masked avengers. A handful of horse owners disclosed they were involved in the night patrols.

About a week after the Rodney's funeral, *Channel 4* began running a public service announcement that was benevolent in tone but surreal in content. A local farmer, about sixty years old, was framed in a medium shot. He wore a green DuPont hat and collared work coat. With his friendly voice and demeanor, he came across as a friendly neighbor who would help anyone in need. A tractor was parked behind him and beyond that was sprawling farmland. While he spoke, he gestured with both hands as if he were holding an idea the size of a volleyball.

> Hello friends. My name is Jim Baxter. I've lived here in Grant County my whole life. I used to be a wheat farmer. Like you, I do what I gotta do to get by. I'm here to talk about the badness that's goin' around. I know you're God-loving, decent people and violence isn't part of your nature. But we've got to defend ourselves, each and every one of us, if we wanna survive. Protect what's yours and together we'll protect what's ours. Our country, our families, our way of life, and our values are under attack. You need to get out that ol' huntin' rifle or pistol if you got one and get it cleaned up real good. Make sure you got the right ammunition and get yourself comfortable using it. If you're not, call a neighbor. Be brave and be strong. If you don't shoot, they will.

I couldn't believe what I was seeing. It was part of a regionwide effort to "fight back." To be fair, it might have been as much about appearances as intention: a message to thieves.

With each passing week, life in the countryside was feeling more pressurized. My view on rural crime hadn't changed. It was being grossly exaggerated. Kat and I didn't see eye-to-eye on this matter and it quickly became a source of tension. Meeting her halfway didn't seem to help. We secured her work shed and the barn and brought valuable items inside. Through a government program launched a few weeks earlier, we acquired two light bulbs, one for the front porch and the other for the kitchen window (inside so it couldn't be stolen).

The incessant radio exhortations about horrors lurking in the darkness were chipping away at my sense of security. Not that I thought bands of malevolent criminals were prowling the countryside. The constant exposure to conflict—voices steeped in fear and outrage—was corrupting my ability to separate fact from fear. I often lay awake listening to nighttime creaks and clicks, expecting at any moment to hear a door rattling, a gunshot, or a distant scream.

Not long after the television PSA first aired, we received an unexpected visit from a local man. It was late Sunday morning. I could hear the motorcycle coming from miles away but I thought little of it until the rider turned into our driveway. Nobody ever visited without a dog or cat.

Through the narrow front door window, I watched the man dismount. He had a buzz cut, a short beard trimmed to a point, and his ears were bright red from riding with his head uncovered. He wore heavy beige work pants and a matching jacket. There was nothing conspicuously threatening or unstable about him but I felt on guard when I opened the door.

"What can I do for you?" I asked, trying not to sound distrustful.

"Morning," he said before he walked up the porch steps. "Sorry to bother you. My name's Rick Ballard. I live about five miles from here, south of 160. Me and a bunch of others are going around talking to folks about what's happening out in the country." He noticed Kat standing in the office doorway and seemed to glean our uneasiness. "I'm one of the good guys, trust me. You all heard about what happened last night near Johnson City? Well, somebody broke into an old couple's home and held them at gunpoint. The man's heart seized up and he died. All for a couple pieces of jewelry and a few dollars."

"Oh my gosh!" Kat exclaimed and cupped her hands over her mouth.

"There's wickedness going around. We gotta protect ourselves because the government ain't gonna do it. We're on our own out here." He spoke politely but his unblinking eyes bore down on me with disturbing intensity. "There are simple steps you can take, alright? If you're out driving, get home before dark. Lock your doors, windows, outbuildings."

"We've already done that," I said.

"Do you own a firearm?" Ballard asked me.

Before I could say no, Kat enthusiastically answered yes.

"What?" I asked with surprise but she was already inside. Hurried. She returned a moment later with a black revolver I had never seen and knew nothing about. "Where did that come from?"

She walked past me and handed it to Ballard. After briefly examining the gun, he looked at me as though he was already pissed about what he was going to say. "If there's anyone on your property, at your window, on your front step, out by your vehicle, or wherever—you shoot first and ask questions later. It's your duty to your country to shoot. It's the only way we're gonna stop this insurgence. We gotta fight back. It's all connected—burglaries, the killings, the terror, drug wars. You understand?"

"Connected in what way?" I asked.

"Oh, come on!" Ballard snapped. "Where've you been the past year?"

"What's the law on shooting someone if they're on our property?" Kat asked.

"Self-defense," Ballard answered.

"What if they're unarmed?" I asked.

"If anyone goes to jail for shooting one of those demons, there'll be an uprising that'll raise the dead. We gotta have each other's back if we want to survive this. They're not coming; they're already here." He frowned at the .22 caliber pistol, turning it over in his hands. "It's accurate, at least. You know how to use it?"

"The store owner showed me but I haven't tried it yet," said Kat.

"First of all, you gotta keep it close at night. When you go to bed, take it with you." He opened the empty cylinder. "It needs to be loaded at all times, alright? Just don't point it at anyone unless you plan to shoot. When it goes down, you're gonna be scareder than you've ever been. You don't wanna mess around trying to load this. Remember to take off the safety. Find your target."

He raised the pistol, and with his arm bent at the elbow, he pointed it over my shoulder toward the back wall. I stepped to the side.

"Take a breath. Let it out halfway, then pull the trigger nice and easy without jerking. Bam."

His menacing gaze lingered on his felled victim. He had the look of a man who'd killed before or had gone through the contemplative process of deciding he would.

"No one's gonna be here to help you. You call 911, it'll be an hour if you're lucky. You're alone out here. Your neighbors can't hear you. You gotta save yourself. If they get you, they get her. This is survival. You kill them or they kill you. They'll take anything that's yours." He looked me in the eye and glanced at Kat.

In the days to come, loathing for Ballard—what he represented—would fill my entire being as his visit cycled through my mind. I was face-to-face with a force that perpetuated power and domination. Just like Clint Emmett. Ballard might have sensed my condemnation. As he was leaving, he stopped and looked back at me. "I'm a survivor. I hope you are too." His scowl made it clear he didn't think I was.

"That was weird," I said to Kat after he was gone.

"No, that was neighbors looking out for neighbors," she replied. "You always complain about not having a community. Well, that's our community."

"That was someone going door to door trying to get people to shoot other people."

"This is the world we live in," she said. "This is our reality and we have to adapt."

"I'm not sure I want to adapt to this craziness."

"You'd rather be shot? Or me? Think about that."

"What did Tom say when you talked to him?" I asked with overdone calmness. "That you should arm yourself for battle?"

"Of course he didn't say that."

"Don't you think he'd warn you if there was any real danger?"

"Roman, did you not hear what that man said about the old couple? Johnson City is thirty miles from here. Someone else was murdered fifteen miles from here. Another just over the county line. Murdered. Mr. McCrary, less than a mile away. He's our closest neighbor. My grandparents knew him. This isn't happening somewhere else. You think those ranchers would hire my uncle if

there wasn't real danger? You need to wake up. It's like you're
entertained by it all. It's just material for your book."

"So what do you want me to do?"

"Open your eyes."

"Okay," I said with eyes sprung wide.

Kat shook her head and walked away.

"Where did you get that gun?" I asked.

She stopped and turned around. "At a gun store."

"Why?"

"You really have to ask?"

"You think you can shoot another person?" I asked.

She walked inside and closed the door behind her.

I wasn't sure of myself anymore. Every night I lay in bed wondering
if it would be the night my crisis—to kill or not to kill—would
culminate in a moment that would define my life. To spill blood and
splatter the side of the barn with muscle and tissue would endear me
to many people. I would no longer live in opposition to Rick Ballard
and the others who shared his values. But even with the blessing of
my community, I couldn't see how once you killed another person,
your world would not become bound in a putrefying atmosphere
where torment rose in the east, and when it set on the western horizon,
guilt hovered like a lightless moon, ever-present but rarely visible.

Violence and killing are pervasive in American culture.
Perhaps it was naïve to believe my choices alone spared me from that
side of America. I was lucky but it was closer than I had realized.
Now, it seemed my time had come and there was no escaping the
volition of primal man that reaches hundreds of thousands of years
through time and deadens consciousness, making us as myopic and
tribal as our ancestors. With reason and empathy came love but with
reason and fear came sophisticated warfare and systemized
oppression.

I find it surprising so many of us can reach across psychological lines of demarcation and sympathize with even the most corrupt and malevolent. This could be evidence of an evolutionary force shrinking the ancient brain and our capacity for malice. For me, at that moment, it felt as though ancient man had a foothold and was pulling me and the rest of us backward into chaos. Maybe the IBS pundits were right and we really were caught in a "plague of iniquity."

ECONOMIC SUMMIT

The Independence Economic Summit, what organizers billed as a "coming-together of the nation's business leaders and sharpest entrepreneurial minds," took place in Liberal over a mid-February weekend. It received moderate coverage around the country, except on IBS stations, where the event was given such weighty significance that one might have thought it was the modern-day equivalent of the Council of Nicaea.

IBS owner Bill Tyson made his first public appearance when he was spotted entering the hotel conference center. He was a heavyset man and wore a white suit with a black bowtie and used a cane to steady his gait. The cameras clearly made him uncomfortable so he avoided eye contact. On the second night, it looked as though someone advised him to improve his public image because he kept his head up and waved at reporters.

Other attendees included Grady Washington; Ted Wilkerson, his former Commerce Secretary; Buddy Hagar, one of the biggest contractors in the country; Shay Connor, owner of Independent Alchemy, the country's largest foundry; a handful of congressmen;

and prominent agricultural figures. The exclusion of Gonzalez administration members was noteworthy.

Reporters weren't allowed inside the summit but a spokesman addressed the media all three nights. These briefings were short on substance but heavy on verbosity about the failing economy, struggling families, and untapped capital. The lone Windsor founder who attended the summit, Mark Carter, joined the spokesman on the last night. He read from a prepared speech.

"Our economy, security, and energy prospects are dying. If they fail, then so does all hope for Independence. Although we have little time, we have the right people to lead a three-pronged attack to save our country. Foremost, we must secure our borders against the infiltration that continues to this day and we must fight the existing forces inside. To do this, we need a strong, proactive NIA. For this, we need Major Krug.[19] He can bring together our forces and resist the evildoers but only if we released him from the chains that hold him down. To accomplish our goals, we need fuel, the cornerstone of our security and economy. Everything depends on fuel. Everything. Right here in this building, we have the people who can make that happen."

No one I knew expected the impact this conference would have on Independence. It would be irresponsible to suggest a nefarious conspiracy was hatched that weekend but it inspired a movement powered by IBS. I didn't think anti-Gonzalez sentiment could be any stronger. Boy, was I wrong.

---

[19] The Krug-run National Security Department had a reputation for being the least transparent of federal agencies. On the campaign trail, Gonzalez hammered Washington and the NSD for its opaqueness. President Gonzalez shocked his allies and adversaries by keeping Major Krug on as NSD Secretary. At the press conference, Gonzalez rattled off Krug's accomplishments: heading the NSD, "a department he created from scratch"; developing unspecified national defense programs; spearheading the NIA; and being the "ultimate hero and patriot." It was believed that keeping Krug was a political move, the first step in winning certain voters' trust.

On the last night of the conference, Bill Tyson appeared on *A Clear View* with Edmund MacAllister. The one-on-one interview show debuted on IBS a month before *Full Report* and was the first nationally televised primetime show. The stage was dressed with two comfortable leather armchairs, a large Venetian rug, and a side table with a lamp, creating an intimate setting.

MacAllister spoke in a warm 1950s television voice that bid for viewers' trust. This was the first time the public heard Tyson speak. He talked with a high-pitched and whiny Texas twang that at first seemed at odds with his gruff demeanor.

"I don't know what the president's problem is. Here we are trying to build a bona fide fuel plant, something this country desperately needs—I mean, desperate as in live or die—and he's doing everything he can to stop it. What he wants to do, and he doesn't hide it, is nationalize energy. He's working with radical members of Congress to revoke our land leases and repeal our development contract. He's also ordered an investigation into my business affairs to smear my reputation. I say let the people of Independence decide what they want. This is a democracy, right? If the people don't want me and what I offer, I'll go. It would be disappointing but I'm a democratic man; I get it. In that case, I guess the entrepreneur isn't welcome here."

All week long, Maude Grese echoed and elaborated on summit talking points.

MAUDE: Gonzalez is trying to turn our hard-fought democracy into a communist state. He toured the country, aggrandizing his social programs and taxation. Does he think we're stupid? We know what that means. Big government! What they want to do is create a culture of entitlement so the higher up the government chain you are, the better off you are. The power gets concentrated at the top. That's fascism. You might say, that ain't gonna happen here 'cause this is Independence. Well, it's happened before in modern history and you better believe it can happen again. If you have a depressed economy like we do now, insecurity like we do now, low morale like we do now, food shortage and fuel shortage, what do you get? Think about another country that had all those features. They were isolated by their neighbors, their morale was blown all to hell by war, inflation was out of control, and bread lines wrapped around the block. What did that produce? Hitler. Economic instability led to Mussolini. How did the most socialist president the U.S. has ever known come to power? The Great Depression. People need to wake up and see what's happening.

CALLER: I've heard impeachment mentioned. Maybe we should all be talking about it.

GRESE: You better believe you'll hear it this weekend. All over the country, people are coming out to speak against the Gonzalez agenda. I will be in Dalhart at eleven on Saturday and Dumas at two. I want to see everyone—and I mean everyone—who believes in freedom and who believes in our country. There will be free buses throughout the lower counties.

These were being promoted as "freedom rallies to resist and retaliate." The events were broadcast live for those too far away to make the trip. I tuned in to the Dalhart event on Saturday morning.

People gathered on a wide swath of open land that flanked a lifeless rail yard. A modular stage was assembled in front of the Union Pacific building. A generator behind the building powered a four-piece country band that played songs of freedom and self-reliance. Demonstration signs bobbed above the crowd. Someone had drawn a Mexican drug cartel family tree and pasted a headshot of President Gonzalez over the leader. As the camera panned the gathering, I spotted posters with graphic beheadings and mutilations from Mexico. There was a sign with Gonzalez in Nazi regalia and a Hitler mustache. It wasn't the first or last time I saw this depiction.

Two commentators passed the time on-air while waiting for the rally to start.

"I remember coming down to the rail yards as a kid."

"Back in the Dust Bowl?"

"Ernie, you're what I love about Dalhart. Got a sense of humor about you. No, I'm talking about a time when America was the greatest nation on Earth. When hope and opportunity abounded. We felt safe. We cared about each other. These rail yards were busy. Freight trains were filling with our grain—"

"Sorry to interrupt you, Dick, but we got two more buses coming in. I think these are the last ones."

Yellow school buses had been bringing rural residents in from six local counties. Each has its own sponsor displayed on the sides of the buses. *Citizens For Economic Progress; Independence Liberty Alliance; Independence Against Dependence; People For Prosperity; Guardians Of Freedom; Descendants Of The Revolution* (which one?)*; The Foundation For Energy And Economics; and The Center For Responsible Politics.*

After the last passengers disembarked, the rally began. The master of ceremonies was a local businessman with a flat-top cowboy hat and black leather pants. "Helloooooo, Independence! You know this is where it all began for Dalhart. They used to call this Twist Junction. That was a time of expansion when folks were following their hopes and dreams. Even though we Independents didn't have to travel thousands of miles, we also said goodbye to our old lives to follow our hopes and dreams. We didn't abandon these rail lines or businesses along this corridor. We left the old way of doing things to work out a better way to live.

"Now, we got to be diligent and make sure no one swindles us into doing things the old way. You all remember when it felt like somebody was always looking over your shoulder, making sure you were living life the way *they* wanted you to live? There was always someone reaching into your pockets with their loooong fingers and taking *your* money? What was that name? That's right, I heard some of you say it. Big government!"

Local politicians and personalities rehashed these themes for the next hour.

"As your congressman, I wanna know who here is okay with Gonzalez raising your taxes? Let me see a show of hands. Huh, I don't see any. Then let me hear you if you got a problem with Gonzalez taking your money?" He had to shout over the zealous callback. "I said it before and I'll say it again, over my dead body! Over my dead body!"

This set the stage for Maude Grese. She was the most prominent media personality in the entire country and she was especially popular in the south, where people had been listening to her show since the early days of independence. She waved to the energized crowd as she crossed the stage in tight blue jeans, cowboy boots, and a long denim saddle coat.

"Wow, look at this crowd! Did you all see those 'Vision of Dependence' rallies they're touting on northern media? They'd get a couple hundred people and call it big news. Ha! This right here is what happens when you threaten our freedom. We all come out. Gonzalez drove down here and tried to convince you it was in your best interest to let the government have your money. Who does Gonzo think we are, a bunch of ninnies who need an udder to suck on? Gonzo, we don't need your big 'ol government cow. Take your commie agenda and get out! This is the most corrupt president this part of the world's ever seen. He's a racist and a flaming liberal. It's sickening. Boy, I'd love to take a swing at him."

She laughed at this thought as she took the microphone off the stand and began pacing on the stage. People in the crowd shouted how they would also love to take a shot at the president or see Maude take him out.

"They caught us off-guard in the elections last year. They beat us at the ballot box but if these transgressions continue, we'll have no choice but to beat them with the bullet. This is our country. We ain't gonna let nobody take it from us. If I go down, it'll be with guns blazing."

BANG, BANG

Cold rain had turned to sleet. I shook off my poncho, hung it on the door handle, and left my muddy galoshes on the back step. Kat came in from her office to look at the plywood signs I staked outside. TRESPASSERS WILL BE SHOT; BEWARE OF DOG!; IS THIS WORTH DYING FOR?

"None of it's true," I said.

"That's what you've decided?"

"Oh, come on. You're not going to swagger out like Joan Crawford and start shooting at the bad guys. It's not going to happen. Let's move on to what we can realistically do."

"This is reality, Roman. You can't wish your way out of it."

"You're talking about a Hollywood Wild West version of reality."

"What are you going to do? Run upstairs and hide in the closet?"

Mimicking a John Wayne-like tough guy, I snarled my upper lip. "It's a man's job to do the killin' 'round here, ain't that right?"

She stood there with her hands on her hips, staring at me as if I were a pathetic excuse of a man. "I don't expect you to do anything," she said at last. "You find a place to hide and I'll protect us and our home."

"You'll just charge out there if someone's poking around the barn? What if there's more than one person? Will you gun them all down like Billy the Kid?" I pretended I was slinging six-shooters. "You think you can kill a person? Imagine the person you shot lying on the ground, struggling to breathe, gurgling blood that's oozing through his fingers, staring up at you with mortal terror in his eyes. Will you stand over your victim and watch him die?"

"Don't put this on me," Kat said in a quivering voice. "I'm not the trespasser."

"What you're talking about doing will change you forever. People are insisting we have to go to war but we still have a choice."

"We don't have a choice."

"Right now, at this moment, there are people in Hugoton marching for peace, protesting the violence. They're making a choice."

"I understand where you're coming from but none of it changes our circumstances. We have to be ready. That's all I'm saying."

"You'd be lucky to get a shot off," I grumbled.

Kat walked to the china hutch and took the pistol from the drawer. With both hands gripping the handle, she pointed it at me. "What's so hard about it? Bang, bang." When she saw my utter shock, she lowered the gun with a bashful smile.

"Are you out of your fucking mind?"

"I was only showing you it's not hard."

"Your finger was on the trigger!" I shouted.

"I was pretending! Don't get so mad."

"You could have fucking killed me! People die all the time from gun accidents."

She marched back to the hutch and tossed the gun into the drawer.

"Oh my god, don't throw it!" I yelled.

"Stop yelling at me!"

In a measured tone, perhaps a bit too didactic, I said, "You never play around with guns, especially one that's loaded. And never, ever point it at someone."

Without missing a beat, Kat took her great-grandmother's antique ceramic teapot off the hutch and dropped it on the floor. The shattered pieces ricocheted off chair legs. The fragments crunched underfoot as she stormed to her office.

"This is just great," I said, throwing my arms in the air.

A few moments later, Kat marched out to the closet, yanked her coat off the hanger, and left.

When she returned in the evening, we didn't bother greeting one another. "Did I get any calls?" she asked in an icy tone as she hung her coat in the closet.

"Nope," I replied in kind.

Out of the corner of my eye, I could see her looking at the hutch. "Thanks for cleaning up the teapot," she said in an agreeable tone I suspected was setting up an unapologetic apology. "I'm sorry I pointed the gun at you but you didn't have to talk to me like a child."

"It was upsetting having a gun pointed at me!" I snapped. "I'm sorry you didn't like how I spoke after you almost killed me."

She rolled her eyes. "Let's just forget it happened."

That was an absurd suggestion and didn't deserve an answer. "I don't believe in this shoot first, ask questions later crap," I said.

"It's not something you believe in," she said without emotion. "You do it to survive."

"If there are people so desperate they're willing to rob someone in the middle of the night and risk their life, maybe we should reach out to them instead of waiting for them to show up so we can kill them."

"Look, I know you're not a violent person but the situation is dictating our actions. At the very, very, very least, we have to be prepared."

Juan Diego stayed with us that night. He was in Hugoton covering the "March for Peace." Per Kat's order, when I spoke with him on the phone the day before, I advised him to get to our place before nightfall. Kat promptly scolded him for arriving two hours after sunset.

After he finished apologizing to her, I called him over to the china cabinet and showed him the pistol. He gasped as if it were a vial of uranium. "Where did that come from?"

"Ask Kat," I told him.

"We have no choice," she said with exasperation. "We have to protect ourselves."

Juan Diego stared at the gun sorrowfully. I immediately felt bad for letting him see it. He wasn't himself that night. He had made the hour-plus trip to Hugoton because he felt it was important to give oxygen to voices that were countering the proliferating messages of fear and violence. What he didn't expect was hostility directed at the marchers who were heckled for the entire march by competing pro-militia rally-ers.

In truth, Juan Diego had seemed out of sorts since the new year. I suspected he was worn down. Not only did he work tirelessly covering nearly every election race in the country, but I don't think he'd taken any time off since secession. He was committed to objective journalism and equally devoted to the country and its cause.

I put the gun away and cooked an enormous frozen pizza Kat brought home. One slice was almost a meal in itself. For once, Juan Diego and I avoided talking politics, and not just for him, but for myself and Kat as well.

"Where's Tommy?" Kat asked him.

"He's down south peddling his booze."

"How long have you known each other?" I asked.

"Since high school. But we weren't friends back then. We were both very different."

"I remember him being a troublemaker," Kat said. "How does that happen when your dad's the sheriff and your mom's the principal?"

"That's how it happens," Juan Diego said. "He felt he had to come across as anti-authoritarian or else he'd be seen as a narc."

"In junior high, he was suspended by his own mom," Kat said with a laugh. "I can't remember what he did."

"He wore a t-shirt to school with Frank Zappa sitting on the toilet. His mom ordered him to take it off but he refused. He claims it didn't break the school's dress code. When he got home, he hid the shirt so his mom couldn't find it. The next day, he hid it in his pants and put it on again when he got to school."

"What a naughty kid!" Kat exclaimed.

"Hey, he earned the reputation he wanted."

"He's still got on edge," I said.

"Even though he comes across as serious and intense," said Juan Diego, "inside he's a sweet person. He moved back here the day before the border closed. It shows he cares about his family and friends."

After Kat returned to her office, I asked Juan Diego what was weighing on him. "You seem down."

"I'm just tired," he said.

"Do you ever feel trapped here?" I asked.

"I wouldn't use that word. We've all made sacrifices. I'd like to go places, see my mother and sisters, but I made a commitment to be here."

"What makes it worth suffering for?"

"David versus Goliath," Juan Diego answered without missing a beat. "I want to be part of the stone that slays the giant. What the U.S. has done to us with the embargo is unforgivable."

In 1948, the United Nations adopted the Universal Declaration of Human Rights. It stated that every person has the right to life, liberty, justice, food, shelter, and government participation. It's not unfair to say the U.S. has been one of the biggest offenders of this humanist manifesto by way of fraudulent wars, toppling governments for not conforming to market capitalism, and pernicious embargos.

This dark side of America isn't exactly hidden. It's glossed over with patriotism and propaganda with phrases like "American interests," "democratic values," and "national security." A government is not representative or participatory if it's bought and paid for by overlords.

Juan Diego believed if Independence failed, it would bode poorly for the world and the ideals of liberty and justice. The U.S. would make a big to-do of coming to the rescue, showing the world how generous and forgiving it was, like a parent taking in her misguided children. After so much suffering, who wouldn't be happy to return to the old ways?

"But if we succeed," Juan Diego said, "it changes everything. We could change the world." He couldn't hold this optimistic note for long. He sighed. "I miss my mom and my sisters. Last time I saw them was right before I moved here. It's been even longer for my dad. He should've gone back before the border closed."

"Do you really believe this country can succeed?" I asked. Few Independence citizens anticipated how far the U.S. would go to prevent the nation from flourishing. Independence was carved out by the powers that opposed its existence. When I met with Paul Gray, Director of Consulate Affairs, he was not exaggerating when he said the country was created to be an example of what happens to those who oppose American power.

"I used to say we shouldn't be afraid to fail," Juan Diego said. "But how bad will it get? That's what I'm afraid of now."

"Farmers and townspeople are getting better at making fuel. I've been hearing the food shortage isn't as severe as previous years. Is it possible things aren't as bad as it seems?"

"The murders, the violence, the rhetoric, the NIA—"

The office door opened and Kat came out. "I'm going upstairs to read," she said with a yawn. On her way through, she stopped and took the pistol from the drawer and placed it on the cabinet top. "Don't forget to bring this with you."

When I heard the bathroom door close upstairs, I turned to Juan Diego. "I'm losing my mind out here. There are commercials on the radio and TV and people going door to door telling us the danger is so real and so close that if anyone even steps foot on our property, we should shoot to kill."

"Geez," Juan Diego said with dread. "I wish you had told me that before I showed up."

"Did you hear about the man out by Johnson City who died of fear?" I asked. "There was no one outside! It was just the wind.[20] Tell me if I'm mistaken, but it seems clear that fear is our biggest threat. Daniel Velasquez was most likely killed by vigilantes afraid the country's being invaded by foreign criminals. Jesús Criollo was shot in the back, unarmed, in the middle of nowhere. Zero evidence of criminality—ever. Everything we know about Rodney Cohoon's death makes it look as though he charged the rider, who in turn shot the kid in self-defense. We hear about sightings and reports of burglars but where are the documented cases? Even the McCrary

---

[20] The county sheriff didn't find any evidence of a break-in attempt and the man's wife later told the local newspaper she didn't believe there was anyone on their property after all.

break-in wasn't as random as people made it sound. Am I stuck in my own way of seeing things?"

"The problem is we don't have arbiters we can all agree on," Juan Diego said. "Irresponsible reporting has spoiled the entire barrel. Help is coming, they say."

"From where?" I asked.

"The Justice Department is sending detectives to understaffed counties."

He was referring to a plan to deploy detectives and law enforcement personnel from large departments—Capital City, Dodge City, Dumas—to places like Ulysses, where Sheriff Bradley operated with a skeleton crew. Juan Diego thought it might also cut into the "reality gap" if law enforcement could begin sorting out rumors and false reports from actual crimes.

"What about the early days?" I asked. "When they were stealing beets and breaking into fuel sheds in your neighborhood, were people calling for the execution of the perpetrators?"

"Back then, we didn't think we were being invaded by the cartels. People were desperate after the supermarkets and gas stations closed. It was a shock to the system. Now they can go to a community center for help. When people lose their way, they just need help finding their way back. That'll happen here."

"I like your optimism," I said.

"You think I'm optimistic?" he snapped, surprising me.

"You believe people are inherently good. I appreciate that about you."

"People are collectively good," he clarified.

"Then society is inherently good."

"If its leaders and government are of the people and constitute a real democracy, then society too is good."

I thought about this for a moment. "What would you say are the absolute worst acts of immorality?"

Juan Diego counted on his fingers. "Murder, rape, torture, kidnapping—"

"All universally condemned, yet so pervasive in the world. If a society genuinely believed that killing another person was a grave unpardonable sin, and they faced the real possibility of killing someone, wouldn't they do everything in their collective power to find a solution?"

"It's not society, Roman. It's a few people we're talking about."

"Do those few people telling us it's our duty to kill trespassers have no conscience or are they as deeply conflicted about killing as I am? I want to know. If I hear someone breaking into the shed, do I just open a window and start shooting? That's what they're asking us to do. If someone came into our house...I don't know what I'd do. In the heat of the moment, maybe I'd shoot because it's expected of me. It's what I've been told to do. But what would that look like? What if you had to stand there and watch a man bleed out on your floor? Or a sixteen-year-old choke on his own blood while he looked you in the eye? Something happens to people when they kill. Something vital is killed inside of you." I paused and added, "So it's not just a moral crisis, it's an existential one."

"What if they come to kill?"

"I would defend myself. But even if I succeed, a part of me will have died."

Juan Diego looked at me with pity. "Do you ever get out of the house? What else do you do?"

"Nothing." I wasn't joking, nor was there anything humorous about it.

TOM JONES

Juan Diego was right about the reinforcements. Investigators were deployed to rural sheriff departments in need, which included Grant County and three adjacent counties. Lo and behold, the following week, Sheriff Potter of Stevens County arrested three men for the murder of Jesús Criollo.

The detainees were Clint and King Emmett and Travis Kuhn. Nationally this was big news but locally it was earthshaking. Duane Emmett's family had been ranching in the county for four generations. West of Ulysses, they owned a massive feedlot (now empty) with an enormous sign towering above silos that bore their name. There were even town streets and county roads named after them.

Tom Jones resigned as resident security man two days after the arrests. I called him at home. He picked up as I was leaving a message on their answering machine. After some small talk, I asked what he thought of the recent arrests. "They were the ones you were watching in Ulysses," I said.

"Mmm," Tom droned musingly. I visualized him pensively brushing his thumb over his mustache. He was reluctant to discuss his involvement until I promised I wouldn't disclose anything that could be directly tied to him.[21]

While patrolling county roads late at night, he had a run-in with King and Travis. Tom was tracking a vehicle he spotted from one of his perches (various rooftops where he would sit with his binoculars) and stopped to examine mud tracks on the road. He said he might have noticed the pickup parked in the shadow of a farm shed close by. But if he did, he would have assumed it was junkyard

---

[21] Much later, he gave me permission to include our conversations in this book, as I had hoped all along.

material. As he surveyed the farm grounds with his flashlight, his gaze fell on the truck. He trained the light on it. Silhouetted figures in the tinted windows shocked him. "And I don't scare easily."

The truck started up. Tom jumped into his little green car, prepared to follow them. Instead, they pulled up behind him, so close he braced himself for impact. Tom had a gut feeling the driver would use the truck as a battering ram if he got out. He drove away and they followed.

After a couple miles, he'd had enough. Tom stopped in the middle of the road, got out, and confronted the men. From the driver's side, Travis sneered insolently while Tom did most of the talking. King wouldn't even look at him. "Go back and do your job where you belong," was all Travis had to say.

Tom noticed two hunting rifles in the gun rack. He wasn't able to inspect them but one appeared to be the most popular lever-action 30-06 rifle ever made. He could also note certain details about Travis's truck.

Three days later, he was driving south from Ulysses on Highway 25 when a Chevy truck similar to Travis's passed in the opposite direction. They both slowed down to observe one another. Even though it was dark, Tom identified the pickup by distinguishing features he noticed the night Travis tailed him.

What made this noteworthy was Travis and King lived in the Northeastern part of the county. If they were guarding their property, they were a long way from home. When they crossed paths that night, they were within a mile from where Jesús Criollo's vehicle was found the following week.

When Tom received a phone call from a former colleague who had knowledge of the Criollo autopsy, he decided to share his thoughts with Sheriff Bradley. The sheriff invited Tom into his office. Three men from the local militia were also there.

"Tom Jones," Bradley said with performative flair for the militiamen. "To what do we owe the pleasure?"

"I was passing through," Tom said. "Just curious if you saw the autopsy report for the Moscow victim."

"You confusing me with Sheriff Howell?" the sheriff replied. "I have my own case to deal with."

"I was hoping I could talk to you about a few things."

"Yeah, what?"

"Probably best in private," said Tom.

"Don't worry about them," the sheriff said. "They're allies. Local militia. These are good men. You can trust them."

"No offense, but I'd feel more comfortable if I could speak to the sheriff alone."

The militiamen filed out, unbothered by the request. The door closed behind them and Tom got right to it. "There were multiple fractures on the left side of the Criollo's body—femur, pelvis, knee—like he was struck by a vehicle."

"Last I heard, no one knows where or when it happened."

"It makes no sense to believe he'd leave the vehicle when he had a blanket."

"It was cold! One blanket's not enough."

"That wool army blanket would've kept him warm."

"What's your point?" Bradley asked. "Like I said, it's not my case."

"He ran out of gas. The militias and non-militia civilians are driving around at night. One sec." Tom opened the office door and asked the militiamen, "If you came across a vehicle parked on the side of a county road, at the very least you'd stop and check it out, right? Shine a flashlight in to see if anyone was in there, maybe in need of help."

One of them shrugged and answered, "Yeah, sure."

Tom closed the door. "There's a decent chance someone came across Criollo. They spooked him. He jumped out of the car and ran. The truck that had stopped on the road hit him. Those skid marks weren't from stopping. They're from rapid acceleration. The truck peeled out, knocked Criollo off his feet, most likely. He got up, climbed over the barbed wire fence—his pants were torn inside the thigh and inner cuff. Skin ripped up pretty good. They tracked him and caught him at the farmhouse. Might have been multiple parties searching for him.

"That's a whole lot of conjecturing, Tom. Why are you telling me this?"

"Because you're the sheriff of the county where the victim's car was found. If it originated here—"

"Listen, I respect you came from the largest department in the country but you need to understand there's a big difference between there-and-here and then-and-now. Until they send me the investigator from Cap City they've been promising, it's just me. So when I say I got my own murder, I mean that's as much as I can deal with. You're coming in here theorizing about matters that aren't my concern."

"Remember I told you Travis Kuhn and King Emmett followed me one night north of Big Bow?"

"You didn't tell me where you were, but okay."

"Their ranch is eight miles northeast of that. A few nights later, I'm pretty sure I saw them down south on 25, about a mile from where Criollo's car was found. In the middle of the night, both times, nowhere near their land. What are they doing?"

"Emmett's got land all over the place. At least three counties. In fact, I think he owns some old oil wells down there."

"That first night, I chatted with them. Yep. In their gun rack they had what appeared to be a Browning thirty-aught-six. I'm sure you know what cartridge they found at the scene. And the owner of the farm said the suspects were driving…same make."

"There's a thousand and one Chevys around!" Bradley whined. "And a lot more of those rifles. I don't have time for this. Go tell it to Howell."

It was all circumstantial. Tom was aware of this. He didn't doubt the two sheriffs knew their business but Tom felt morally obligated to share his observations. The encounter that night with Travis and King stuck with him. It wasn't just the violent manner in which they followed him. He got the sense that intimidating people had been fine-tuned over the course of their limited years. Irreverence never bothered Tom too much. Disrespect is woven into the fabric of some people. But others have a look in their eye that can make the most poised feel uneasy. King Emmett gave the impression of someone who would cross the line at any moment and break laws, reason, and bones without even flinching.

Tom briefly met Sheriff Howell at the crime scene near Moscow. He was less hospitable than Sheriff Bradley. Speaking to him was out of the question. Anyway, he had an investigator from Capital City assisting him. The reason Tom went to see Bradley was more about the future than the past. It's highly unlikely their brief discussion aided the investigation, even if he had reached out to Howell. Tom thought Bradley told the militiamen present that day about their conversation. The day after the arrests, Tom got a call from Duane Emmett. He wanted to talk.

They met at a roadside steakhouse the next afternoon. When Tom arrived, he found Emmett already seated at a corner table. Being midday, they were the only diners there. After a little chitchat, Emmett got down to business.

"My sons are in jail for the murder of somebody in a different county."

"I heard."

"I heard you were there the morning of," Emmett said.

"The crime scene? Briefly."

"I also know you gave Doug Bradley information. I know people everywhere, Tom. My family's been here since before the Dust Bowl."

"I talked to the sheriff for all of five minutes—"

"It doesn't matter how long you talked," Emmett snapped. "What matters is the information you conveyed, Bradley shared with that fat-ass sheriff in Hugoton."

"We discussed the autopsy report, that's it," Tom said defensively. "I didn't put the puzzle together. I didn't arrest anyone."

"Well, they're in jail now and we need to get 'em out."

"I'm not a lawyer," Tom said.

"My two youngest, they got a reputation. They can go off half-cocked but that doesn't make 'em criminals. There's a whole lot of badness going on in this country. Those boys have been going out there night after night defending our land. We're putting the wrong people away. They're full-blooded Independents. And good blood." He banged his fist on the table like a gavel. "People ain't happy. I ain't happy. Their brothers and family ain't happy. Hell, the whole county ain't happy. Tom Jones, you don't represent the law no more. Your job, what we're paying for, is to protect our interests. All you gotta do is point out the errors they made. We'll do the rest after that."

The aroma of incoming steak stole their attention. A gray-haired cook with a dirty apron set two plates of thick ribeyes with diamond grill marks and huge servings of mashed potatoes with pools of brown gravy on the table. Emmett ogled his food as he unrolled his knife and fork. "Don't wait til it gets cold."

Emmett cut into the medium-rare meat and took a bite. When satisfied with the preparation, he turned his attention back to Tom. "You can help by showing how the pieces don't fit together."

He said this in a way that suggested Tom should read between the lines. "Whatever you saw that morning. If you have new evidence for them, I can make sure Howell's more receptive to you this time."

"I don't have any evidence," Tom said firmly.

"If all else fails, you could write a bit in the paper. Whad'ya call that?"

"An op-ed?"

"You can write an op-ed about how they bungled the investigation and arrested patriots. You might wonder whose side Bradley and Howell are on. You could mention a few things you saw when you were down there and how it don't line up with the sheriff's take on it." He took another bite and chewed on a thought that turned bitter. "What right do they even have? We have to hire our own police. Sheriffs don't cut it anymore. No wonder they're getting rid of 'em." If this was a shot at Tom, he didn't acknowledge it. "They can all go to hell." He used his knife to rake the potatoes onto his fork and lowered his mouth closer to the plate. "Maybe you have a better idea."

Tom chewed his steak and then took a drink of root beer. "Hmm," he murmured. Emmett plowed through his steak and potatoes. After he scraped up the last remnants, he dropped the fork and knife on the plate and leaned back with an air of satisfaction with his palms resting on his gut.

"You need a lawyer," Tom said between bites. "There's nothing I can do."

"Will you get off your high horse? You ain't the sheriff no more. What do I have to do to persuade you to take up the righteous fight? We're the good guys!"

"You and me?"

"And my sons, who are wrongfully in jail. There's a war goin' on," Emmett rasped. "Our own president cares more about the Mexicans than us. He cut down the NIA and left us alone to do the fighting. It's unholy to prosecute people for defending their property and their country. I want them out and I want you to help."

"I can't do that."

"I don't mean maybe." Emmett's lips trembled. The bags under his eyes darkened and swelled. "If you're not on my side, you're against me."

"I'm sorry then."

Emmett's face twisted menacingly. He reached across the table, yanked Tom's unfinished lunch away, and dropped it on the adjacent table. "Git out of here 'fore I kick your ass all the way back to your shit town."

Tom calmly folded his napkin, placed it on the table, and rose. He stood there, looking down at the rancher's discolored, swollen face. As he walked away, he steadied himself for parting shots sure to come.

"I promise you're gonna regret this," Emmett yelled after him. "You fucking washed-up civil servant."

"Can you believe that man was on a *Peace* Council?" Tom asked me.

We talked for over an hour that day and then longer a few days later. At first, he spoke cautiously, as if contemplating the ramifications of what he was telling me. But the more he talked, the more comfortable he became. Mentioning the Peace Council offered a segue into the previous year.

"They approached us about being part of that," Tom said. "Well, technically, it was Gail they wanted. I got a call from Wayne Montgomery in the middle of the night." He was the county commissioner who appointed Tom to his position. "He showed up an hour later with a Presidential Hall official. Gail came down in her robe and we talked about this Peace Council they were literally coming up with overnight."

"Why'd they want Gail?" I asked.

"Successful Independence businesswoman. Former school principal. Respected in the community. And of course, she's married to a former sheriff who served for twenty-seven years. She was going to do it in spite of me. Felt it was her responsibility to take part in anything that might bring the sides together. She's a good person in that regard."

"You were against it?"

"I was," he admitted. "I thought the whole thing was a joke. 'Council of Peace' sounded like a PR ploy. Gail didn't care how it looked. Her take was she had lived here her entire life and had never witnessed such unabashed cultural hostility. She told me pointblank that they asked her, not me, and she was going to do whatever she could to help. I get where she was coming from but this council was put together by the same administration that straight-up lied about my dismissal. Accepting the invitation would've signaled those lies were true. It would make it look like we were all buddy-buddy. In the end, she agreed with me."

"Who fired you?" I asked as though I'd forgotten.

"The Deputy Attorney General. I went to talk to him about the NIA detainees. They brought in those suspects bound and hooded. It was a shit show if I've ever seen one. Mitch Black and his people were mad at me over a comment I made to a local reporter."

"I remember that well," I said. "It heard it live on the *Gazette Radio Hour*. How come you never came out and gave your side of the story?"

Tom sighed. "So many reasons, Roman. For one, Wayne Montgomery was working to straighten it all out behind the scenes. He was more upset about it than I was. To him, it wasn't merely a violation of our laws. It betrayed the principles of this country. I was hoping it would be resolved and I could continue my job without turning it into a public fiasco."

It obviously didn't pan out. In the end, they determined the Home Defense Act empowered the attorney general by giving him broad authority to "appoint officials to detect and prosecute crimes." And it gave him the right to dismiss or reappoint anyone under the AG's authority.

"What was their reason for dismissing you?" I asked Tom.

"Impeding federal officers, which is ridiculous. Those agents refused to follow even the most basic booking steps. No names, charges, affidavits, mug shots, nothing. They wouldn't even show their warrants. When I asked for their badges, all I got was a folded-up xerox."

"Is it true you wouldn't let them keep the suspects there?"

"A toothless threat. They'd already housed their suspects in a cell block reserved for federal prisoners. It'd never been used before."

"I still don't understand why you didn't put up more of a fight," I said. "Publicly, I mean."

"The NSD, Major Krug, to the president—they would've supported Mitch Black and portray me as the bad guy. It wasn't worth it. I didn't want to be part of an inept or corrupt system. But I suppose by walking away, I let their lies stand as truth."

"Not everyone believes it's the truth," I pointed out. "You never felt obligated to speak out for the truth?"

"Maybe that's why I'm talking to you, Roman."

ARRESTED GOVERNMENT

The Southern media's relentless denunciation of President Gonzalez intensified each week and Maude Grese led the charge. *"He is the most corrupt, most despicable, most incompetent president in the history* of North America. Since he took office, the country has fallen under a spell of malice and hate. With him at the helm, there's no hope."

What Matters host Davey McGraw was more nuanced in his approach. "*We can't take back the election or call a redo. But it illustrates major flaws of national elections. They play on emotions and force the candidates to be caricatures of themselves. That's not how we should go about picking the best person for the job. We need the top candidate for the top position in our country. I believe—now, hear me out before you blow a gasket—the president should be appointed instead of elected. Leave it to Congress to hire the right person. Seriously. They know what it takes to be a leader. It could be done behind closed doors with serious interviews and discussions without the big sideshow we all hate.*"

Bill Tyson and his allies rolled out a massive advertising campaign promoting themselves, their economic and political ideals, and their endeavors. This television commercial ran nationwide and prompted rumors that a U.S. or other foreign marketing firm produced the spot. The rumors reflected the production quality. Apart from its somberness, it could've aired during the Super Bowl.

EXT. BLIGHTED NATION
Mournful chamber music plays over a montage of shuttered gas stations, desolate streets, and police vehicles blighted by rust and flat tires.

Voiceover: *Our future and our independence are in danger.*

Ominous rumbling sounds give way to an optimistic melody.

EXT. CONSTRUCTION
The picture cuts to images of razed land in the beginning stages of construction.

Superimposed: FUEL PRODUCTION

EXT. MONTAGE OF RENEWAL
The next image is a sketch of the finished refinery with a large sign in the front: CERES ENERGY

This dissolves into a colorful illustration of a gas station packed with happy drivers filling their shiny new vehicles.

Voiceover: *Our future. Our independence. Our Nation.*

INT. GAS PLANT
Video clips show the inner workings of a natural gas plant with blue-collar and white-collar types working together.

Superimposed: NATURAL GAS

Voiceover: *Together, we're finding solutions to power our nation. Tell your legislators, "Don't let politics get in the way of progress, our future, or...."*

Superimposed: OUR FREEDOM

Less than a week after this glossy commercial debuted, fifty-seven congressmen calling themselves the Coalition to Fuel Independence walked out of Congress, shutting down the legislature. At a press conference in the Congressional Hall lobby, Senate Leader and walkout participant Phil Mooney spoke to reporters.

"Independence has prided itself in being the world's only non-partisan democracy. It saddens me more than you know to stand here and tell you there's a leftwing faction attempting to fracture our unity. They're sabotaging Congress with an unethical gas bill and making it impossible to get anything else done. They've refused to participate in governing until their cause is taken up by the rest of us. They have blurred the line between truth and propaganda and they must be stopped. This is a critical moment for our nation."

Sixteen senators and forty-one assemblymen fled the Plaza. In both chambers a simple majority was required for a quorum, which meant the twenty senators and fifty-nine assemblymen still on the Plaza could bring a vote to the floor. A reporter pointed this out to Senator Mooney. He replied, "The spotlight is shining bright so all of Independence can see who their oppressors are."

In the following days, demonstrations outside Presidential Hall called for Gonzalez to do the right thing and put Congress back together by scrapping his energy bill. He didn't respond to the legislators' walkout. In fact, he hadn't appeared publicly in a week. For a president who had so far delivered on his promise to be visible and accessible, this was unusual. A rumor he was vacationing in Mexico (with some callers suggesting he was meeting with cartel types) spread across the talk radio spectrum.

During the second week of the president's absence, things took a strange turn. At a media briefing at Presidential Hall, the press secretary spoke to reporters. "The president has been battling an illness. He thought he'd be back by now." His voice was devoid of spirit as he woodenly read from cue cards. "Alas, government business must go on. We have urgent security issues that warrant immediate action. So...." He cleared his throat before continuing. "Major Krug has appointed a new NIA director to help our law enforcement in this time of need. So without further ado, here is National Security Secretary Major Krug and former Attorney General Mitch Black."

The brief uproar from off-screen correspondents surely mirrored the reaction of Independents everywhere. This was the first time anyone had heard of an NIA director. Appointing a controversial figure from the previous administration in Gonzalez's absence was shockingly brazen.

Major Krug appeared in his fancy military coat. He was followed by Mitch Black, who wore his customary black flat-top cowboy hat, bolo tie, and Western-style suit. Krug stood next to the podium with his hands clasped behind his back and his chin high as he looked over the press corps with a satisfied, if not smug, smile. He took a step back, and with a hand gesture, presented Black.

"Thank you, Major Krug," Black said. "The savage lawlessness going around is unacceptable. These acts have been enabled by our crippled law enforcement. Hear me when I tell you, the buck stops here. The violence, the savagery, it must end now! I've had many conversations with Major Krug and his deputies. They made it clear they want our intelligence operating at full capacity. We will stop these heinous acts. We will not be deterred and we'll use everything in our power. Our hands will not be tied. To all my rural brethren: help is on the way."

WHITE CATERPILLAR

A terrifying cry shredded the otherwise placid afternoon on the farm. It sounded like a ferocious, wounded animal. It jolted me head-to-toe, causing me to knock my empty lunch plate off the desk, breaking it in two. When I turned off the radio, my ears rang in the dead silence.

I ran down to Kat's office and threw open the door. Papers were strewn across the floor. The cordless phone was lying in the corner with its battery and lid close by. Kat was sitting with her forehead on the desk.

"What happened?" I asked. "Are you okay? Kat, are you okay?"

"Go away," she commanded in a strained and muffled voice.

"What the hell just happened?"

"Leave me alone."

"I need to know you're okay," I said with as much authority as I could muster.

She lifted her head but her hair still covered her face. It was a dreadful sight. "Go away."

I did as she said and returned to my office but I couldn't focus on anything. A hormonal stress cocktail had run through me, leaving a wreck in its wake. My mind probed in vain for the cause of Kat's gut-wrenching distress. Right or wrong, I kept coming back to her divorce—her marriage—her husband. Since I wasn't gifted with visionary abilities, there was no hope of gleaning the source of her anxiety. Yet I couldn't stop trying.

An hour later, Kat came upstairs. After a light knock, she opened the door. "Sorry about that," she said. "A deal I really needed fell through."

"What deal?"

"For supplies," she said.

I didn't hide my indignation. "It was *that* important?"

She looked around the office, ignoring my question. "I've decided to turn this into a sunroom," she said with finality. "It has the most windows and sun exposure than anywhere in the house. I can extend my growing season."

"Say what?" I struggled to shift to this new topic. "Where am I supposed to go?"

"In the other room."

"What other room? You mean the storage room? It's the size of a closet."

"That's because it's full of stuff," Kat said impatiently. "It's not a closet, it's a bedroom."

"It's dark and cold."

"You're a writer, not a CEO. You don't need all this space."

Space I used and had become accustomed to. Windows I contemplatively gazed out of every day. "When do you imagine this happening?" I asked, hoping her idea would never come to fruition.

"Now."

I spent the next two hours moving boxes of clothes and keepsakes from the small bedroom to the basement and then consolidating everything onto sheets of plywood set on two-by-fours. As I was moving the last box off the dirt floor, an ancient vacuum cleaner fell through the bottom and crushed my foot. I fell to the ground, rocking in agony.

"What happened?" Kat called down.

With clenched teeth, I held back a storm of expletives.

Kat worked the rest of the day setting up the sunroom. She brought in small planters and muffin tins she used for seedlings and hauled soil up in five-gallon buckets. I spent the rest of the day on the couch with my foot elevated. When she came down later, she found me settled into the cushions with my foot propped up and a bottle of whiskey on the coffee table.

"The entire bottle's almost gone!" she exclaimed.

"So is my will," I said.

Post-news static was playing on the television. Kat turned it off. She had just missed the news. As she was walking away, I mentioned one story was about veterinary and medical supplies confiscated at the border. When I pushed myself up and peered over the back of the couch, she was standing a few feet away, eyes fixed on the dark television screen. "Did it have anything to do with your deal?" I asked.

"What happened?"

"Two cars full of medical supplies were stopped at two separate crossings."

"Do they know who was involved?"

"I don't think so."

"Weird," she said. "I don't know."

That's all she ever said of the matter. I never found out for sure if there was a connection. It's difficult to believe it was mere coincidence. After being shut out by the Vet Alliance, I could understand her desperation and frustration. Her penchant for secrecy vexes me to this day.

The next morning, my foot was black and blue and swollen twice its normal size. I tried to work in my new office but the pain amplified my frustration with the gloomy space.

"Kat," I called down the stairs. "Kat…Kat."

"What?" she yelled impatiently from the living room.

"Do you have appointments today?"

"Why?"

"I'd like to lie on the couch."

"What for?"

"My foot."

She came to the bottom of the stairs. "What if I have a walk-in?"

I had no choice but to make the bed my temporary workstation. I set up my laptop and radio and propped my foot on two pillows. Within seconds of getting situated, I realized I'd forgotten ice.

"Kat," I called out. "Kat. Kat."

"Now what?"

"Will you bring some ice for my foot?"

Five minutes later, she came up with ice packed in a nylon makeup bag.

"Will you please not shout down the stairs," she said. "I'm working."

"I'm working too."

"You're lying in bed."

"With a broken foot."

"When I go to work, I *go to* work." She looked down at me with her hands on her hips as if she were scolding a child. "Would you call me for ice if my office was twenty minutes away? No, you'd go downstairs and get your own ice."

"I just need a little help," I said in a patronizing tone meant to match hers.

"You have nothing else to do," she snapped. "Go slow. Take your time. I'm busy working for our income. Show me a little respect for once."

264

"If anyone is treated with disrespect around here, it's me!" I erupted, surprising Kat.

"You have all the time in the world to work on your writing. You have food and shelter. You have your own office—"

"Closet, you mean."

"And that's how you show your appreciation. I've asked for nothing and all you show me in return is this—this meanness. It's like I should be thankful to serve you."

"We live under the same roof and share the same bed but it's like being alone. You don't ever want to talk about anything. When you're not working, you're checked out."

"I work hard," she said with a trembling voice, "and I get criticized for it by you. I'm exhausted at the end of the day and I get criticized for that too."

"Whatever happened to being open with one another? It's turned into the exact opposite. Instead of facing our fears, fear has become the code we live by. Instead of seeing our insecurities—"

"You want to talk about fear? I sleep with a gun next to me. People are being murdered and our government's falling apart. We're running out of food. We're out of fuel. We're on the brink of collapse."

"The real crisis is inside." I pointed to her chest.

"You are such an asshole. I hope your foot falls off." She slammed the door behind her.

I dozed off in the afternoon and woke up at dusk. The only light in the room came from a shimmer on the horizon. Feeling disoriented, I swiveled off the bed onto my good foot and hobbled to the bathroom to rinse my face.

Kat was having dinner at the dining table. She was bent over an enormous veterinary book. She didn't even glance at me as I limped down the creaky steps.

"I fell asleep," I murmured groggily. "Haven't done that for years. Must have needed it." Kat ignored me. "What are you having?"

She didn't respond. On the kitchen counter was a tamale on a small plate. "Is this one for me?"

"Freezer," she responded icily.

I sat at the table and watched Kat take another bite without acknowledging my presence. "I had a bizarre dream," I said, suddenly remembering it. "There was a white caterpillar under a shady tree." I looked out the window to see if that specific tree existed outside. "It grew larger and had long silky white hair, like a—what are those dogs called—a shih tzu. It kept growing until it must have been six feet long. It had a round, flat face at the tip of its body with an expressive mouth and eyes. It was a little cartoonish. Like a snake, it raised its head off the ground and was watching me with a little smile that was sort of cute and innocent but I was afraid of it. I didn't trust it. I sensed it was dangerous. You're not even listening, are you?"

"Dreams are only interesting to the dreamer."

"In the same way screams are only interesting to the screamer?"

She was about to cut into the tamale when she shifted the butter knife into her fist and slammed the end of the handle down on the plate, cracking it in two. She glared at me, still gripping the knife with white knuckles. For an instant, I genuinely feared she would do to my skull what she did to the plate. For the first time, I could see suffering deep in her eyes. It was as if she had inadvertently bared her inner self by unleashing her emotions. Sensing the breach in her defenses, she dropped the knife on the broken plate and ran away to her office.

"Just let it out," I called after her. I'm afraid this came out cruel and mocking. It wasn't what I intended.

The American Secession Movement (Crisis) was comprised of many movements with a multiplicity of ideologies and aspirations. The upheaval was anxiety-inducing. Friction between the concurrent movements and those inclined to the status quo might have fueled the sense of instability in the country as much as anything. Tension between those parts was (still) playing out in Independence and our rural household. Individual desires within our relationship were in constant opposition. Kat and I resisted one another's needs because it required change—altering the status quo.

An underappreciated aspect of human nature is our resistance to change. It's as if our compulsions and general view of reality are physically imprinted in our brains, like cutting fresh grooves in a vinyl record. The brain is formed and re-formed by shifting perspectives so it makes sense that changing one's mind can seem like moving mountains.

If Kat and I lived anywhere other than Independence, our relationship might've been less pressurized. My world had become so small. It wasn't until much later I realized how preoccupied with Kat and our relationship I had become. It's what I lived every hour of every day. I suppose I eventually would've learned to live with it. The mind has ways of adapting. Perhaps I would've become emotionally calloused as people do when mired in circumstances beyond their control.

Kat's tremendous fixation on her work never made sense to me. She devoted herself with unbending determination. The type of success she strove for seemed more of an American ideal, where one's human value is determined by income or career advancement. I still wonder if her marriage was the driving force behind her preoccupation. Something happened—regret, rejection, or even trauma—and it wouldn't loosen its grip on her. The broken plate and shattered teapot were evidence Kat intuited what needed to be done more keenly than I. It might have illustrated how desperately stuck she felt—in our relationship and her life.

I was just finishing my dinner when she emerged from her office. Masa had fused onto the biggest segment of the broken plate with loose strands of pork dried deep brown, almost black. It was an unpleasant sight and I refused to clean it up. She sat down and pushed the pieces aside. In her defeated and haggard face, I caught a glimpse of her as an old woman.

"We can't go on like this," she said in a forlorn voice.

"What should we do?"

She stared off to the side as if waiting for the answer to appear on the floor.

"Remember that evening when we were sitting on Johnny's porch?" I asked. "You told me about your parents' big fight and how it ruptured their marriage."

"What about it?"

"What if that night is so deeply engraved in your mind that it plays over and over so you're constantly reliving it? You can't help but act it out sometimes. Like tonight. You can't be content in a relationship because you unconsciously need discord."

"What about you?" she asked. "You act like you had a perfect family. You never even knew your father," she said spitefully.

"That wasn't my fault."

"And neither was my parents' separation."

"That's not the point."

"No," she said. "The point is you're always turning everything against me. Anything I do, past or present. So let's flip that around. Not knowing your father. It's sad. I'm not being cruel about it but it's left you…." She paused, fishing for an idea. "Not having a father figure…." Again she stopped, unable to make a connection. "You never learned how to treat a woman."

"Oh, please," I groused. "I do have a mother, in case you forgot."

"One who was never around," she said in an accusing tone. "It makes sense why you became a writer. You want to be left alone because that's all you know."

"Now you're just throwing anything to see if it sticks!" I tempered my outrage. "Look, all I'm trying to say is today at the table—"

"You need to stop!" Her nostrils flared. "Your obsession with my past ends right here, right now. All that matters to you and me is what happens from here on out."

"So we can't talk about what happened today or anything that's ever happened that may have created a misunderstanding between us?"

"That's right," she said tersely.

"That makes no sense."

"Because you live in the past."

"We are the product of our past," I said. "If we can't figure out what went wrong, we're doomed to live out our mistakes forever."

"If you want to be here, you need to be here in the present." Her authoritative tone reminded me of a witchy schoolteacher I had in elementary school. "Is living in the moment too hard for you?"

"I want to talk to you about the night of Independence Day so I can apologize and explain why I reacted the way I did. But we can't do that because you short-circuit when I bring up anything in the past."

Her eyes filled with anger but then quickly glazed over. I don't know if she was upset because I defied her by talking about the past or if bringing up that night caused the embarrassment, disappointment, or something else she experienced to resurface. As quick as lightning, she sprung to her feet and walked away. When she reached the stairs, she turned back. "You can sleep on the couch."

Kat's mother grew up on the farm where we were living. Coincidentally my mother grew up on a farm in Oklahoma. She never took me to visit her parents but my understanding is it wasn't much different from where Kat and I lived. It was impossible to imagine my mother in that environment. They were incompatible realities. If you met her, you'd never guess she wasn't born into a cosmopolitan life. Her parents were poor and I think she was ashamed of that. Sadly it permeated her entire life.

When she was seventeen, she left home. With all her worldly belongings packed into one suitcase, she caught a bus to Santa Fe. As an aspiring artist with no experience outside her rural milieu, the New Mexico town was the nexus of her dreams.

Her parents must have been scared as hell. Their lives were confined to their farm and local community. Leaving home to become an artist wasn't something folks did. But for reasons my mother never shared with me, they didn't prevent her from going. Maybe they thought she just needed to get it out of her system.

Her time in Santa Fe wasn't what she hoped for and she left after three months. She thought the world would conform to her desires and she would be lifted to her rightful place. She blamed the selfish, insular community (but years later, she wasn't complaining during her frequent trips to Santa Fe as an established dealer, staying at cushy hotels and dining at the best restaurants).

Something about San Diego caught her fancy so she packed her suitcase and caught a westbound bus. That's where she met Jim, my father. She characterized their relationship as a fleeting youthful romance, which means it amounted to little more than a one-nighter. She couldn't even remember his last name. He was a Navy man and he shipped out shortly after they met. Where to, she didn't know. It wasn't until she moved to San Francisco that she discovered she was pregnant.

My mother was eighteen years old when I was born. Who can raise a child at that age without family or a close-knit tribe? Having a kid wasn't part of her life plan and it didn't dissuade her from pursuing her career ambitions. My earliest memories are of her working in the studio—the corner of our living room—while I sat in front of a little television set nearby. My earliest impressions are of being the object of resentment. I don't say this to be self-pitying. She was deeply driven and devoted all her time and energy to her work.

That mother and child are like people I once knew long ago. It's more of a lingering sense of anguish and anger. I had to confront it when I was a teenager. Only after reading through this section did I realize the resentment still existed. Kat took the full brunt of my indignation. I refused to give in to her. Refused to give her any sympathy until she apologized. It earned me a spot on the couch. If I had only recognized the parallels between Kat and my past/mother.

DISAPPEARANCE AND DEPARTURES

I woke up on the sofa to Kat stomping around upstairs. A few minutes later, she came down the stairs with her suitcase thumping behind her. My first thought was that she was leaving me, even though it was her house.

"What's going on?" I asked.

"Chance is gone." Her voice trembled as she spoke.

"Gone?"

"Disappeared," she said from her office.

"He disappeared? What does that mean?"

"It means he left in the middle of the night and nobody knows where he went."

That's all I got out of her before she left for Gail and Tom's. I had to call Juan Diego to find out what was going on. He told me Chance had been arrested a few days earlier for alleged involvement in the burglary of a rural feed store a few miles from the Jones's home. This was shocking. Chance seemed like a good kid. The crime didn't match his spirit. But then again, I'd spent all of one day with him.

The theft was unspectacular, according to Juan Diego. There wasn't much to steal at the store. The kids came away with engine grease, expired gummy worms, and vehicle air fresheners. But they trashed the place by knocking over displays and shelves and spray painting *ACHTUNG* on the wall. Weird, but it seemed like something kids suffering from perpetual boredom might do.

The interim county sheriff served as Tom's undersheriff for fifteen years. They met before arrest warrants were issued. Tom agreed to bring Chance in the following day. He and three of his friends, ages twelve to fifteen, were booked, questioned, and released.

The store owner would recommend dropping charges if the boys would somehow make amends. But Chance and his friends wouldn't talk to the investigators, interim sheriff, or even their parents about what happened. Their collective silence was making the families and lawyer uneasy.

Chance disappeared the night before his arraignment in court. A vehicle idling near the house woke Tom. By the time he got to the window, the car was already driving away. Thinking they had been burgled, he rushed outside but nothing had been broken into. When he and Gail returned to bed, they discovered Chance wasn't in his room. It didn't take long to put two and two together: he ran away.

Kat called for client messages but there was never any news to share. Our conversations were brief and to the point. I didn't believe it was possible to be more bored. I was wrong. The tire tubes on the Almira Gulch bicycle were beyond repair so I couldn't bike to town. Writing, listening to the radio, deciding what to eat—everything I did became frustrating.

About a week after she left, I heard the answering machine in her office. *"Roman, pick up…. Are you there?…. Roman."*

"Am I here?" I yelled down the stairs. "Where else would I be?" After a calming breath, I answered the phone in a voice as pleasant and silky as a Bora Bora hotel agent. "Hello."

"Have you heard from Juan Diego?" she asked.

"Not for a few days."

"Tommy said he's leaving the country."

"To do what?" I asked.

"Leaving as in moving away."

"I don't understand." No one left Independence unless they could afford the exorbitant airfare to Mexico and Juan Diego wouldn't just up and leave like that.

"I don't understand," Kat pleaded. "You need a special permit. He doesn't have the money for that, does he?"

"What makes you think he's suddenly leaving the country?"

A few minutes before she called me, Tommy was on the phone with Juan Diego. The way Kat described it, he completely lost his shit. He exploded out the front door. Gail came running down the stairs. Tom followed her outside. In the middle of the road, Gail tried to calm Tommy while trying to find out what had happened. Tommy was inconsolable.

Kat was still shaken as she recounted the episode. Every waking moment since Chance left was filled with anticipation of news of his whereabouts. Along with Gail and Tom, she couldn't help but think Tommy's despair was connected to Chance. Everyone thought something horrible had happened.

It was an immense relief to discover the source of Tommy's angst was learning Juan Diego was flying to Mexico. It was unclear to me if Kat was distressed about a friend leaving us or the unfairness of it. Either way, I was certain it was a misunderstanding. I told Kat I'd call her back.

For hours, I tried to reach Juan Diego. I even called the *Gazette* to see if anyone there had seen him. Colm O'Brien was out and no one there knew anything. Then out of the blue, he showed up at the house that evening.

"Your ears have been burning?" I asked as I met him at the door. The expression went over his head. "I've been trying all afternoon to get a hold of you."

"I'm sorry," he said. "I should've called to tell you I was coming."

"Come in, come in. No need to apologize."

While he took off his layers, gloves, and hat, I put the kettle on the stove.

"Any news about Chance? Kat doesn't tell me anything."

"Oh," he said, surprised. "The Black Hand?"

This meant nothing to me. I heard it as *his* black hand, as if Chance had marked or smudged it.

"That's who Chance was involved with. They were behind the break-in. Now the police are calling it an 'act of disruption.'"

Perhaps the fathomless boredom and general discontent I'd been suffering had hollowed my comprehension faculties. All I could think of was the secret Serbian society that may have been responsible for starting World War I. In my defense, I had no context to understand what he was saying. Juan Diego did. He knew about the Independence-based Black Hand group.

Then it hit me. At the American Legion meeting the previous spring, a man in the back kept yelling, "The Black Hand." Afterward, I gave it no thought and I never heard the name again until Juan Diego broke this news.

Little was known about the group except that they were anti-secessionists. Days later, we'd learn The Black Hand was a militant secret society. They didn't advertise themselves or seek public attention. A few months earlier, Gail caught Chance wearing a shirt that said "Unification or Die." This was their motto and another name often attributed to the Serbian group.

Its members wooed Chance and his three friends in front of the same store they broke into. They gave them gas for their motorcycles (two of them owned little 50cc dirt bikes). Gave them candy, money, and ham radios so they could communicate with the group.

When the kids joined, they swore allegiance to the group and its cause. The consequences of spilling the beans must have been severe because none of the four kids buckled under pressure from police or parents, even though they were told they could be tried as adults and sentenced to jail. It was the youngest of the group, an eleven-year-old, who cracked after Chance disappeared. Unfortunately it didn't lead authorities to his whereabouts.

"The real reason I came out today...." Juan Diego sighed.

"You're worried I don't have enough human interaction?" I interrupted in a lame attempt to diffuse the gravity of the moment.

"The State Department granted my dad and me travel permits."

"So it's true."

He nodded. "We're leaving tomorrow."

"Tomorrow!" I couldn't conceal my disappointment. "But why?"

"My dad needs to go back to Mexico. My mother and sisters are there. I'm afraid if I don't go now, I'll never see them."

"Wow," was all I could say.

"I'm sorry," Juan Diego said. "I know I'm letting everyone down."

"Just like that, they said you can go?"

"On the application, I wrote we needed to get back to our family. They called me the next day for an interview. I was ready to get on my hands and knees to beg them to let my father go, but I didn't have to. They approved us both."

"It was that easy? Everyone says it's impossible to get a travel visa. You told me that." I realized I sounded like Kat did earlier. It's not that I was envious he was being allowed safe passage to greener pastures. Juan Diego was one of my few real friends in the country. Selfishly I didn't want him to go. But it made little sense they were letting him leave. "Sorry, I don't mean to sound resentful. I'm happy for your father, especially. What's the trick to get approved?"

"Roman, I'm afraid they're letting me go because I'm a journalist."

"They're expelling journalists?"

"I'm not saying that but they knew everything about me and my paper and what I'd written. The consular actually said to me, 'You're not a big fan of our country, are you?'"

"That's ridiculous!" I snapped. "You're more of a patriot than anyone I know—wait, who'd you meet with?"

"Paul Gray. He knows we know one another. He even asked about you."

Struck by a vision of ICE agents coming for me, I looked out the window.

"Don't worry," Juan Diego said, seeing my discomfort. "They don't know you're still in the country. He asked about your article. I told him it hadn't been published."

"I'm sorry to see you go. You have to do what's right for you."

"I don't feel good about it, to be honest."

"Has your faith in Independence been broken?" I asked.

Juan Diego looked away. After a long silence, he said, "I want you to have my scooter. It's my gift to you and this country."

"What about Tommy?" I asked.

"I'm leaving him my dad's electric car. Roman, I still believe in Independence and I want this country to succeed. I can be an advocate from the outside. Independence needs more of that. And the country still has you. You're not just a third-party observer anymore. You have a stake in this." This surge of inspiration quickly evaporated and his despondency was more acute than ever.

"You're flying out tomorrow?" I asked.

"It was the most expensive fare you've ever seen. We also had to pay the thousand-dollar application fee. It used up all my father's savings. We're leaving with nothing."

"At least you have the means," I said, trying to cast a positive spin.

"I was hoping Kat could come by my house before I leave. I want to say goodbye."

"Why don't you ride out there?"

"Tommy doesn't want to see me." This visibly pained him. He quickly changed the subject. "I'd like to give her gas and the rest will be for you. There are instructions for how to make more if you want."

Over dinner, we talked about a better future and kept to practical matters concerning the present. It was uncertain what would become of his house, which he acquired through the Homestead Act. For the time being, I was going to stay there, at least part of the time.

With the setting sun at his back, he rode away. From the porch, I watched until he was a small plume of dust on the horizon. Walking inside, I felt a sharp and distinct pang of loneliness.

Kat ended up taking Juan Diego and his father to the airport early the next morning. From there, she drove straight home. I came out to the front porch when I heard her car. It had been a week since she left but it felt like months. Seeing her in person was strange.

"Hey," I said from the doorway.

She saw my packed bag at my feet. "You ready?"

"Yeah."

"Let me grab something inside." As she walked past me, she averted her eyes. A minute later she returned.

"It's a nice day," I said as we pulled onto the dirt road.

"The sun is nice," she said.

"Will it last?"

"I heard it might snow in a few days."

It was a twenty-five-minute drive to Highway 83, where I was catching the Independence Arrow up to Capital City. We drove without saying much and arrived at the bus stop early. It was just a highway junction surrounded by tilled fields of dirt that were never replanted. The land—surely there's none flatter—dulled my mind.

The bus appeared earlier than expected. "You sure you'll be okay?" I asked.

"I'll be fine."

"Alright. See you soon."

We leaned over the console and kissed. Just a peck.

"Hey," she called before I closed the door. She stretched across the passenger seat and handed me a sealed envelope. I didn't have time to ask questions so I took it and ran across the road. When I looked back from inside the bus, she was still there. I waved. If she waved back, I didn't see because of the glare on the windshield.

Inside Juan Diego's house, books, and papers were neatly stacked on the small, round dining table. The harvest gold stovetop and counters were sparkling clean. In the refrigerator, he'd left a half dozen eggs, a couple of blocks of cheese, jars of pickled vegetables, and various homemade condiments.

After looking around the house, I was ready to sit down with Kat's letter. I cut open the sealed peak of the flap. Inside was a single folded sheet of paper. I was expecting a multi-page letter describing the failings of our relationship and me. When I opened it, three one-hundred-dollar bills slipped out and landed on the table with a click. The clean and crisp bills stuck together.

Instead of a long letter describing her feelings, desires, needs, and fears that had been dammed up for so long, I received a blank sheet of paper. It was a letdown. As much as I feared it would mark the end of our relationship, intuitively, I welcomed it. The yearning for her rejection ran deep, as though I'd been waiting all my life for that moment.

The cash was confounding. Spending money was stressful for Kat. Three hundred dollars was a decent amount of cash in Independence, especially for pocket money. It was generous. The mint-condition bills suggested there was more from where those came from.

MAUDE'S MOB

I was in town the same weekend Maude Grese was holding a rally at the National Fairgrounds. Radio ads had been airing for weeks. *"My rowdy ladies and roughneck men, I'm giddier than a cock in a henhouse to announce I'll be heading up north this Saturday. Get yourselves ready 'cause Maude's Mob is taking the capital by storm. Get out and come out and don't be left out. We need everyone there."*

After the Southern anti-taxation events, where she was a featured speaker, she continued making appearances at similar gatherings. Maude's Mob was a boisterous group of followers growing exponentially. These rallies were adding up to a movement and showed how the Independence sociopolitical spectrum was transforming.

As mentioned earlier, there were no political parties and it was uncivil to refer to others or their beliefs as liberal, conservative, bourgeois, and so forth. Constitution Committee member Stanley Carlton told me the campaign against political labels came from a fear of people "subscribing to pre-packaged bundles of political convictions."

At the historic National Assembly meetings of the French Revolution, supporters of the monarchy sat on the right side of the presiding president and supporters of democratic empowerment on the left. The world's been fighting over the rights of citizens ever since. Although various forces were pushing and pulling Independents in different directions, I think it's fair to characterize the divisions as Left and Right.

This struggle took discernible form during the election season when Albert Gonzalez proclaimed that the nation's resources inherently belonged to the people. Bill Tyson represented the age-old establishment of sovereignty—the control of resources and therefore the wealth and power. Maude Grese was unabashedly camped on the right. Although she was still seen as a pundit and entertainer, she had become the vocal leader of a political movement. She was essentially arguing on behalf of the feudal rights of nobles and aristocrats.

IBS had been expanding into the Northeast. Maude, Davey McGraw, and the other radio hosts didn't have as significant of a fan base in the North (Grese was disliked for being divisive and illiberal), the television shows *Full Report* and *A Clear View* were more popular than people admitted.[22] Maude's Capital City rally was part of their effort to gain a foothold in the nation's political center.

The year-round Saturday Market at the fairgrounds was located on a grassy area near the rodeo grandstand. When I arrived, a crew was finishing setting up Maude's stage out on the huge asphalt parking lot, two hundred yards from the market. I came early, hoping to find Tommy, a regular at the Independence City Artisans stand. He wasn't there.

There were dozens of Grese fans at the market, identifiable by the slogans taped or painted on their backs—MAUDE'S MOB; GONZO'S GOTTA GO; LIVE FREE OR SHOOT YOUR WAY OUT. I spotted Todd Leiker and Carey Dobbs passing by with canvas bags packed with supplies. As a crew struggled to moor Maude's banner against the brisk wind, the Legionnaires were gathering near a big metal convention building nearby. It looked as though they were mounting a counter protest. I was salivating for what was sure to be an entertaining show.

Just before Grese took the stage, two men ran through the market. I watched them beeline toward the Legionnaires. Whatever they conveyed caused visible distress among the group. I saw one man toss his picket sign onto the ground. Another woman turned away from the others and wrapped her arms around her head. Something was amiss.

Maude's Mob began cheering for their champion as she appeared on stage. "Hello, Capital City!" she shouted into the microphone. "This is a great day. Have you heard the good news? Come on and gather round. This is a historical day. Mark my words,

---

[22] Even after the overwhelmingly negative public and critical response to *Full Report*, people in the north were still watching these shows. In part, this was because of their high production qualities and the dearth of entertainment options. The lure of IBS's glitzy visuals was stronger than many expected. It's worth noting *Full Report* toned down its egregious political bias as the network expanded northward.

this is the turning point we've been waiting for. Listen up. Alberto Gonzalez has resigned and will no longer be our dictator! Gonzo is gone!"

Her words sent a shock wave through the crowd. At the back, where I was standing, there were gasps and outcries. People turned to one another, unclear whether this was one of Maude's stunts.

"This is a great day for Independence," Maude continued. "A great day for the people. You should feel good. Turn to the person next to you and shake their hand and say, 'I think it's gonna be okay after all.' God has given us another opportunity to right this ship. This country was created for people willing to sacrifice everything for their freedom. We let our guard down in a big way and allowed a leftist faction to slip through. By taking the power away from the people, they took away our freedom. Government tried to take our voice away. They didn't want us here today. Wouldn't give us a permit. Thank God we have Major Krug. He stood up for us and said, 'Nuh-uh, these are the good guys.'" A chant broke out, "Krug, Krug, Krug," and quickly petered away.

Out of the corner of my eye, I spotted the Legionnaires on the move. With their banner before them—MAUDE'S THE DEVIL— they were marching across the empty lot toward the stage. Many in the crowd, including myself, couldn't help but laugh.

"Ha!" Maude shouted when she spotted the oncoming marchers. "Look at those liberal monkeys. This is the problem with these lefties. Nothing real to say." She took her virtual rifle and pointed to the Legionnaires. "Boom, boom, boom."

Carey Dobbs raised a bullhorn as they approached. "Friends, this woman is poison. She's an extremist. She thrives on anger and bitterness."

The Mob yelled for him to shut up and leave. Maude agreed. "You can have your little commie party but do it in private so no one has to see it. It's disgusting. There's room back over in the pigpen."

"Extremist!" Dobbs and his companions shouted.

"Liberal," Maude fired back.

"Fascist," Dobbs replied.

Maude laughed again. "Like I said, nothing of substance to say. Yada yada yada."

The opposing groups shouted at one another from a close distance while Maude shrieked over the PA and Dobbs yelled into his bullhorn.

"With Maude Grese, it's always about what *they* are doing to us. She spreads fear and makes you angry at *the others* who are coming to get you. She's a wedge that's driving us apart. What's your real name, Maude? Tell them what it is," he implored his people.

"The Devil," they roared.

By now, the groups were within spitting distance as they hurled invectives at one another. A man whose face was red and twisted with rage confronted Dobbs. "Go apologize to her! Go apologize!" He got right up in Dobbs' personal space. "You go apologize to her right now!" Dobbs refused his demand and took it a step further by listing reasons she was the devil.

Up to this point, I hadn't noticed his adversary was carrying a walking cane, even though he was plenty young and didn't seem to need it. While Dobbs counted on his fingers the indictments against Maude, the man wildly brandished the cane, causing everyone close by to jump back. Before Dobbs could react, the man struck him in the lower back. As he fell to his knees, the man swung the hooked end as if he were launching a wiffle ball off a tee. Dobbs launched himself backwards, avoiding the hit. The crowd tightened around them but I could see Dobbs on the asphalt, propped up on one elbow, trying to protect himself with his other arm until Leiker one elbow, trying to protect himself with his other arm until Leiker and others swarmed the attacker.

Policemen came out of nowhere and pushed their way through. The two sides were separated. The Legionnaires' banner was used as a stretcher to carry Dobbs away. That was the end of Maude's rally.

A PRESIDENTIAL VOID

The press secretary made it official later that day. "It has fallen upon me to inform you President Gonzalez has resigned his presidency. It's been increasingly obvious to those around him, and for the president himself, that he cannot fulfill his duties because of unexpected and pervasive health issues. With deep regret and a heavy heart, he bids you farewell."

It also fell upon the press secretary to inform the public that Vice President Jarvis Wilson was stepping down as well. Wilson, a sixty-year-old African American man, was about as non-public as a public figure can be. The former college professor never appeared on television and communicated with the press with written statements. When Gonzalez disappeared, so did Wilson.

There wasn't much time to absorb the shock of the mysterious resignation as the media focus shifted to who would succeed him. The Constitution stated that the line of succession after the Vice President was Senate Pro Tempore Phil Mooney. Because he was part of the coalition that left the capital weeks ago, his absence made Assembly Speaker Marcia Mendoza the next in line.

The assemblywoman lacked national recognition but in Capital City she was known from the two terms she served on the city council. Later that evening, the press corps assembled inside

Congressional Hall. Assemblywoman Mendoza came out, flanked by two dozen of her colleagues. Light bulbs flashed as she stepped to the microphone.

"It's with a heavy heart I come before you, the People of Independence, to acknowledge my duty as determined by our Constitution to take the oath of Office of the President of—"

Commotion off-screen interrupted the press conference. The camera whipped around to reveal Senator Mooney and a company of congressmen charging in through the main doors. "Just hold it," Mooney yelled. "I'm back."

The media's attention swung from Mendoza to the senator. Wearing a navy suit and crimson tie in the tradition of U.S. congressmen, Mooney spoke to the cameras and reporters. "Ladies and gentlemen, with me are thirty-six members of Congress who fled the capital earlier this month to save our beautiful country. Well, we're back!" His contingent cheered.

"You abandoned your country!" a woman in Mendoza's group yelled. "You abandoned your position! You shut down Congress." This was true. After the initial walkout, two more senators joined, which meant the Senate did not have enough members present to vote. "It's too late for you, Mooney."

The groups began shouting at one another and it soon escalated. Reporters were caught between mostly middle-aged men as they grabbed, flailed, and shoved one another in a frantic and sloppy display. It took a group of coolheaded congressmen and women to separate the parties and bring order to the lobby. The two sides retreated but not without parting shots.

The camera panned to the *Channel 7* reporter. He swiped his tousled hair off his forehead. "Phil Mooney or Marcia Mendoza, who will be our next president? Reporting from Congressional Hall, I'm Pax Armstead."

I walked over to Zapata's, the little bar where I first met Juan Diego. The owner, José, was leaning against the back counter, working a toothpick in his mouth as he listened to two men at the bar discuss the day's news.

"Just by looking at him, you could tell he took care of himself, ate the right way," one man said. "He was fit as a fiddle."

The other man, hunched over the bar, shook his head with remorse. "If it can happen to him…." He shook his head before he guzzled the last of his pint and set the glass down. "It don't make me feel so good."

"Benji, you're doing just fine," José assured him.

"Here's to your health," said Benji's companion, who turned out to be his nephew, Javier.

At the end of the curved bar, a woman named Carolyn, wearing overalls and had her hair tied back with a striped ribbon, was listening skeptically with her arms crossed. Leaning back on the bar stool, she grinned at the men. "You believe all that crap? He disappeared just like that"—she snapped her fingers and sat up—"because of poor health? Never seen again. Not at home, not anywhere."

"You trying to say he was abducted or something?" Benji scoffed and grabbed his glass, which he forgot was empty.

"By aliens!" Javier added with a snort.

"They wanted him gone more than anything!" Carolyn exclaimed.

"She's right about that," said José.

They were referring to the president's most bitter and vociferous enemies, who saw Gonzalez as the biggest obstacle to their seemingly monopolistic dreams. True or not, it was already growing into a widely held suspicion, if not a firm belief. One couldn't help but wonder if Gonzalez was pushed out. As Carolyn said, one day he was out and about, speaking at public events, and the next day, gone.

"What's your pleasure?" José asked me.

I nodded to the neon sign in the window. "You have *Tecate*?"

"That's just an antique," he said.

"Guess I'll have whatever you're pouring."

I placed a crisp hundred-dollar bill on the bar. José stared at it and appeared uncertain about whether to accept it. He squatted down and rummaged through a cabinet and stood up with a counterfeit pen.

"Haven't used this in ages," he said as he marked the bill.

Irrational thoughts of Kat giving me fake bills caused a sinking feeling in my stomach. Despite whatever misgivings I had about her at the moment, she wouldn't do that. José slipped the bill inside the cash register and gathered a stack of ones and fives.

"You live around here?" he asked after he closed the drawer. "Don't think I've seen you before."

"I've been living out by Ulysses since last summer," I said.

"A lot of crazy shit happening down there," Javier said as he leaned forward to get a better look at me.

"You don't look like a farmer," said Carolyn. "No offense."

"You'd be surprised," said José. "Homestead farmers aren't what you're used to."

I stared at the pint of beer in front of me and thought about that vast, arid, lonely countryside. For a second, I couldn't remember why we were ever there.

José must have mistaken my momentary withdrawal as evidence of agronomical failure because he said sympathetically, "It's not easy to learn if you haven't done it before."

"We had a garden," I said. "That's it."

I briefly explained why we moved out there: Kat's veterinary aspirations and my literary ambitions. I told them how I came to the country a year earlier to write a magazine story. "To be honest, it was just a way in." I surprised myself with this admission. It must have been the months of isolation and introversion. Speaking my thoughts aloud had become involuntary.

"Are you saying you came here for a woman?" Carolyn asked.

"And stayed for her," I answered.

"Stayed?" José asked with a crooked brow. "As in, you gave up your U.S. citizenship?"

"Yep."

He burst into laughter. "She must be a goddess!"

"Oh please," Carolyn said to him, shaking her head. "You don't have a romantic bone in your body, do you?"

"I'm just messing with you," José said to me. "It's not so bad here. People talk about things they don't have. To me, all that stuff is a lot of extra baggage. Life is easier here if you figure out a few things. You don't need a lot. A little money, food, family, friends. Everyone's got a place to live. We have heat in the winter. We have water. Plenty of sun. I love it here."

Benji and Javier nodded like they hadn't ever thought about it that way. The conversation shifted to life in Independence versus pre-secession. In my experience, these discussions would end in frustration about everything that was lacking. On this day, however, they all agreed life overall was easier.

"Just getting by and living a decent life wasn't good enough back then," José said. "Always something you thought you needed even though you didn't."

"Getting by and living a decent life wasn't easy," Benji lamented. "Here, if you're short on cash or whatever, you don't get punished for it. They won't fine you for going through a tough

A New America

stretch, making it harder for you. Back in the day, they'd take your home away, kick you to the curb! How is that humane?" You could see he had suffered these miseries, if not directly, through someone close to him.

"They're ruthless," Carolyn said with disgust. "Good riddance."

"Money," José said. "That's what we all lived for, right?"

"Yep," Javier said. "We're better off for sure."

Even the fuel shortage had its upside that day, as they agreed it was healthier to walk more and drive less. But it brought them back to the current and unhappy state of political affairs.

"What's to become of us?" Carolyn asked. "We live in a country where a rightly elected president just disappears. In place of who we voted for, we get what we voted against."[23]

As José nodded his head in agreement, his eyes fell on me. "There isn't any actual evidence suggesting foul play, is there?" Perhaps this was a proprietor's inclination to be diplomatic to avoid alienating customers.

"The man is human," Carolyn said about the former president. "Any of us could find out tomorrow—"

"We know, we know!" Benji snapped. "Enough already."

All this time, a group had been playing at the pool table in the corner. One of them came up to the bar for a refill. He stood close by, leaning on his pool stick with both hands.

"I overheard you say you got stuck here," he said to me. And then in a confidential tone, "I know someone who can get papers. Visa, passports. It's the real deal. Ain't cheap, though."

"How much?" I asked.

"A grand."

"How would I get in touch with him?"

---

[23] She was referring to Grady Washington ally Senator Mooney. Two days later he was sworn in as the nation's third president.

"His pager."

I didn't have the cash and I wasn't looking to leave the country anytime soon. I still felt compelled to look into it. I borrowed a pen and wrote the number on my hand. When I returned to Juan Diego's house later, I called the number. The forger called back fifteen minutes later.

"I heard you were the man to talk to if I had urgent business on the other side of the border," I said.

"Depends how urgent," he responded.

"Not very, to tell you the truth. Are you open to trades?"

"Depends what it is."

"A 50cc scooter. Gets great gas mileage."

"I'm coming through Cap City tomorrow. I can stop by and have a look."

THE FORGER

The next morning, I slept until ten o'clock. I attributed the deep, untroubled sleep to not having a loaded gun in the room. After a late breakfast, I walked to a bookstore where I found a musty first edition of *In Cold Blood*. It had belonged to a local school. The due date card was still in its pocket. It cost five percent of all the money I had but I couldn't pass it up. It seemed fitting my only copy should originate from there.

When I passed through Independence Plaza, hundreds of people were gathered outside Congressional Hall, demanding that Senator Mooney step aside and allow Assemblywoman Marcia Mendoza to assume the presidency. Like-minded demonstrations were happening around the country. Their shared view was that Mooney's ascension was not aligned with the will of the people, especially given that Gonzalez was still in the first hundred days of a four-year term.

Mooney and his allies had no interest in fairness. He announced he would "fulfill his obligational and constitutional duty." The next day he was sworn in. Nationwide protests grew but he never blinked. With Maude Grese leading the way, his media supporters repurposed the anti-Gonzalez script to rage against the "treasonous," "lawless," and "Godless anarchists": the protesters. The groundwork was being laid for what would surely be a turbulent four years.

I was relieved to see Carey Dobbs at the demonstration. He was the spitting image of a wounded soldier, head bandaged and hobbling on a single crutch. If I hadn't seen him pummeled, I would have thought it was a prop. People lined up to give him their best wishes so I didn't have a chance to talk with him.

The document forger was waiting outside Juan Diego's house. He was a Native man with pock-marked skin and a pair of those big protective sunglasses people wear after eye surgery. I got the key from inside and met him at the garage.

"So where you trying to get to?" he asked as I unlocked the door.

"I don't know. Haven't thought about it. Mexico, maybe." I said this because I promised Juan Diego I'd visit someday.

"You said you live out on a farm but you're not a farmer? How's that going?"

"Not so great," I said.

"It's important to have community. When you're isolated, you live only for yourself and none for you. You know about Black Kettle? I live there most of the year. There's plenty of space but nobody's too far away."

He took the scooter for a test ride around the block and returned a few minutes later. "Alright," he said as he dismounted. "Even trade. I'll make a travel permit and a U.S. special passport."

"Does it always work?" I asked.

"Perfect track record. Choose the right port of entry. They're cracking down at the southern crossings and Las Animas. I recommend the northern stations. You'd need someone to drop you off and pick you up on the other side because there's nothing there. If you went through Eads, I could probably arrange a ride. You could visit Black Kettle on your way. You don't have to be Cheyenne or Arapahoe or Indian at all."

I told him I'd think it over. As he was leaving, I asked how much an additional set would be.

"A thousand."

NO GOODBYES

I sacrificed a certain degree of my freedom to remain in Independence. To be honest, I didn't believe the punishing blockade could last. I thought better angels would prevail over the brutal politics of geopolitical systems. So I didn't fear the prospect of being trapped in the country long term. After a year, I wasn't so certain about this. When the opportunity to leave (or go to jail trying) crossed my path, I seized the moment.

The scooter was a high price to pay. It would have given me the independence I desperately needed to move freely throughout the country. Although, if I lived in Capital City, I could get around on a bicycle and the national bus system. Before I decided, I needed to talk to Kat and confront our relationship, face-to-face, as I proposed on my first night in the country: without fear.

I left a message telling her I was coming back sooner than planned because of an opportunity I wanted to discuss in person. The next morning, I rode out to the farmhouse. Her car wasn't there but luckily I had my key. Stepping inside, I was struck by the house's unique odor. It was like seventy years of dander and body oils filled the air with decay. It had only been a few days since I left.

Regardless of how our conversation went, I planned to return to Capital City for another two weeks. So I went upstairs to pack more clothes into a backpack I'd found at Juan Diego's. As I entered the bedroom, I immediately noticed Kat's side of the closet was open and empty except for a few work shirts on hangers. Her suitcases were gone. Shoes were gone. I opened her dresser drawers: empty.

I was stunned. I didn't see this coming, although maybe I should have. Now I understood why she gave me the money. It was a farewell gift. Starter cash, I suppose. She was giving up on her rural practice and giving up on us. It was bewildering she would end it without a word or hint of her intentions.

As I lay on the bed gazing at the ceiling, my eyes fell on a hat in the back corner of the upper closet shelf. I swung myself off the bed and stretched on my tiptoes. It was the one she wore at La Serena but it wasn't the Stetson with a turquoise-and-sterling band I'd always imagined. It was a straw sun hat with a wide brim and a colorful woven band. Strange, the misremembering.

I packed my clothes and all the food I could fit and tossed the rest of the perishable items into the compost bin behind the barn. Before I left, I entered Kat's office. Voluminous veterinary books were still on top of the metal cabinet. Its doors were open, which was unusual. She always kept it locked. On the shelves were rolls of gauze, packets of ointment, and her tinctures and herbal blends. Underneath the cabinet, I spotted a mustard-colored slip of paper. When I picked it up, I saw it was a strap used to bind 10,000 USD bundles of hundred-dollar bills.

After an entire winter of having our impending financial collapse drilled into my head, all I could do was laugh. If anyone had walked in at that moment and found me on the floor howling like a lunatic…. Moments later, I was nearly in tears—of rage. I gathered my belongings and left.

Before I drove away, I looked back at the farmhouse for the last time. It would take another year for the anxiety that tormented me there to loosen its hold on my memories so I could appreciate the unique experience. Reading through my shockingly confessional notes was difficult. There were days when our relationship matched the passion and focus we shared at La Serena but those were far and few between. Unfortunately we never came close to the intimacy of our letters. That confounded me as much as anything. Affection came easier for her than the scenes in this book might suggest. Intimacy did not.

On my way back to Capital City, a million thoughts flitted through my head. A random image came to me of my mother wearing a fedora like the one I imagined Kat wearing at La Serena. I must have been ten or eleven when she brought me along on a business trip to Santa Fe. Alma, our live-in au pair, was away for the week and my mother couldn't find anyone to take me. I remembered her wearing the hat with a matching turquoise-and-sterling necklace and bracelets. The sun was high over the arid land and the air itself seemed to pop with light. My mother was smiling as she fraternized with patrons and dealers. I can't recall another time from my childhood when I was as happy as that moment.

This memory was anything but pleasant. It was disconcerting to think that my idealistic image of Kat in her sun hat was connected to childhood emotions. To this day, I'm unsure what to make of it but it's hard to dismiss as coincidental.

THE JONESES

Tommy returned my calls a few days later. He had just gotten off the phone with Juan Diego. Our friend was doing well. His family was reunited at last. Tommy's family, on the other hand, was not in a good place. Chance was still missing and they had another major problem: Tom was in jail.

The week before, Tommy had gone out on a bicycle he and his dad had outfitted with a trailer. He spent three days traversing county roads between Capital City and Dodge City, posting flyers on mailboxes and utility poles. He ended this first phase at his home in Independence City and was planning to set out the following day.

> MISSING 14 year old boy - Caucasian - Brown eyes - Sandy brown hair - Freckles on cheeks and nose - 5'3, lean - Last seen north of Capital City in a red Chevrolet Cavalier, two door coupe with chrome spoke wheels and tinted windows - If anyone has information on the whereabouts of the boy or the vehicle please call 775-6785

Two days into Tommy's excursion, Tom got a call from an aging farmer named Arnold, who said he knew of a vehicle that matched the description. Tom drove out to a house near the Finney-Gray county line. He knew from Arnold that the owner was a youngish man who bought the property during the Transition. He moved there with his girlfriend, sister, and brother-in-law. None of them had any farming experience. Arnold told Tom their undertaking was a failure. The man who drove the Cavalier was the only one who still lived there.

Tommy didn't tell me exactly what happened between his dad and the failed farmer but things got ugly. Tom believed he was the one who took Chance away. He tied him down in the bed of his pickup to deliver him to the authorities in Capital City. He didn't make it far before he was stopped by a caravan of trucks blocking the road. A group of armed men released his captive and Tom was tied down in one of their trucks. They took him to the Law Enforcement Center, where he was arrested and charged with assault and kidnapping.

The next day's front page of the *Capital City Gazette* featured a triptych of Tom: 1) lying in the back of the pickup grimacing in pain; 2) sitting on the tailgate with a swarm of policemen around him; and 3) being led away handcuffed.

Tom won a bail appeal and was released the next day. As you might expect, he had a lot of friends at the law enforcement center. His former undersheriff launched an intensive investigation. Much of it was done off hours by investigators. Tom's captors ended up being the link to Black Hand members. Chance was found six weeks after he disappeared. The charges against him and his friends were eventually dropped.

When I asked Tommy how Kat was doing, he went silent. The subject made him noticeably uncomfortable. I assumed she was staying at Gail and Tom's cottage. Turned out she hadn't been there since I last saw her. Tommy told me she had moved in with another man.

Jody Thornburg was his name. He was an assemblyman from Lakin. He was married and had four kids. Gail thought Kat tried to leave the country but was turned back at the border. She ended up in Lakin with no gas and nowhere to go. She spent the day at a diner we had been to once. The place looked like it came out of the fifties. The waitresses even wore frilly pink outfits. That's where Kat ran into Thornburg.

The two of them attended the same high school but were a couple of years apart. According to Gail (according to Kat), they had only seen one another a few times since. How they ended up moving in together the following week is still a mystery. With Colm

O'Brien's help, I later found out the congressman told people close to him his wife and kids were staying with friends down south. But unofficial hearsay was they flew to Mexico, the one and only flight destination, and re-emerged in Oklahoma City, where the congressman's in-laws lived.

Whether these were partial truths, it made for a workable version of reality. It dramatically altered how our relationship existed inside of me. My opinion and feelings about Kat soured even more. The thought of being intimately involved with her repulsed me. I wanted to get away—as far away as possible.

You couldn't walk a block without seeing posters promoting the First Annual Freedom Fair. Radio advertisements were ubiquitous throughout the country. It seemed like the perfect way to spend my last weekend in Independence—or out of captivity if my papers failed.

Like the anti-Gonzalez rallies in Dumas and Dalhart, a mobilization of natural gas-powered buses brought people to the National Fairgrounds. The previous effort was a trial run, in comparison. On Wednesday afternoon, yellow school buses began dropping people off at the park across from the fairgrounds. This continued all day Thursday and Friday. In addition to the buses, there were dozens of fueling stations around the country where vehicles with four or more riders could get a fill-up while supplies lasted. These were community efforts made possible by farmers.

By the time the fair kicked off on Friday, there were thousands of tents throughout the park. Smoke from grills and campfires filled the air. Out on the massive asphalt parking lot, there were more vehicles than I'd ever seen in Independence.

The weekend events included steer rustling, bronco busting, puppet shows, gymnastics, and shooting events. They held swine, goat, and sheep shows in the agricultural buildings. The 4H building featured home supplies, home tools, farm tools, alternative adhesives, textiles, fuel, feedstock, standard crops, diverse crops, seeds, flowers, and more. Next to the rodeo arena, more than a dozen militia groups set up tables for people to donate money and supplies. There were also prominent groups from the Flatland Revolution, such as the Ulysses Justice League, Meade County Brigade, and Krug's Guardsmen.

The event was not without its detractors, nor the effusive patriotism without dissenters. The protest movement against the Mooney presidency had not abated. In the weeks leading up to the fair, violent clashes had broken out between protesters and their counterparts. Many officials (mostly Mooney supporters) called for the protesters to respect the Independence Constitution and end the divisive demonstrations. Some were even calling on Major Krug to "put down the treasonous rebellion."

The protest leaders were clear about their demands. They wanted Mooney's inauguration voided or proof that Albert Gonzalez left of his own accord. They wanted to see the former president on live video. If he was "free of shackles and coercion" and he or his wife could testify that he willingly left office, the protests would end.

There were few violent encounters that weekend. The most notable confrontation happened Saturday night between a flash mob and a hooded man on horseback posing as a mysterious nightrider that had become the face of rural terror. A black sheet was draped over his broodmare. Across one side, LIES was printed in red, and on the other, FEAR. The mob pulled the rider to the ground and unmasked a middle-aged man. He was taunted and pushed around, which led to a sloppy fistfight that police quickly broke up.

The large convention building housed the National Exposition, where federal departments, government organizations, and private companies (e.g., Ceres Energy) had set up stalls. A stage at one end featured speakers throughout the day. Late on Sunday afternoon, the booths were cleared out for the finale.

Congressmen, church leaders, civic leaders, and media personalities took the stage. Fuel insecurity was a popular topic. So were crime and national security. Mitch Black, who was now the official NIA head, and had been given the title of Federal Marshal, told the crowd they *should* be afraid.

"The cartel incursion caught us unawares. We had to work our butts off to catch up. Right when we were getting a handle on things, right when we were getting the borders shored up, their access routes cut off, their supply chains destroyed, their hideouts and bunkers turned inside out—right when the battle was turning in our favor, what happened? We became careless. Why'd we lose track of the cells operating inside our borders? I'm not here to answer that because it's a matter of politics but I am here to tell you that this country faces grave, grave threats. That's just the reality of it. Remember in the elections, all the people talking about how President Washington and others were sowing fear in the hearts of the people? There's too much fear in our media, they told us. People, listen to me. Don't run from fear. Embrace it. Embrace it!"

President Mooney took the stage late. "Things are going to be different in Independence from here on out. Things are changing and we have a plan. There will be more barbecues, more dances, more music and fairs. There will be restaurants with menus you can afford. We're going to create jobs because jobs is what you've been asking for and so that's what you're going to get! You shouldn't have to deal with the crime and the scum that's plagued our land. We have a plan for that. We're going to power your vehicles so you can power your life. This isn't a third-world country. We need fuel and we know the people who will make that happen. And you do too! Folks, this is just the beginning."

The enthusiastic audience ate it up. Mooney introduced the next-to-last guest. "I know you remember this guy. I'm proud to introduce this distinguished member of the Freedom 5, Jerry Hickman! Give it up for him!"

The crowd roared with applause. The Flatland Revolution star wasn't forgotten after all. Hickman walked on stage with an acoustic guitar strapped over his shoulder. His beard was trimmed down to a point and he wore a t-shirt that read CITIZENS RECLAIMING GOVERNMENT, which, of course, was the banner he and his cohorts hung from the courthouse they occupied.

"Thank you very much." Hickman looked overwhelmed by the reception. He nodded appreciatively to different sections of the audience. "This is a song I wrote. It's called *Independence Through and Through*." He strummed a single G chord and sang the first verse a cappella.

Well I grew up believing
In red, white, and blue
That freedom and country
Meant the same to me and you

Those were only two choices
Just like night and day
Drive a Chevy or drive a Ford
Pay your taxes or get locked away

Still I lived my life day to day
I loved my TV, loved being me
But I realized I had two choices
Neither one meant being free

I used to bleed red, white, and blue
Now I'm Independent through and through
I believe in our country
I believe in God too

I used to bleed red, white, and blue
Now I'm Independent through and through
I believe in freedom
I believe in you too

Then one night at the bar
I saw the news in Bonner's Ferry
They'd shut down the town
The time had finally come

They said to hell with your choices
We can't live like this no more
To hell with this country
We don't bow to King George

You've robbed us of dignity
You've stolen our pride and joy
Founding fathers'd be ashamed
You've sold our country for a lie

I used to bleed red white and blue
Now I'm Independent through and through
I believe in our country
I believe in God too

I used to bleed red white and blue
Now I'm Independent through and through
I believe in freedom
I believe in all of you

Independence, I love you
Independence, we're all for you
Independence, this is true
Independence, means you

I believe, I believe in you
Independent through and through
I believe in freedom
I believe in God too

The hall roared with applause long after he left the stage. Then the lights dimmed as Mooney returned to the spotlight. "Ladies and gentlemen, fellow Independents. THE one and only, Maaajooor Krug!"

Krug walked onto the stage in his decorated uniform and brimmed hat and carried a 12-gauge shotgun with both hands. Halfway to the microphone, he turned to the back, and from his hip, shot into the air. The crowd exploded as he pumped the shotgun and fired again. Smoke rose above the stage as he took a cob pipe from his shirt pocket and plugged it into the corner of his mouth.

"KRUG, KRUG, KRUG," took hold. Thousands of people packed inside the building, and a thousand more outside the open garage-style doors pumped their fists in the air in unison. "KRUG, KRUG, KRUG, KRUG, KRUG, KRUG…."

BURNING FLAGS

During my conversations with Tom Jones, he explained his reluctance to respond publicly after he was fired. Simply put, he didn't want to be part of what he saw as blatantly corrupt governance. But he left out an interesting detail.

Soon after he was let go, Gail received a generous government contract that included NIA and border patrol uniforms. She had never placed a bid for these contracts or even knew the opportunity existed. One day, a government official showed up out of the blue and dropped off documents for her to sign. It didn't take long to realize they were bribing them for Tom's continued silence.

She signed the contracts and began work a few weeks later. It also included national flags. Gail sewed the country's first flag by hand. A colorful patchwork of the thirty-six counties that form Independence were centered within the old state borders and lightly traced with black thread. On both edges were alternating red, white, and blue stripes. For all I know, it's still displayed in Presidential Hall.

Her seamstresses continued to make replicas that were distributed to government buildings around the country. The final flags that Jones Outfitters produced have a special place in the nation's history. During the weekend of The Freedom Fair (Chance was still missing and Tom was in jail), Gail erected a laundry line post next to the road. On the crossbar, she hung a flag so that it dangled vertically. Whenever a Freedom Fair Express bus appeared on the road, she would set the flag on fire.

This is the last image I took from Independence. It was on the front page of the *Capital City Gazette*. It was an excellent photograph. Black-and-white and shot with a long lens, it shows the flag ablaze in the foreground, with the oncoming bus prominent in the background.